"I've never seen anything so incredible,"
Emily whispered.

Bering agreed, but he was watching her, not the deer ouside the cabin.

They stayed silent for a long time. He wanted to take her hand, to take her into his arms. Instead, he willed himself to get ahold of his emotions.

It was too late, he realized. He was owned by Emily Hollings, a smart city girl who worked for the enemy. He began to wonder about his resolution to remain only friends.

Was there some way he and Emily could be more than just friends? He wasn't sure which to listen to—his heart or his head—but he knew he couldn't touch her again until he had an answer to that question....

Dear Reader,

This is my first novel. Not just my first for Harlequin, but my first published work ever, and I am so very excited that it's a part of the Heartwarming series.

Growing up in a small town is truly life-defining. No matter where you go from there or what choices you make along the way, it just...sticks with you. And yes, there is much about it that is annoying—seeing the same faces day in and day out, unbearable people, gossip.... But there is also a lot that is wonderful about it—seeing the same faces day in and day out, incredible people, gossip.... But no matter how you look at it, when it comes right down to it we love our small towns—just as they are.

So what happens when the face, the very character, of one special small town in Alaska is threatened irrevocably? I know you're thinking "This is a romance—it's love that happens," right? Eventually, yes, of course. But not without a rousing battle of wills and wits between two headstrong rivals complete with all the fun that the advantages and frustrations small-town life can bring. I hope that you are as taken with the charming little town of Rankins and its inimitable characters as I have come to be.

Thanks so much for reading,

Carol Ross

HARLEQUIN HEARTWARMING

Carol Ross

Mountains Apart

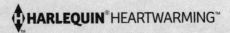

Recycling programs
for this product may
not exist in your area.

ISBN-13: 978-0-373-36670-5

MOUNTAINS APART

Copyright © 2014 by Carol Ross

Printed in U.S.A.

www.Harlequin.com

CAROL ROSS

lives in the Pacific Northwest with her husband and two dogs. She is a graduate of Washington State University. When not writing, or thinking about writing, she enjoys reading, running, hiking, skiing, traveling and making plans for the next adventure to subject her sometimes reluctant but always fun-loving family to.

For Paul,

My champion–I will miss you always.

CHAPTER ONE

SOMEONE NEEDED TO invent a new word, Emily decided as she stared out the window, glaring really, at the three-foot-long icicles hanging from the eaves. *Cold* just didn't cut it. *Cold* was "don't forget your jacket because a chilly wind is picking up." *Cold* was that bite in the air that made you wish you were wearing jeans instead of a skirt. This place was so far beyond *cold* that not even *freezing, frigid* or *icy* could do it justice. *Chilly, nippy, cool—* what a joke.

She'd read one time that Alaskan Natives have numerous words for different types of snow, so maybe they could just borrow one of those. Whichever one referred to the eyelash-freezing, nostril-frosting, step-outside-at-your-own-risk-because-you-may-die-of-hypothermia type would be perfect. Although to be fair, Emily wasn't actually cold *now*. Nope. In fact, she was currently sweating like a flyweight boxer in the middle of the tenth round.

It was approximately ten degrees below zero outside, and in between appointments she was running around in bare feet and a thin skirt and tank top. Because, like every other piece of equipment in this run-down, antiquated, tin shack that was currently serving as her office, the thermostat was on the fritz.

To make matters worse, a skull-splitting headache had begun to form directly behind her eyes and the pressure was now so intense. She tipped her chin down and pressed the heels of both palms hard against her eye sockets for several seconds.

She removed her hands and spotted the pills that her assistant, Amanda, had dropped off at her desk earlier. She scooped them up, peered at the tiny yellow tablets nestled in her clammy palm and wavered for a few seconds. Normally she didn't like to take medication of any kind, but Amanda had insisted that these would knock her headache clear to Skagway, wherever that was. She had no clue. With a grimace, she tossed the pills into her mouth and gulped them down with what was left of the tepid water in the now-soggy paper cup Amanda had deposited along with the pills.

Just then Amanda's voice came on the intercom along with a healthy dose of static.

What Emily heard was "Misst ollinsss, your nexx ssex appointment issst ere."

She reached down and hit the call button only to be met with a loud, static-filled shriek. "Amanda?" She pounded on the speaker and fiddled with the buttons. She leaned over and shouted her name again. "Amanda!"

"Hey," Amanda said, poking her head into the office. "Did you get that?"

Emily nodded and smacked the now-buzzing intercom, which was already dented on the top from, she assumed, the last frustrated owner who had finally had enough and heaved it against the wall. The faded drywall opposite her desk had a conspicuous indentation that appeared to exactly match its dimensions.

Emily answered, "My afternoon trick has arrived?"

Amanda cocked her head, amusement splitting her lips into a wide grin. "What?" Amanda enjoyed Emily's hilarious impromptu interpretations of the static-prone intercom.

"My next sex appointment is here?"

"Exactly," Amanda confirmed with a smile. "Do you need any help getting ready?" This induced a full-blown bout of laughter.

She stepped into the room and shut the door behind her.

Emily attempted to grin as she yanked some tissues out of the box on her desktop. She wiped her brow and then mopped at her cleavage. She pulled her suit jacket on over her clammy shoulders. "Yes," she said, adjusting her lapels and straightening her shirt, "but it's becoming increasingly clear that I need help of the kind that only a skilled mental-health professional can provide. But for now, could you please see if you can get something even remotely resembling a copy out of that...that...machine in the corner? I can't get it to do anything but light up like a Christmas tree, and I didn't make enough copies of the report, although how I was to know that every local yokel from the neighborhood barbershop, Laundromat, karaoke bar and pool hall was going to come straggling in and ask for a copy of it is beyond me. I swear I've never seen anything like this town in my entire life...."

She continued muttering as she turned toward the vintage-looking behemoth that was supposed to be acting as her computer and began banging on the keys. An error message, approximately the seventy-eighth one of the day, flashed across the screen. She exclaimed loudly.

Amanda threw a startled look her way. "You okay, Em?" She walked over and hit the escape key, then rapidly tapped several keyboard commands, causing the screen to dutifully display the document Emily had been seeking. Emily then watched, amazed, as Amanda turned toward the copy machine and effortlessly print out page after page of the requested proposal and then began to efficiently staple the crisp pages together. Emily had also tried to use that implement earlier and would have sworn it was out of staples.

Amanda, in direct opposition to Emily, was already in love with their "Alaskan adventure," as she'd fondly dubbed their pseudo-exile to these ice-encrusted ends of the earth.

"Yes, I'm fine, Amanda." Emily tentatively pressed a couple buttons on the keyboard and watched as the screen went black again—and then promptly remained that way. She thumped loudly on the side of the computer and this time added a colorful string of frustrated protestations.

"Moose what?" Amanda asked with a bark of laughter.

"Nuggets," she repeated in a tired voice. "Moose nuggets."

"Wow. Nice," Amanda said.

"Thank you. At least I've managed to pick up some of the local vernacular. It's charming, isn't it? How long has he been waiting?" She gestured toward the door, where she knew yet another irate citizen was waiting to verbally abuse her.

"Only a few minutes, and he knows he's early."

"Good." Emily looked down at the papers in front of her and could not for the life of her remember what she'd just been looking for. "What am I doing? It's so hot in here. And this headache…" She began absently patting at her desk hoping to somehow solve the mystery.

"Emily?" Amanda said.

Emily looked up. "What? Oh. This Mr. Bearing is another business owner, right?" she asked.

"Um, yes, but actually, it's Mr. James."

Emily's face twisted with confusion. "What?"

"James," Amanda repeated. "Your appointment is with Mr. James."

"What do you mean James?" Emily looked down at her planner and back up again. "I have *Bearing* written down here. He runs a guide and outfitter service?"

Amanda nodded. "Yes," she said. "That's right, but his last name is James. His first name is Bering—Bering James."

"Oh, my—" Emily said with a groan as she reached over and whacked the intercom, which had started buzzing again. "You're kidding me. Where do these people get these names for their children anyway? Already today we've had a Grizzly, a Rock, a Scooter and a Bean. And now Bearing? What in the world kind of a name is Bearing? Where does one come up with a name like Bearing, I wonder? Like, ooh, watch out, there's an iceberg bearing down on us." Emily gestured wildly and continued with her rant. "His mother is probably one of those iceberg-crusher boat captains, or whatever they call those barges that break through the ice. Ha! Yeah, and she probably wears an eye patch and curses like a sailor."

Amanda arched her brows in surprise at Emily's emotional, and very uncharacteristic, outburst. "Actually, Em, it's *B-e-r-i-n-g,* Bering, like the sea."

"Bering, like the seeaaa, he-he-he." Emily repeated the words with a weird, mental-patient kind of cackle. She scowled at the now-fizzling intercom and then turned around and tugged the cord out of the wall.

"Um, Em, are you sure you're okay? And you should know that Mr. James is a very influential figure here in Rankins."

"Pfft…" Emily spit out the noise and took a swipe at her desk. "I'm not scared."

Amanda chuckled. "I know you're not scared, but you don't seem to be completely on your game here, either."

Emily shrugged and made a face.

"Seriously, why don't you let me reschedule this one? You, uh, you don't look very good."

"Who cares? These people don't exactly stand on ceremony, in case you haven't noticed."

"No, I mean you don't look well. You look ill, actually. Like you could pass for Morticia's little blonde sister. Your skin is as white as that snow falling out there." She pointed out the window.

"Hmm. Well, pale is the new tan. Did you know that? I just read that the other day. People are embracing their natural skin tone these days."

"Ok, but—"

"I'm serious, Amanda. That's a quote. And personally, I think it's great. This skin-cancer thing has nearly reached epidemic proportions. I'm in style without even trying." She pointed at her face and smiled happily.

Amanda looked dubious but said, "Okay, sure, you've convinced me—pale is in vogue. But what I'm saying is that maybe you and your fabulous vampirelike complexion should go home and get some rest."

"Home? Home," she repeated. "Oh, I'd love to go home, Amanda. And I'm not talking about that igloo that we are currently camped out in. Nope, I'm talking about my brand-new town house back in San Diego that I've slept a total of, what, six nights in? But then again, there's nothing really there for me, either, is there?"

"Emily, I…"

Emily inhaled a deep breath and then let it out slowly. "I don't expect you to answer that. And no, I don't want to *re-skoodle,*" she slurred. "I mean re-sched-ule," she enunciated carefully. "Just send him in so I can get it over with."

"O—kay, I'm going to tell him to come on in, and then I'm running down to the café to get some coffee. Do you want some?"

"Coffee? Gads, no, I'm burning up. How about an iced tea? No, no, make that a slushy—you know those kinds you can get from those machines in the mini-marts? I like blue raspberry." She grinned goofily up at Amanda and then frowned down at the floor as she wiggled her sticky feet into her expensive beige pumps. She shuffled through the messy stack of papers on her desk, looking for the report that she'd had Amanda copy only moments before. The papers swam before her eyes and she blinked hard to clear her vision.

She pinched her fingers over the bridge of her nose and closed her eyes for what she thought was just a few seconds. But when she opened them there was a very large man standing very quietly in front of her desk. He was tall and so broad-shouldered that Emily took a second to wonder how he'd managed to fit through the doorway. His dark brown hair curled on his forehead and around his ears. He had a sprinkling of stubble on his strong square jaw, and Emily stared up into his brown eyes just long enough for an awkward moment to coalesce. He cleared his throat, which finally prompted her to rise clumsily to her feet and extend a sweaty hand. She tried inconspicuously to blot her palm on her skirt before offering it again.

She swallowed, or tried to anyway, because...

What in the world was wrong with her tongue? It felt absolutely enormous in her mouth, which had suddenly gone dry.

"I, uh, hello, Mr. James? I'm Emily Hollings. It's a pleasure to meet you. Uh, have a seat."

He nodded and smiled a stiff greeting that didn't even come close to dampening the intensity shooting from his eyes. His handshake was firm but quick. He lowered himself into the chair directly across from her, leaned back, folded his arms over his chest and then didn't utter a single word.

Oh, great, another hostile, Emily thought dejectedly. She didn't know if she had the strength for yet another confrontation. Ever since she'd arrived in Rankins, she'd been met with fierce resistance and resentment from the local community. In spite of the huge opportunity for economic growth that Cam-Field was offering this little town, a vocal and powerful coalition of the local population appeared to be staunchly opposed to the development of the oil and gas deposits hidden beneath the waters offshore. She'd fought some tough battles during her years with Cam-Field, but she had a feeling this one was shaping up to be one of the most contentious. And normally she would relish the challenge, but right now she just wanted to get through this meeting.

She stiffened her spine and said, "Okay, then, Mr. Buh, er, James, let's just jump right in here, shall we? I'm assuming that you are going to want a copy of the economic projections as well as a summation of the estimated environmental impact of the potential oil extraction and pipeline infrastructure—"

"You're assuming wrong, then, Ms. Hollings," he interrupted smoothly. "We both know that that report is completely disingenuous."

"Excuse me?" Emily replied, trying to sound surprised, even though she knew very well where the conversation was now headed—due south. Come to think of it, that was where she should be—south, way down south, all the way to Mexico. Warm sun, white sand, cold, fruity drinks—now, *that* was where ice really belonged, in a blender with fruits and juices....

"You heard me," he said. "That report is dishonest, deceitful and embellished. It means nothing to me and to the rest of the community, for that matter."

Emily furrowed her brow as if thinking hard about what he'd said. In reality she was stalling, trying to gather her thoughts and her argument—Cam-Field's argument—together for the development of this little Alaskan village. But for some strange reason, she was finding it rather difficult. Emily excelled at her job as vice president of North American operations, and this was her element, normally anyway. And she should have had this presentation memorized by now. But… And why was it that she couldn't seem to keep a thought in her head?

She attempted another swallow, but there was now a large lump in her throat, a perfect match to her oversize tongue. Amanda was right; she didn't feel good. She probably should go home and…and…get these clothes off. Yes, definitely! She would feel so much better if she could just cool off. She was literally burning up.…

Mr. James shifted in his seat, reminding her that in order to do that she first needed to deal with this combative man perched in front of her.

"Um …what?" she asked.

Bering leaned forward and placed his forearms on his knees. The movement seemed to bring him about ten feet closer but Emily resisted the urge to scoot back in her chair. What was that old saying about never letting them see you sweat? Well, that might not be literally possible for her at this moment, but she certainly wasn't going to act intimidated. She steeled herself and tried to concentrate on the subject at hand.

"That report is gibberish—it's bogus, crap,

bunk. It's not worth the paper it's printed on. I take that back—Tess down at the Cozy Caribou is making targets for the dartboards out of them, so I guess they're worth, what?" He answered his own question with a careless shrug. "About two cents a sheet."

"Is that why everyone and their uncle, or some other shoestring relation, has come into my office over the last week requesting a copy?" Emily countered smoothly, relieved that she'd managed such a snappy retort.

"Probably," he shot back. "The old targets had so many holes in them you could barely see the bull's-eyes anymore."

Emily smiled faintly and then met his eyes, and the sarcasm in his tone. "Well, Cam-Field is eager to help the community in any way we can, Mr. James, even its most desperate of dart-throwers. But what I really meant is, if the report is so worthless, then why is everyone so eager to read it and then discuss it with me?"

Emily saw a muscle twitch in his jaw and guessed that Mr. James was struggling to keep his anger in check. He was obviously passionate about this quaint piece of primitive hinterland. He could have it as far as she was concerned, but of course that wasn't the position that she'd been sent here to advocate. Which reminded her, she also wasn't supposed to get into a verbal sparring match; her job was to win him over.

"Because, Ms. Hollings, it's the only thing they can think to do. This community feels threatened, and don't think I don't know exactly what Cam-Field's strategy is in handing it out so freely. By issuing this report, Cam-Field is trying to make people think that they have some control over the situation. It's an illusion created by you, by Cam-Field, to pull the wool over our collective eyes. You will say and promise anything necessary until the town council passes your resolution and then you will do whatever you want—including destroying the environment and this town along with it."

Emily plastered on a benign smile and said calmly, "Come on, Mr. James, don't you think you may be overreacting a bit here? Cam-Field only wants what's best for the citizens of Rankins. And we—"

Bering interrupted with a snort of disbelief. "No. And I mean no to both of those ridiculous statements. What Cam-Field wants is what is best for Cam-Field—money. You may be able to bamboozle a few ignorant fools and some desperate souls around here with the sheer abundance of dollar signs in that report, but just so we're clear here, Ms. Hollings, it's my mission to get the facts across to the good people of this community. And by the time I'm through, you—and the rest of your Cam-Field crew—will be nothing but an unpleasant memory that we'll all shake our heads and share a chuckle over."

Emily had heard similar arguments before and she automatically opened her mouth to deny the accusation. But for some reason, this time the words wouldn't come; she knew that what he said was largely the truth.

Cam-Field's operating strategy was, essentially, just as Mr. James said: to get the community on board for their development projects with help from a carefully executed marketing plan. They would send in a "landing party," in this case her and Amanda, to feel out the local opinion and ingratiate themselves into the community. Their usual procedure included holding and attending public meetings, issuing informational brochures and reports about the exciting improvements Cam-Field would bring to the community, outlining exciting job opportunities, and quoting generous estimates of the amount of money that would be poured into the economy. If things proceeded well, the communities would be nearly begging for Cam-Field to come in and "save" them. If not, as appeared to be the case here in Rankins, it took a bit more convincing. And while the economic projections were essentially accurate, it was true that after Cam-Field was through, Rankins as it currently existed would cease to exist.

Emily raised her brows in a maneuver that she'd perfected during her long tenure with Cam-Field. The gesture was intended to express concern and convey empathy—and innocence. "I'm not sure what you're suggesting exactly, um, Mr. James?" she said, but she was having a hard time keeping her thoughts focused. "And please, call me Emily."

Bering rolled his eyes. "I'm not suggesting anything, Ms. Hollings," he replied, pointedly ignoring her attempt at informality. "I'm stating it outright. Cam-Field has skewed that report, emphasizing the positives and completely and purposefully understating the negatives. But you're in for a big surprise here because you're going to find that Rankins is different than other places. Money doesn't mean so much here, Ms. Hollings. Not like it does to you city slickers anyway. Here it means a roof over our heads, food on the table and coats on the backs of our children. You know, not everyone who lives here does so because they don't have any other option. We have a quality to our life that is unmatched anywhere in the nation—probably the world, for that matter, certainly as far as most of us are concerned—and which I'm sure that you and your Cam-Field cronies know nothing about. We're more than just a community—we're a family. We choose to live here, and I will not sit idly by and watch while Cam-Field Oil & Mineral destroys what we, and our friends and family before us, have built over the last one-hundred-and-some-odd years. So you'd better come to your little town-hall meeting with a whole lot more than what you've got in that report because…"

Emily tapped a finger to her chin and tried desperately to concentrate on his words. But her head felt as light as the cottonwood down that used to blow from the trees and float through the streets of her childhood home. She almost grinned as she pictured it in her mind, her head floating up, up, up and away like an errant helium balloon. She resisted the urge to reach up and pat it to make sure it was still securely anchored to her neck; she entwined her twitchy fingers tightly on the desk in front of her.

She forced her eyes to focus on something, and for some reason they landed upon the deep cleft in his chin, which was slightly off-kilter, she noticed, and yet not…unattractive. It was a physical trait that she'd always found appealing in men…

Emily felt the fog closing in around her again, stealing her attention, until finally it seemed as if she had come loose from her moorings and really was floating. She looked down and saw a smartly dressed, albeit rather rumpled and inattentive, corporate executive being lectured by a burly outdoorsman who didn't seem to adhere to the popular rule of watching his tone in front of women. In her experience, country boys were usually rather careful when speaking to the opposite sex, but Mr. James was now delivering his speech with ever-increasing volume, although like a gentleman he'd yet to throw in any profanity. She should share her *moose nuggets* with him, she thought, and fought the urge to giggle again—wait, maybe she was giggling a little bit. She definitely needed to stop that. She did her best to compose herself; she pressed her lips together and sat up straighter in her chair. But now her head felt really heavy, so she rested her chin on her intertwined fingers.

He certainly was eloquent; she was sure of that even if she wasn't quite getting the gist of what he was saying. And he really wasn't bad-looking, either. In fact, he was quite good-looking, she thought, or he could be—with a shave, a haircut and a change of clothes. A nice Italian suit or maybe even some pressed silk trousers—anything but this denim and flannel that these people seemed to think was fashionable for absolutely any occasion…

"Would you agree with that assessment, Ms. Hollings?"

Silence ensued as Emily found sharp eyes piercing hers. She almost flinched, or maybe she did flinch.

"Um, what?" She'd missed the "assessment" completely, but it wasn't her fault, really; it was getting impossible to think in this…this sauna. She grabbed another tissue and flattened it against her brow. She pulled it away and stared down at it. Strange, she thought, that it didn't appear to be damp with sweat. How could that be when she was so hot? She dabbed it on her forehead and looked at it again. She patted it with her other hand— dry. *Huh. Weird.*

"THIS IS RIDICULOUS," Bering said crossly. He stood to leave and then added, "I can see that I'm wasting my time here."

And he was perturbed. The woman was

clearly and deliberately tuning him out. And now she was just sitting there spacing out. He'd known when he'd been out in the waiting room that it was probably going to be a waste of time, but he'd also known it was a necessary first step to meet with Cam-Field's representative. And he had to admit that he'd been hoping he could have a reasonable conversation with this Emily Hollings because he knew exactly what Cam-Field was going to do to this community—his community—if they won approval for their proposed "oil extraction and development project." And he knew the long-term dangers such development would bring with it.

He had been a young boy when the worst oil spill to ever hit Alaska's coast had occurred. His dad, uncle and several other family members had dedicated months of their lives assisting in the cleanup. Bering had grown up hearing the stories about the devastation and the impact it had had on Alaska's coastline, marine animals and the state's fisheries. An environmental disaster of that nature would have a similar impact on his business, not to mention his quality of life and the lives of the entire community.

As a result, it had become an important part of his life's work to prevent that sort of destruction from happening again anywhere in Alaska, and especially right here in his hometown. But he could see that discussing it with their front person wasn't going to do a bit of good. The woman was obviously incompetent. Bering turned to go, but her bizarre question managed to stop him.

"Why aren't you sweating?"

"What?" he snapped.

"Why aren't you sweating? Aren't you hot? I mean, you're wearing that fuzzy shirt for goodness' sake, and you're just standing there like it doesn't even faze you. And I'm...so... so hot." She tugged on the lapels of her jacket. "I'm burning up!" She squirmed in her seat and continued mumbling incoherently.

Bering thought he heard the words *moose* and *beach* and *smoothie,* but he couldn't be sure. He watched as she then shrugged out of her jacket and dropped it on the floor. Her tank top was nothing but a flimsy scrap of silk and Bering could clearly see the outline of her bra underneath. What in the world was she doing? Was she out of her mind?

Bering answered himself with a definite yes, as she then swiveled in her chair and kicked off her shoes. They twirled through the air and thudded one at a time against the wall behind her desk. She turned back toward him and he watched transfixed as she reached up and with one fluid movement stripped off her top.

Next, she stood abruptly and kind of lurched to one side before clumsily regaining her balance with the aid of the desk in front of her. She reached her hands behind her, unzipped her skirt and began wiggling her body in an effort to loosen it from her hips. It fell to the floor with a quiet swoosh. She stepped out of it, leaving her in nothing but a lacy pink bra and matching panties. And Bering could only assume that eventually she would have ended up stark naked—if she hadn't passed out first.

CHAPTER TWO

BERING QUICKLY DIALED 911 and waited impatiently at Emily's side for help to arrive. His cousin Tag was a paramedic and Bering knew he was on duty. The minutes seemed to crawl by until he finally heard a noise in the entryway. He yelled, "Tag, in here!"

"Emily?" a voice called from the next room. "What's going on?"

Bering looked up to see Ms. Hollings's assistant standing in the doorway, an insulated drink cup in each hand.

"What are you doing to her?" Amanda demanded.

Bering saw it through her eyes: a strange man crouched in front of her nearly naked boss, who didn't appear to be moving at all. He hoped she wasn't packing. It was not at all unusual for women he knew to carry a handgun with them at all times. He rushed to explain, "I'm... She—"

"What have you done to her? Get away from her, you freak!" Amanda shrieked.

"I'm calling the police." She plopped the cups down on the desktop and reached for the phone.

"An ambulance is already on the way," Bering replied calmly. He gave Amanda time to absorb the scene, hoping she'd note that while Emily was only partially clothed, he was completely presentable. He reached out and placed two fingers on Emily's neck, feeling for her pulse. Was it his imagination or did it seem kind of weak and thready?

He glanced at Amanda and met her worried eyes. Judging by the expression on her face, she was getting it.

"Oh," Amanda said, dropping the phone back onto the desk. She sank to her knees next to Emily's limp form. "What happened? What's wrong with her?"

"I'm not sure." He pinched Emily's arm. "I think she might be dehydrated, though. Has she been sick?" Bering inched closer and was alarmed anew by how soft and shallow her breathing seemed.

Amanda began shaking her head. "No, not that I know of…I mean, she said she had a headache today. And she really hasn't been herself lately, but she hasn't been sick. Did she faint or something?"

Bering nodded, but never took his eyes off

Emily. "She started acting really weird. She said she was hot and then she, uh, she began taking her clothes off, and then she passed out. It scared the heck out of me. I... Where in the world is Tag with that ambulance?" Bering put his fingers on Emily's neck again, the weak, faint thud of her pulse causing his own heart to leap and then thump heavily in his chest.

"Oh, no!" Amanda cried suddenly, springing to her feet. She crossed over to the desk, and as she frantically searched through the messy pile, she let out an anguished groan.

"What is it?" Bering asked her.

"I gave her some pills earlier for her headache. But I told her to only take one or even a half to start with, but it looks like she took them all. They're prescription and they're really strong, and I don't think she's eaten anything all day. She hasn't eaten much at all since we've been here, actually, and..." Amanda was rambling now as she rushed back toward Emily. "Like I said, she really hasn't been herself. She's been through so much and she..." Amanda broke off with a sob, dropped to her knees and grabbed one of Emily's limp hands. "Emily, honey? Wake up, Em, please," she pleaded. "Wake up."

Bering heard the ambulance crew bust into

the reception area. "Finally," he muttered in relief and then shouted, "Tag, in here." The paramedic team came charging through the door and Bering had never been so glad to see his cousin in his entire life.

"I FEEL SO SILLY," Emily said much later as Amanda helped prop her up against two wonderfully fluffy down pillows. She'd awoken and oddly enough hadn't been all that surprised to find herself in the hospital. She had vague and hazy recollections of an ambulance ride and voices coming from very far away. There were also remnants of vivid dreams swimming in her head, of strong hands running a cool cloth over her skin, and warm fingertips caressing her face and hair. But of course that was crazy. She'd obviously been delusional.

Amanda's face split into a wide grin. She set the paper bag she'd been holding on the bed beside Emily. "I'm just glad that you're going to be okay. What did the doctor tell you?"

Emily made a face. "That I was dehydrated, undernourished, exhausted, anemic and stressed-out, and on top of all that I was then, apparently, drugged."

Amanda winced. "I'm so sorry about the

pain pills, Em. I should have only given you one."

"Amanda, clearly it wasn't your fault. I was out of my mind. The doctor also said I am overall generally unhealthy." She scrunched her face into a doubt-filled expression and asked, "Do you think I'm unhealthy?"

"Honestly?"

"Yes, honestly."

Amanda began ticking things off on her fingers. "You don't get enough sleep. You don't get enough exercise. You work all the time. You never eat very well—I've been telling you that for years. So, yes, I'd say it doesn't surprise me that the doctor says you're unhealthy."

Emily shrugged and said defensively, "I don't have time."

Amanda looked at her doubtfully. "You don't have time?"

"To eat healthy and stuff."

"You have just as much time to stop at Whole Foods in the morning as you do the bakery. You have just as much time to eat a banana or some oatmeal as you do an apple fritter. You have just as much time to walk through the salad bar at Trader Joe's as you do the drive-through at Chicken Little."

"I don't like hummus," Emily said with a curled lip. "Or wheat germ."

"No one is suggesting you eat hummus, and I would be willing to bet you couldn't identify a germ of wheat if your life depended on it."

"That's probably true," Emily conceded with a grin. "But you know what I mean—I don't like slimy, wheat-germy-type things."

"Wheat germ isn't slimy. But look, Emily," Amanda said and then took a deep breath. "I know you don't like to talk about this, but ever since the promotion-Jeremy thing, you haven't been taking very good care of yourself at all—worse than normal. All you do is work. All you talk about is work."

Emily folded her hands neatly in front of her. "Hmm," she said thoughtfully. "Amanda, I know I've probably been awful to work for—"

"No, no," Amanda said, "you are, and always have been, the best boss in the world." She reached down, took Emily's hand and squeezed it. "But right now I'm talking to you as your best friend. You need to pull yourself together. You need to start taking care of yourself and thinking about yourself first, before your job—before even your stepfather and your mother, and definitely before that worm Jeremy."

Emily bobbed her head agreeably. "You're right. I know you're right. I'm going to. I will."

"I'm sorry, Em, if I sound harsh, but you have no idea how worried I've been about you."

Emily felt a surge of guilt well up within her. How selfish of her not to realize what Amanda had gone through, too.

"Oh, Amanda, I'm so sorry." She reached over and enfolded Amanda's hand in hers. "Yes, I promise I will get my act together. I will get better and healthy and eat raisins and vitamins and do yoga and become a hummus-eating vegan. And you know what? I'm thinking about starting my training for a triathlon the minute I get out of this hospital bed."

Amanda let out a bark of laughter. "Let's not get carried away here. It's important not to set our expectations too high."

"You're right. I won't, because I'm not eating any raisins. I'm not eating anything that looks like a dead bug. And I'm really not a strong swimmer, so that triathlon thing might be a tad unrealistic."

"I'd settle for a brisk fifteen- or twenty-minute walk on the treadmill." She let go of

Emily's hand and then reached into the brown paper sack sitting on the tray table and pulled something out. She placed it on a napkin and set it on Emily's lap. "Here, try this. It's one of the most delicious things I've ever eaten."

Emily grimaced at it. It was some sort of biscuit covered with purplish-brown polka dots. "What is it? Wait, Amanda, is that a raisin?"

"Those are huckleberries. It's a huckleberry scone. Just try it," Amanda coaxed in a motherly tone. "Stop looking at it like that. I swear they aren't raisins and there's no wheat germ or anything healthy in it. I don't even think it would fall into the 'healthy' category at all."

Emily looked skeptical. "I'll try it later, okay? I'm really not hungry right now. Now tell me exactly what happened after I passed out."

Amanda ignored her attempt to change the subject. "Emily, you just told me you were going to do better. You promised. And the doctor says you have to eat if you're going to get out of here today. And judging by your tray, you skipped breakfast."

Emily crinkled her nose at the congealed cheese-and-smoked-salmon omelet and slimy canned fruit that lay untouched on the cart next to them. An apple fritter sounded good, or even a couple Oreos.

"Just try a bite," Amanda encouraged.

"Fine, if it will make you happy." Emily nibbled on the edge of the flaky biscuit and was immediately overwhelmed by its luscious texture. She took a real bite. Sweet, fluffy dough met tart berry in a delectable combination. Her stomach lurched painfully and then growled in anticipation of more. She took another bite and this time she savored it.

"That's really good. I feel like I haven't eaten in days."

"You *haffen't*" came the muffled reply as Amanda's mouth was now also stuffed full of scone.

"What?" Emily answered. "I had that candy bar, let's see, when was it? Yesterday morning? I guess it has been a while."

Amanda shook her head and swallowed. "Nope, that was the day before yesterday. You've been asleep since Friday."

"What?"

"Today is Sunday. You were out of it all day yesterday."

Emily stared down at the scone in her hands and reeled over the fact that she'd lost almost two whole days out of her life and hadn't even realized it. She thought hard for a moment. The last thing she remembered was a meeting with a Mr. James. She'd had a terrible headache, and she'd been really hot and…and he'd seemed angry with her—the memory of his deep voice reverberating in her brain made her cringe—and then she'd…

"I wouldn't eat all of that if I were you," that same voice suddenly called from the doorway. Emily shot a startled glance at Bering James as he strode into the room. She definitely remembered that voice. His hair was too long and rather unkempt, she thought, but he looked and smelled freshly showered, Emily decided as a few more steps delivered him right beside her bed. Her body tingled in memory of…what? Possibilities sent a shiver skittering uncomfortably across her skin.

It was just his close proximity making her feel overheated and self-conscious, she decided, pulling the sheet up to her chin. Bering ran one hand over his mouth and it looked to Emily as if he was smothering a chuckle. What was funny, she wondered irritably, and what in the world was he doing here?

"Your stomach might tell you it wants all of that," he said, gesturing at the scone in her hands. "But if you eat that much, it might turn around and change its mind on you. It's awfully rich." He smiled at her, and Emily had the distinct feeling that he was going to reach out and touch her. But he didn't.

"I'm glad to see you're finally awake, Ms. Hollings. How are you feeling?"

"I, uh, I'm fine, I guess, Mr. James. Thank you so much for stopping by. If you want to talk to Amanda here, she can reschedule our meeting. I really have to apologize. I'm afraid I don't remember most of our first one."

"Emily," Amanda began, "Bering hasn't—"

"It's okay, Amanda," he said, cutting her off. "I would be happy to reschedule—but later. The doctor is going to be in to see you again in a few minutes. But first, here you go. Drink this." He reached into a pouch on the side of the backpack he had slung over his shoulder and removed a plastic bottle filled with a thick liquid. He inserted a straw and placed it in her hands.

Emily held it up—it looked like a smoothie. She hadn't had a smoothie in so long that the mere thought of it caused her mouth to water. But she had to ask, "It's pink—please don't tell me it's some kind of liquefied salmon drink?"

"What?" Bering said with a surprised chuckle. "No, it's peach."

She took a sip from the straw and the taste of fresh peaches drenched her taste buds.

"Mmm, oh, my goodness," she said with a groan. "This is even better than the scone. It's the best thing I've tasted since I've been here. Where did you get it? Because I know there is nothing even resembling a proper juice place in this town."

Bering grinned at her. "I made it. And my mom made the scones, and I'll be sure to tell her that you think my smoothie is better than her scones. The smoothie is very healthy. So drink it, and I'll see you later." With that he turned, his long strides carrying him swiftly from the room.

Emily gaped toward the door and then gaped at Amanda. "Amanda, what the…?"

Amanda patted her mouth with a napkin and Emily was struck with the notion that she was swallowing a chuckle, too.

Several minutes later, she decided that that was exactly what she'd been doing, as had Bering James. As Amanda filled her in on the details of the past couple days, she knew it wasn't the richness of the scone that had her feeling nauseated. She pulled the cool sheet up to cover her now-flaming face.

Amanda seemed to be enjoying her mortification, however, and continued torturing her with more details.

"Okay, okay, I get it," she finally said, lowering the sheet enough to reveal her eyes. "I had some kind of psychotic break. I just haven't been hungry since we've been here. All this seafood..." Emily scrunched up her face distastefully. Then she lowered her voice to a whisper and said, "I've got to get out of here, Amanda."

"The doctor said he's going to release you today. But you have to take it easy, get some rest and eat something. You need to get your strength back. You've got your first presentation in two days, but the town-council vote isn't until the twenty-third, so that still gives us over a month to prepare."

A month suddenly loomed before her like a giant and hulking mountain, and just the thought of trying to scale it was exhausting. She wished she could curl up and rest somewhere for a while, somewhere warm and preferably for the rest of her life.

"No, no, I mean I've got to get out of this place, this backwoods...frozen...wasteland." Emily felt her lashes thicken with moisture. "I want to go home." A single tear broke loose and trickled slowly down her cheek. "I hate it here, Amanda."

"Emily, listen to me. You can't quit now. We can do this. We can. We've faced worse. Remember that weird town in Northern California that everyone said was impossible? We did it, remember? And what about that ranching community in Texas? We had death threats there, but we won them over. Oh, and who could forget that little Molotov cocktail thrown through our window in Oklahoma? They almost burned down our house. Come on, Em, this place is going to be a cakewalk compared to some of the jobs we've been on."

Amanda took a deep breath and continued, "I know you've been struggling and I know you haven't wanted to talk about it, but I think you need to hear this. You need to be successful on this job, Em. It wasn't right that Franklin promoted Jeremy over you, but you did the right thing by breaking up with him. The guy is a leech. He would never have gotten the job if it wasn't for you, and now you need to show Franklin what a colossal mistake he has made. This is your opportunity to prove how valuable you are to this company. Without Jeremy here stealing your thunder, Franklin will have no choice but to see it. So, we're going to do this, in your kick-butt efficient and effective Emily Hollings manner—just not at the expense of your health."

Emily snuffled into a tissue and then wiped her eyes. Amanda was right. This was what she did—no one did this job as well as she did. She really didn't know what it was about this place that had her so out of sorts. It was just so cold and isolated and wild and... intimidating. Kind of like Bering James, she decided. Yep, the man personified the place. She was suddenly struck by an image of him hovered over her and holding her hand. *Oh, no...*

"Amanda, was Bering James here at the hospital earlier?"

Amanda leaned forward and lowered her voice conspiratorially. "He stayed here the entire time. I mean, he barely left your side until this morning. You came to really early and the doctor said you were going to be okay, so he went home to take a shower, and apparently whip up a little peach power drink, and hightailed it back here. He was gone for maybe an hour, tops."

Emily's cheeks grew warm again. She cooled them with the smoothie, holding the cup against one cheek and then the other. "I wonder why. I mean, why did he stay?"

"I don't know. Maybe he was hoping for a repeat performance of your impromptu strip-tease?" Amanda teased.

"Very funny."

"Emily, he was worried about you, obviously. And I was worried, too. And to tell you the truth, it was really a comfort having him here."

"Ugh," Emily bemoaned, "I can't believe that that man saw me almost naked."

"Don't worry about it. He wasn't the only one. But hey, between him and that cousin of his—I would let either one of them see me naked."

"Cousin? What cousin?"

"Oh, man, Bering's cousin is the paramedic that brought you in. And phew, talk about a hottie. I have half a mind to strip down later and fake passing out." She tapped a finger thoughtfully against her pursed lips and then asked, "How do you fake a heart attack, I wonder? I should probably be wearing something lower-cut, right? Maybe instigate a little wardrobe malfunction?" She tugged down on the collar of her shirt. "Whaddya think? Would that be too much?"

"Amanda, be serious." Emily winced. "So, there were actually two men that saw me in my, um, semi-dressed state, then?"

"No."

"Thank goodness." Emily breathed a sigh of relief and then realized that couldn't be true. "But wait, you said—"

"It was more like six or seven if you count the doctor, the nurses, the ambulance driver and the other paramedic guys. The whole crew, they were *all* men—how weird is that?"

"Oh, Amanda, what am I going to do?"

"Quit worrying about it. I'm sure it's routine for these guys. They see naked people all the time. They probably didn't even notice, really...."

BERING COULDN'T GET Emily Hollings out of his head. He'd come home, returned several phone calls, attempted to catch up on some paperwork and then decided to take a quick nap before he went out to meet Tag for dinner. It was like the lost-puppy syndrome, he decided, as he stared up at the cedar-planked ceiling in his bedroom and thought it over.

Granted, it had only been a matter of hours since he'd left the hospital and he was tired and his brain was thoroughly scrambled. But sleep was out of the question—he could see that now—because Emily Hollings looked so much different than a puppy. But it wasn't her partially clothed state that had him out of sorts, although he didn't think he could ever get tired of looking at her....

There was a vulnerability about her that spoke to him. He was drawn in by it, and he couldn't shake the sense that she needed help. What kind of help, he didn't know, but for some inexplicable reason, he wanted to be the one to give it to her. He took a deep breath and exhaled slowly. He obviously needed to get a grip. He needed a distraction, something to take his mind off her.

But what was a woman like her doing working for Cam-Field Oil & Mineral anyway? She certainly didn't seem like the kind of executive they would send to do a job like this. She didn't seem as if she could handle the kind of intense pressure such a job would entail.

Although, to be fair, he hadn't really met her under the best of circumstances. And according to her assistant, she really hadn't been herself. And now that he thought about it, Amanda had mentioned that several times over the past two days. Now Bering couldn't help but speculate as to what she meant. What was Emily Hollings really like? And he knew, even as his good sense warned him it was a bad idea, that he was going to find out.

BERING STROLLED INTO the Cozy Caribou an hour later and spotted Tag already sprawled out in a booth at the back of the restaurant. The Cozy Caribou was more than a restaurant; it was a family-oriented establishment and an unofficial gathering spot for the community. There were booths running along both sides of the wide building with tables scattered between. The place was essentially two sections divided in the middle—one part restaurant one part bar. Huge chunks of a spruce tree—cut, sanded and polished smooth, then formed into a U-shape—served as the divide between the restaurant and the bar.

A wide doorway complete with a set of antique saloon-style swinging doors led into the back, where alcohol was served. Stools carved from the same spruce trees were set into the floor around the bar, one side for diners and the other for drinkers. It was Tess's rule that drinkers could dine but diners couldn't drink. She was very strict about this and didn't even allow drinkers to use the same door as diners.

"So, you finally came up for air, huh?" Tag asked as Bering slid into the seat across from him.

"Mmm," Bering answered vaguely. He took a sip of the water that was already waiting for him.

"How's the patient doing?"

"She's going to be fine. Or she will be if she starts taking care of herself. But after talking to her assistant, I have my doubts about whether that's going to happen."

"Man, she's sweet, huh? No wonder you were holed up in that hospital all weekend."

He scowled. "Yes, she's beautiful, but it's not that. Something's not right. Emily is—"

Tag flashed his cousin a quick grin. "I was talking about her assistant. Amanda, right?"

Bering nodded absently. Funny, he couldn't really even recall whether Amanda was good-looking or not. And then he remembered that he'd definitely thought so on Friday before he'd met Emily.

"Do you know if she's married or anything?" Tag asked.

"No, Amanda said she was involved with someone fairly recently, though. I got the impression that was part of the reason she was here."

The waitress appeared and delivered two heavy frost-covered mugs of root beer. They placed their orders.

"To see him?" Tag asked.

"No, to get away from someone or something…" He shook his head. "She wasn't really clear on that. She seemed a little uncomfortable talking about it."

"Do you think she'd go out with me?"

Bering choked on his swig of root beer.

"What? Tag," he sputtered, "I don't think that'd be a very good idea. I don't even know if she's out of the hospital yet."

"Amanda was in the hospital, too? What, was it something contagious?"

"Funny," he said with a chuckle, finally realizing what his cousin was up to.

Tag let out a booming laugh.

"I don't know, though, Tag. Something is wrong. I'm worried about her. She's, um… I want her…"

Tag's smile disappeared along with his teasing tone. "You want her?"

Bering looked annoyed. "I want her to get well, Tag, is what I'm saying. She needs help."

"Well, you're definitely not the one to give it to her, Bering. You know that, right?"

"I do. I know that, but I can tell she's having a really difficult time here. If you'd have seen her, and Amanda said—"

Tag interrupted, "Bering, I did see her, remember? I was the paramedic who treated her. The woman was dehydrated. She was drugged and exhausted. But what does that have to do with you?"

Bering shrugged and tried to look nonchalant. "Nothing, except that if you'd seen her in the hospital… There's just something about her that I…"

"Bering, snap out of it, man. Need I remind you that this woman works for Cam-Field Oil & Mineral? You remember Cam-Field, right? The 'corporation of environmental corruption,' I believe I've heard you call it on more than one occasion. The fact that this woman is sad is not your fault, is not your responsibility and has nothing whatsoever to do with you."

"Uh-huh," Bering said absently.

Tag shook his head and said slowly, "Oh. No."

"What?"

"You are asking for trouble here, Bering. Mark my words. Stay away from this woman."

"Trouble, Tag? Don't you think that's a little dramatic?"

Tag was frowning. "No, Bering, I don't. It's not your job to help her. And under the circumstances, I don't even think you should go near her."

Bering took another drink of his root beer and then plopped his mug down on the table. "Don't worry, Tag, I know exactly what I'm doing."

CHAPTER THREE

THE NEXT MORNING Bering ignored the twinge of guilt. He decided it wasn't taking advantage of an unfair situation to visit Emily under these circumstances—even though she had just been released from the hospital and she was certainly not 100 percent physically. She probably wasn't even thinking clearly. He reminded himself that it didn't matter. What was at stake was what mattered: his livelihood, the livelihood of his community, the integrity of the environment and that people were counting on him. He also ignored the nagging curiosity that had him wanting to see for himself that she was going to be okay.

And maybe a more informal meeting could serve a double purpose: checking on her and talking some sense into her—into Cam-Field. He knew the latter was unlikely, but at least maybe he could learn something about what he was facing. Keep your friends close and your enemies closer—wasn't that how the old saying went? He'd never heard anyone specify as to exactly how close but he'd figure that out as he went along.

He took a quick shower and then dressed in jeans and a flannel shirt. He bundled into his down jacket, pulled on his boots and hat, and stepped outside. He started his pickup and let it warm up while he called the Cozy Caribou. He ordered two breakfasts to go, along with two large coffees.

He drove the short distance to the restaurant, picked up his order, then made his way across town and parked in front of the duplex where Amanda had told him that she and Emily were staying. He knocked softly on the door.

A tired-looking Emily opened the door wearing only, from what he could see anyway, a very thin bathrobe. Memories of her scantily clad body swam before his eyes.

"I hope I didn't wake you. I just thought I'd come by to see how you're feeling." He held up the bag he was carrying. "And I brought you some breakfast. The doctor said it's important that you eat."

Emily smiled warmly at him and Tag's words of warning coalesced in his brain. But how could someone who smiled like that possibly be trouble? But as quickly as he wondered, an image of the Trojan horse flashed

across his consciousness. Tag was right—
he needed to remember that she might be a
pretty face, but she was still the face of Cam-
Field.

"And did the doctor also say that it was
your responsibility to feed me?"

"No, but you said that the food here was
terrible, so I thought I would see if I could
prove you wrong."

"You already have," she said, "and I'm
afraid I didn't thank you properly the first
time."

Bering realized then that she was shivering from the cold, and it was no wonder what
with that thin piece of silk that she was trying to pass off as a robe.

"If I could come in for a minute then I'd let
you take a shot at that."

EMILY HAD BEEN AFRAID he was going to say
that, and she thought it was probably a bad
idea. She took a few seconds to remind herself why it was a bad idea. First of all, the
man had seen her naked (mostly naked, but
still…) Secondly, he was clearly a part of the
unswayable opposition in this town, and to
socialize would only be a waste of time, not
to mention the probable cause of further con-

flict and embarrassment. And third, he'd seen her mostly naked.

She felt herself blushing, and for the first time since she'd arrived in this stupid town she was grateful for the cold. Why was she waffling like this? She was never indecisive. She prided herself on always knowing what to do, but ever since she'd arrived in Rankins, everything seemed to be completely out of her control—including her emotions and, apparently, her ability to think rationally.

Her current predicament illustrated this point perfectly. Reading people had always been one of her strengths. It had served her very well in her tenure with Cam-Field. But right now she had no idea what was going on with this guy. What was he doing here? Probably trying to get information out of her, she told herself.

What other possible motivation could he have for being so nice to her? It was a little above and beyond professional courtesy.... It wasn't as if he'd somehow caused her to pass out. In fact, if he hadn't been there, she might have ended up even worse off than she had been. And why had he stayed so long at the hospital? More things that she should probably thank him for...and a reason to invite him in—that and the heavenly odors wafting out of the bag he was holding.

But she didn't need to invite him in to thank him, did she? No, it was definitely not a good idea to invite him in. But it would be rude to refuse breakfast, wouldn't it? Maybe she could take the opportunity to state her case—Cam-Field's case. She had managed to win over some pretty tough rivals in the past. Shouldn't she at least try to sway him, too? After all, that was her job. Now, that was a reason to invite him in. She ignored the niggle in her brain that suggested she may have tried overly hard to come up with a reason at all.

"Sure," she said, standing back from the door to allow him in. "There are a couple things I'd like to talk to you about anyway."

EMILY USED THE LAST bite of biscuit to sop up the last bit of the creamy sausage gravy. She stared at her plate and then looked up at him. "I can't believe I ate all that. You were right, it was absolutely delicious. I had no idea there was food like this in this town."

"I'm glad you enjoyed it."

"How did you manage to find something without fish in it anyway?"

"You don't like fish?"

Emily crinkled up her nose. "I don't like seafood."

"You don't like any seafood?" he asked skeptically.

"No, and this town of yours seems to be unduly obsessed with the consumption of sea creatures. I actually saw something called a razor clam on the menu at one of your restaurants. Now, tell me there's not a warning in there somewhere?"

Bering laughed and handed her another biscuit, this one slathered with thick jelly. "Here, try this."

"Oh, I don't know if I can eat another bite…mmm," Emily said with a moan as she took a taste of the fluffy bit of heaven. The jelly was tart and sweet and utterly divine. "Where did this come from?"

"The Cozy Caribou," he answered and then took a sip of his coffee. "They make all their own jam," he added proudly. "They also make their own root beer. They serve it cold on tap. It's pretty popular."

"Root beer, huh?"

"Yep. You should try it."

"I might," she said with an agreeable nod. "This is the establishment that is using copies of Cam-Field's community-impact reports as dartboard targets?"

"So, your memory has returned, huh?"

"Somewhat," she said, not quite able to meet his eyes. "Look, Mr. James, I really am sorry about all of this—"

"Bering," he said. "Please, stop calling me Mr. James."

"Okay," Emily conceded. "Bering," she said. It rolled off her tongue and she decided that in spite of her initial reaction to it, she liked it. Which was completely beside the point, but she found herself asking about it just the same.

"I was named after the Bering Sea," he explained. "My father was a crab-boat captain. My mom was pregnant with me when he drowned there in a fishing accident."

Emily stared, trying to take in the implications of such a life-shattering event. She had to ask, "Why in the world would she name you after such a tragedy?"

"She says it was the Bering Sea that brought her and my dad together in the first place. That's where they met, that's where they earned a living and that's where they fell in love. She didn't ever want to forget that."

"What do you mean? How did they meet there?"

"She applied to work on his boat as a deckhand, which she did for quite a while—until they got married and she got pregnant with Janie. She claims she was the best deckhand he ever had. She didn't want her memories of the Bering Sea to be filled with only sadness because it had brought her so much joy, too."

He smiled at that, and even though it had been long ago, Emily thought she saw sorrow there, too. She smiled warmly in return, not wanting to be the cause of dredging up painful memories.

He looked away briefly before meeting her eyes again. "My entire life I could only imagine how difficult it was for my mom because I wasn't even born yet. But I have a much better idea now because my sister, Janie, lost her husband six months ago—and she's pregnant. With twins—that will make four for her."

"Oh, my…but how will she manage—"

It was as if Emily's words flipped a switch in him—from warm and open to solemn and stony in an instant.

"The same way our mom did—with the help of her family and friends. That's how we do things around here, Emily. We stick together in good times, we offer support in bad and we're there for all the challenges in between."

The message was blatant, but he said it with such a tone of confidence that it almost made Emily envious. It must be nice to have that kind of support system, she thought bitterly—personally or professionally. She was suddenly aware of both his intense stare and the personal turn her thoughts had taken. What was wrong with her? She couldn't let him play on her emotions and turn the tables like this.

"That must be really great," she said. "But look, Bering, I invited you in because I feel like I should apologize for the circumstances of our first meeting and I really do want to thank you for...everything."

He shrugged. "No problem."

"Actually, it is kind of a problem."

"How so?"

She smiled thinly. "I don't think there's any point in dancing around the issue of why you're here or why we met in the first place, however unfortunate it turned out to be."

"I don't know that I'd call it unfortunate." His voice was smooth, but his brown eyes danced with some kind of emotion that Emily felt it best to ignore.

"I would, because now I'm in the awkward position of being indebted to you while knowing that we're at odds. And we both know that I'm here to change your town irrevocably. I plan to improve it, build on it, make it better, but I know very well that you don't see it that way and that it's your intention to try to stop me."

"That it is," he acknowledged quietly.

"But you can't."

"We'll see about that." His tone was almost careless as he picked up a biscuit and began to butter it methodically. He added a generous dollop of jam.

"We will indeed, and I'm afraid you're not going to like the outcome. But if you would be willing to open your mind a little, you would find that Cam-Field is going to do some really good things here—"

"Not nearly enough to outweigh the bad."

"But how do you know that? You haven't even heard our plans—"

"I know," he interrupted firmly.

"I understand that you're scared—"

"Scared?" His brows danced up on his forehead.

"Yes, why else would you be here? You are here to try to get a feel for what I have in store for my, um…campaign so you can try to stop me in my tracks."

His lips twitched but Emily couldn't tell if it was from anger or amusement. She guessed it was the latter. She didn't think he was taking her seriously quite yet. And who could blame him given their awkward introduction?

He took a bite of his biscuit and swallowed it. "Maybe I stopped by to see how you're doing."

She scoffed at that. "You're not my mother— a simple phone call could have accomplished that."

His grin made her uneasy. "That reminds me," he said, "my mother is a schoolteacher. She decided she should stick to dry land after she had Janie, so she got her teaching degree." He devoured half his biscuit in one bite.

"Oh? That's nice. I'm sure it must be a very rewarding profession." She smiled politely and took another healthy bite of her own biscuit.

"Not a ship captain."

"Huh?" she said, even as the biscuit slowly turned to sand in her mouth.

Bering smirked. "Yeah, and just for the record, she has perfect twenty-twenty vision—in both eyes—and I've never heard her so much as mutter a curse word."

Emily bent her head. "Oh. No. You heard that?"

"I did," he said. "You have quite an imagination."

"Of course you did—that stupid intercom.

Nothing in that junk heap of an office works properly. Bering, I'm so, so sorry. I can't believe I insulted your mother. That's not... And I'm not... And she made those delicious scones..."

Bering chuckled. "I think you can be safely excused under the circumstances. But what do you mean nothing works properly?"

"Just one of the many problems we've had since we arrived in this town. We thought we were all set up with an office but when we got here nothing was like the property manager claimed. The place is a complete joke. The computers are ancient—seriously, they look like some kind of practical joke—the printer doesn't work, the phones are outdated. And we really need the phones—our cell phones work only intermittently. Of course you know how spotty cell-phone service is, since you live here. Even the copy machine is a piece of junk. And to make matters worse, my laptop came down with a virus the first day we were here, so all my software and work files are inaccessible. I have to use that dinosaur to even get my email. And I can't find anyone in town who can work on it or my laptop. We can't find anyone to fix anything, actually. But it's the heating system that's killing us. There are exactly two settings—iced-over or sauna. And I really can't tolerate iced-over, so…"

Bering rubbed a hand over his chin. "Hmm. Buster Bradbury owns that building, right?"

"That's what we've been told. But we've never spoken with him. He is, apparently, somewhere in Florida this time of year. We've dealt with his property manager, a guy named Oden Franks. He's based out of Anchorage, so there's not much he can do, either, supposedly. He claims he's been making calls and he can't figure out what's going on. The place was supposed to be state-of-the-art. He claims it is—that he personally had it set up for us. But obviously standards are a bit different here."

Bering nodded, his face an unreadable mask.

"If I was a paranoid sort, I'd say we were victims of sabotage."

"Hey, that's my hometown you're running down here, you know."

"I do, and it's unfortunate if you take it personally. But Rankins isn't special…."

Emily saw the narrowing of his eyes, the subtle clench of his jaw, and was reminded once again of the irritable mountain man she'd encountered in her office a few days ago.

She rushed to explain, "I'm not saying that

your little town isn't special. I'm sure it is—to you and to others who live here. What I mean is that I'm no stranger to opposition like we're facing here in Rankins. This is my job. This is what I do. So on the level that my behavior was unprofessional, I am sorry—especially for the intercom thing. In spite of the fact that it doesn't work properly, I should never have said those things."

"Don't worry about it."

"I am worried about it, because I would probably be fired on the spot if my…" Emily was always hesitant to voice her familial relationship with her stepfather boss. It wasn't relevant, other than it colored people's perceptions of her and her job. And nepotism had certainly never played a role in her position within the company. No, that was exclusively Jeremy's department. "…boss knew that I had said that and…done that."

She had volunteered for this assignment, and even though she hadn't thought it through completely, or had the time to prepare as thoroughly as she normally did, she certainly wasn't going to watch it all crumble down around her because of her own imprudent behavior. Her primary goal had been to get as far away from Jeremy as she could. And securing Cam-Field's first holding in Alaska would serve the additional purpose of showing Franklin what an asset she was to the company.

So far she'd managed only the distance part, a feat that could have just as easily been accomplished by a vacation to the South of France. But now that she was here and finally feeling better, she was determined to succeed. Not that Franklin would ever fire her, probably, but it certainly wouldn't be beneath her stepfather to replace her on an assignment.

"Listen," she finally said, "all I can say is that I really haven't been myself lately, although that's beside the point and doesn't excuse my bad behavior. But like I mentioned earlier, the, uh, the heat isn't working in the office, which partially explains my, uh, um…" Emily met his curious gaze.

"Clothing removal?" Bering suggested politely, but Emily could see the humor in his eyes.

Now he was having fun at her expense. She countered in a tone of mock sincerity, "You mean my recent medical emergency? Yes, it probably does."

"Emily, I'm sorry. I—"

She didn't know if his look could be considered contrite, but it was close enough for her. She grinned and said, "I'm kidding. I should have known it was coming. I've suffered from dehydration before."

"Really?"

"Yep, as a teenager—I think I was seventeen or eighteen. I was an assistant to the roustabout on an oil rig and I—"

"You were what?"

Bering looked both intrigued and doubtful. She wanted to assure him that she was no stranger to hard work, but she knew better than to tip her hand in that way. It had been impulsive to share that much with him as it was. She rarely talked about her personal life, unless she could see it as a direct benefit to the job. And intuition told her that there wasn't anything personal she could relay to this man that would change his mind about the job she was here to do.

"The roustabout is the maintenance person who keeps things clean and running smoothly on the platform. I worked for him as an assistant. The pay was good, but it was hot and busy and I forgot to take my breaks. I ended up dehydrated and I passed out then too."

She wanted to laugh at the look of shock on his face.

"Wow...I imagine it was hard work."

His tone was filled with admiration, and

for some reason Emily felt herself warm at the quasi-compliment.

"It was."

"Where did this take place?"

"Texas," she said.

"I thought you were from California."

"I am. But I worked summers in Texas oil fields to help pay for college." She left out the part about her stepfather setting up the jobs for her so she could learn everything about the industry she would eventually be a part of. She'd even worked a stint in one of their mines.

"Is that how you became interested in the oil industry?"

"Basically," Emily said, and hoped he'd leave it at that.

"Where were you born?"

"Crescent City, California."

"But now you live in San Diego?"

"Yes, I moved there when I was young."

"Hmm. What kind of food do you like to eat?"

She answered even as she wondered at the subject change. "The dessert kind," she said.

Bering grinned. "I have a bit of a sweet tooth myself. Chocolate?"

"Sure. And pastries and pretty much anything with frosting."

"Dogs or cats?"

"Oh. No. Please don't tell me you eat those here, too?"

He laughed, and she said, "I like them both, but I don't have time for pets."

"Favorite color?"

"Red."

"Brothers and sisters?"

"One brother—half brother."

"Were you close growing up?"

"Yes, as close as we could be. He's three years older than me. We had the same dad, different moms. So we didn't grow up together— he lived in southern Oregon with his mom and I grew up in San Diego with my mom and stepdad. We did see each other, though, as often as we could. Aidan's mom was great about arranging that."

"Where does he live now?"

"Um, Oregon, when he's not traveling for work…. Why are you asking me all these questions?"

"I'm curious."

He flashed her another smile, and the thought popped into Emily's mind that she liked the way his eyes crinkled at the corners. Curiosity, huh? What did that mean? She knew she couldn't get involved with him, so why she was even speculating, she didn't know. It shouldn't matter. It didn't matter. And, she reminded herself, either way, it was not professional behavior and certainly not professional thinking. And more than likely he was trying to learn about her for the same reason she planned to learn about him....

"Oh, um, why?" she asked, forcing herself back into the moment.

"Because you're new in town, and here in Rankins we are known for our hospitality toward newcomers?" he jested.

Emily made a snuffling sound of amusement and disbelief. They both knew that the welcome she'd received as a representative of Cam-Field had been anything but hospitable.

"Okay, maybe not so much in your case. But I do know that we, meaning you and me, didn't get off to the best start, so I was thinking maybe we could start over."

"Why?"

"I get the feeling that you could use a friend in this town." he suggested.

"Right," she returned sarcastically, "like we could be friends—me working for Cam-Field and you...well, not." But she had to admit that he did seem a lot different than the hostile man she'd first encountered. Had she dreamed up the fierce opponent who had confronted her in her office a few mornings ago? He was clearly a kind, compassionate and thoughtful guy, as evidenced by his behavior toward her the past couple days. And she had been dehydrated, drugged and delusional, and he seemed so harmless now. She met his eyes again and felt a jolt of awareness course through her. Okay, maybe "harmless" was understating the matter slightly. She recalled the passion he had displayed for this town a few mornings ago and his ultimate intentions where Cam-Field was concerned.

"I don't see why it has to be a problem," he said.

"Again, in case you missed it the first time, we are clearly on opposite sides of a very tall fence here."

"But that's just business."

"Just business?"

"Yes, business—it's not personal."

Emily flicked her eyes toward the ceiling.

Bering chuckled. "What?"

"People always say that and it's just such nonsense."

"What?"

"That business isn't personal, but that's really just a way to explain away actions that otherwise would make them feel uncomfortable. The truth is that business is personal. It's one and the same."

"You're joking, right?"

But Emily wasn't joking. Her work was her life, and she'd been working her entire life. As a child she'd begun doing yard work and other odd jobs for money. By the age of twelve she'd had her own paper route, at thirteen she'd begun working with the janitorial staff at Cam-Field and at fourteen she'd landed a job in the mail room. And on it had gone: from assistant roustabout to training coordinator to her eventual position in Cam-Field's upper management. She'd never stopped working.

She'd worked all through high school and college until she'd graduated at the top of her class. And then, while earning her MBA, she'd begun climbing her way up Cam-Field's corporate ladder. She'd nearly reached the top, too, until Jeremy had begun climbing and elbowing his way upward, and as with any good ladder, there'd only been room for one person at the top. Which was why she was here and Jeremy was in San Diego lounging around in her corner rung, er, office.

In spite of her stepfather's wealth, working hard had been the best way of gaining and then maintaining his approval. The only people she'd ever really had relationships with, friendships or otherwise, had been people she worked with. Even Amanda, whom she considered her best friend, was also her assistant.

Now she stated simply, "No, I'm not."

Bering was quiet for a moment before he finally said, "Well, then, Ms. Hollings, I think it's time someone finally showed you the difference."

CHAPTER FOUR

"EMILY, THESE ARE AMAZING. You're like a real artist, you know that?" Amanda was busy flipping through some sketches Emily had done. Since her laptop was still down, she couldn't generate any computer models, so she'd spent a good part of her last two doctor-ordered recuperation days drawing up some illustrations of Cam-Field's proposed development of Rankins. Amanda had emailed Jeremy another request for an arrangement of stock photos they sometimes used in their presentations but she hadn't heard back from him. Emily knew that Jeremy had them on his computer, because she had put them there herself. She had a speech to give the next day to the Chamber of Commerce and she needed something to show them.

She smiled at Amanda's compliment. "I wouldn't go that far, but thank you, Amanda." She did love to draw. It was her one indulgence.

"I love this one of the town and the bay

that you did from above. It looks just…idyl-lic," she said wistfully. "Like a place where anyone would dream of living."

Emily peered over her shoulder to look at the sketch. She had drawn it after a stop at the museum, where she'd learned about the town and its fascinating history: Theodore Rankins, an enterprising businessman, had come to the area during the early gold-rush days. He'd constructed a large rough-hewn cabin and hung a sign above the door that read simply Rankins. He set up shop and the miners who flocked to the area soon came to rely upon Rankins for needed supplies. It was probably inevitable that the town itself would come to share his name, as well.

Theodore had chosen the location wisely. The bay was relatively protected by several small outlying islands yet the deep water al-lowed access for trading ships, and marine life seemed to be thriving in the cold, nutrient-rich waters. The Opal River carved its way through the rugged mountains that served as the town's backdrop. The river slowed and widened before emptying into the waters of the bay, creating marshy wetlands that pro-vided prime moose and waterfowl habitat. The land reaching inward toward the moun-tains was richly forested with spruce, hemlock, cedar and hardwoods, interspersed with lush meadows making it a haven for wildlife.

With mining claims widely established in the surrounding area, Rankins became an essential outpost. Homesteaders moved in and began to utilize other resources that the area had to offer—trapping, hunting, fishing and logging. The settlement continued to prosper and grow into the quaint and picturesque town that it was today.

In a burst of inspired spontaneity, Emily had attempted to capture some of the charm of the historic town with her pencil and paper. She was strangely happy that Amanda could see it, too.

"Unfortunately" Amanda added, "it is totally not useful for our purposes here. This really is a beautiful little town, though." She gave the sketch another admiring glance before setting it aside. She picked up another. "But this one of the community center is perfect. The mom with the kids out front—nice touch. It really humanizes the scene. We can use this."

Much of the initial groundwork had been laid for this project in advance of their arrival, including obtaining federal and state offshore approvals. It was now their job to secure a majority vote from the town council for the remaining permits for the necessary construction within Rankins. After this final step was achieved, Cam-Field would come to town in force: build an offshore oil platform, pumping facilities, a pipeline, oil storage tanks and support structures in the town.

Because of Rankins's unique location, bordering both the river and the bay, all onshore facilities would be constructed within the city limits. The pipeline itself would not only travel through the town but would also transverse the entire length of the valley before eventually connecting to the Alaska Pipeline.

In an effort to make all of this construction more palatable to the townsfolk, Cam-Field would implement "community-improvement projects" in the form of new and improved infrastructure, parks and attractive buildings like the community center she'd drawn, which was slated to include a state-of-the-art gym, rock-climbing wall and competition-size swimming pool.

"Yeah, but I wish I had some real photos to show," Emily said. "Do you think it could be Jeremy?"

Amanda executed an innocent one-shouldered shrug. "I would go so far as to say that old Jeremy is undoubtedly having one heck of a time trying to get anything accomplished right now."

"Amanda…what did you do?"

"What? Me?" she replied innocently.

"Amanda—"

"Oh, Emily, don't worry. I didn't have to do anything. The entire staff can't stand him and it certainly isn't my fault if they've rather suddenly and collectively come up with a bad case of incompetence." She shrugged again and suggested, "I hear it's contagious. I would even be willing to bet that they caught it from him."

Emily stared at Amanda for a few seconds, eyes wide, mouth agape. Her lips were forming words of disapproval, but instead she burst out laughing. She had gotten tired of constantly holding Jeremy's hand herself; she could only imagine how the busy, mistreated staff at the home office felt.

JEREMY STRATHOM WAS PACING in his office, back and forth, back and forth across the two-hundred-dollar-a-yard pressed-wool carpet. Normally he'd be concerned about the destructive impact of such an action upon said carpet and vary his path to avoid an obvious wear pattern, but not now. Not today. His future was at stake here and it was a future which had taken him nearly two years to carefully scheme and meticulously craft.

And now it seemed as if it was all about to tumble down around him like a house of cards in an unguarded sneeze. He walked over to his desk and opened the drawer, extending it nearly to its full length. He stared down at the small velvet-covered box. He'd nearly had everything. He still didn't understand how this had happened. What he did know was that somehow he needed to get Emily back—back into his arms—and more importantly, back into the office.

He'd had no idea that his getting the promotion over her would result in this silly, impulsive breakup. He'd certainly never anticipated her taking off for places far-flung and nearly unreachable. It was unacceptable. The consequences of her actions were nearing disastrous proportions. She wasn't answering his texts, his calls were going straight to voice mail and her emails were strictly business-related.

Jeremy slipped out the door and walked toward his uncle's office. He'd always enjoyed the sound that his handcrafted Italian leather loafers made as they clicked on the marble floor of the hallways at Cam-Field headquarters. And never had he enjoyed it more than the day, a few short weeks ago, that he'd been made senior vice president. But the fact had not escaped him that at some point during the past week the sound had begun to get on his nerves. Clack, clack, clack—it now seemed as if even the floor was mocking him.

"Jeremy, I've heard it through the grapevine that you haven't yet sent the simulations to Emily for her first presentation in Rankins. It seems they are having some equipment trouble up there and she needs them ASAP," Franklin Campbell barked as Jeremy entered the man's huge corner office. Franklin leaned back in his chair and tapped the fingers of one hand on the scarred oak desk in front of him. The man seemed to constantly be in motion and apparently never ran out of energy, a trait he'd noticed that, in spite of there being no common DNA between them, Emily shared.

Jeremy crafted his face into a look of bafflement. "She hasn't received them yet? I asked Kim to email them," he lied smoothly. How did his uncle figure this stuff out all the time? Did he have spies everywhere in this place? Cameras? Bugs? Access to email accounts? What? "Maybe they didn't go through. The internet has been a little unreliable up there, too, from what I understand. I'll be sure to check on that again today."

The truth was the photos hadn't even been put together yet. He'd asked someone in the graphics department to compile them, but no one seemed to know what it was he was asking for. These people were idiots. Not for the first time he wondered how Emily managed to get any work out of them at all, much less the abundance that she did.

"How is the job going up there anyway?" Jeremy asked, changing the subject and hoping that Franklin would say terribly, but knowing that Emily was handling it like she did everything—perfectly. The woman had always made him feel inadequate, and now that she was gone, instead of making it better as he'd hoped, it was worse—much, much worse. He hadn't realized how difficult this job was going to be without her.

"Fine, just fine," Franklin responded flatly, but Jeremy could sense the pride behind his tone.

"Wonderful! " Jeremy said and nodded happily as if delighted by the news.

He caught a glimpse of something in his uncle's eyes. Something, Jeremy thought, like confusion or skepticism. It dawned on him then that he shouldn't have asked how Emily was doing in Alaska; he should have already known. Was that why his uncle was sitting there silently staring him down? What was the old man thinking? It was impossible to tell. Jeremy swallowed nervously as Franklin continued with his wordless scrutiny.

He finally shifted in his seat and his features seemed to soften slightly. Then he spoke. "You must miss her terribly."

"Yes, yes, I do," Jeremy replied soberly. *You have absolutely no idea, old man....*

"You're sure she's going to say yes?"

Jeremy smiled smoothly even as his stomach twisted and knotted painfully. His nerves seemed to have a direct link to his intestines lately. "Absolutely." Another lie—they hadn't ever talked about it, but he couldn't imagine that Emily wouldn't say yes. She had to say yes. He'd already assured his uncle that it was going to happen. And it would. As soon as he could get her back here...

His uncle's tone was suddenly sharp as he asked, "You've got the projections ready for the meeting with Argot tomorrow, I assume?"

Jeremy shifted nervously. "Nearly there. Very close."

"No problem generating the graphics, then?"

Jeremy nearly groaned aloud. *Graphics?* He hadn't even managed to get the final numbers together yet. He had delegated most of it to two accounting people, but they obviously hadn't communicated with each other, because what they'd given him seemed to be from two entirely different sets of data. And in total it appeared to him to be nothing more than a tidy summation of gibberish. Now he was going to have to find someone to stay late to do the graphics? He hadn't been able to get the graphics department to do anything beyond making a new sign for his office door, which now read Jermy Struthorn. He figured that said it all.

EMILY WAS FEELING like her old self as she stepped into the meeting room where she was going to be giving her presentation to the Chamber of Commerce. It was her first official opportunity to try to turn the tide in Cam-Field's favor. Amanda was right, she could do this. She just needed to get her head in the game. Just because she'd never been to Alaska didn't mean that it was going to be that much different than any of the other scores of places she had worked before.

Her sketches did look good and she was glad she had done them. Her computer was still down and she had yet to hear from Jeremy, aside from some weird texts that had come through on her phone telling her how much he missed her, followed by a question about who her favorite employee was in the graphics department. Whatever. He could jump off a cliff for all she cared. She was starting to feel more like herself—much more confident and definitely more in control.

In addition to resting, eating the healthy food Bering had suggested she buy and sketching, she'd spent a great number of hours over the past few days on the telephone, which had miraculously started working to an adequate degree (although she still couldn't put anyone on hold) trying to get to know some of the townspeople. She had purposely arrived several minutes early today so she could mingle and introduce herself in person.

She walked up to a handsome, athletic-looking man wearing dark blue jeans and a long-sleeved flannel shirt. It looked almost crisp and Emily got a kick out of the fact that it appeared to have been pressed. *Perhaps,* she thought wryly, *an iron is what distinguishs everyday-wear flannel from the more professional for-the-office flannel.* She extended a hand toward him and noticed that his thick black hair contained only touches of gray and, along with his trim physique, made him look much younger than he probably was. She'd noticed that wasn't an uncommon trait among the men here.

"Mayor Calder? Emily Hollings. It is so nice to meet you finally. I've so enjoyed our phone conversations...."

BERING WATCHED THE INTERPLAY between Emily and the mayor and was relieved. She really had bounced back. She looked great—stunning, actually—and she seemed well on her way to recovery. There were some smart, tough and stubborn men and women who belonged to the Chamber and he hadn't been looking forward to seeing her get eaten alive. Now, however, that he could see her in full swing, a new kind of concern was creeping up on him. She was good at this, much better, in fact, than he had anticipated.

Which was a relief on one hand, because he could quit worrying about her, but on the other hand, he was beginning to speculate about what kind of fight he was really in for. He might have his work cut out for him after all. And to think, because of his apparently misguided concern, he'd already solved one problem for her....

Bering hadn't thought she was being paranoid about her office sabotage. He'd had a pretty good idea who was behind it all. He was well acquainted with the Bradbury family. Buster Bradbury's son, Brodie, often helped out Oden Franks by taking care of property matters locally, including his own father's rental properties. He was also a well-known amateur computer hacker. And it was no secret which side of the issue the Bradbury family was on.

Brodie and his wife ran the hardware store, which also carried the bulk of the town's office supplies. He'd inherited the business from Buster, and they were all terrified that Cam-Field's development of Rankins would bring in one of those big-box stores and drive them out of business. Bering had quickly discovered that Brodie had taken it upon himself to do his part to prevent that from happening. Bering had convinced Brodie that those kinds of tactics could very well get him into trouble and really wouldn't make a difference in the final outcome anyway.

Though the sensible part of him said that an uncomfortable Emily shouldn't make any difference to him, could maybe even give him an edge, this level playing field somehow made him feel better about the battle he now felt certain was commencing. He absolutely wanted to win—he had to win. The alternative was unthinkable. This town, this valley, was his lifeblood. His living depended on the pristine wilderness—clean, pure water where the fish thrived and the unspoiled country where wildlife teemed. Sure, he guided fishermen to the best fishing of their lives and he helped hunters pursue their dream trophies, but he was careful to do it in a way that respected the ecosystem.

He'd gone away to college in Anchorage and majored in environmental science and business, and he had done so with every intention of coming back to Rankins. He knew how fragile the balance between nature and man could be. In addition to volunteering for environmental cleanups, he also contracted with the Department of Fish and Game for the surveying of big game and predator numbers and the reporting of any threat to them that might arise. Bering was convinced that he'd never seen a greater threat than Cam-Field.

His father and his grandfather before him had made their livings by fishing commercially, but Bering had possessed a different vision from a very young age. He had rebelled against everyone who had told him he could never make a go of a guiding and outfitter business in this remote of a location. But he'd worked hard and he'd done it. And in the process, the business that he'd created continually generated new business for the town. His customers shopped at the local grocery store, they bought gear at Les Hartley's sporting-goods store, they ate at the restaurants, they bought art from local artisans to take back home and on it went. And when they returned to their own unique corners of the world, they talked about James Guide and Outfitter Service, and they talked about the hospitality and the accommodations they enjoyed in Rankins.

Bering had no trouble with outsiders— tourists were his bread and butter. But the kind of people he wanted to come to Rankins weren't the ones who worked for Cam-Field Oil & Mineral.

Now he watched Emily working the room and felt his concern shift solidly back to where it belonged—to Rankins.

Emily—eaten alive? Yeah, right.

Bering stood back and half listened as Wally Crumrind, the town's pharmacist, raved about his new snow machine. He watched from the corner of his eye as Emily approached a small group of Chamber members, a couple of whom also happened to serve on the town council. He thought about going over and smoothly weaving his side into the discussion, but before he could extricate himself from the conversation he was having, he realized that she'd beaten him to it. In fact, he soon saw, they were all talking and laughing as though they were old friends. What was going on?

As the event continued to unfold, Bering felt his concern solidify into something even more ominous. Emily had called it, but he'd been too blinded by something—concern, curiosity, his own confidence—to see it. He was scared. Gone was the inattentive and scatterbrained woman he'd first met a few days ago, gone was the vulnerable and lost girl from the hospital, and gone was the questionably capable business executive with the understated sexiness that he'd come to know in the past few days.

In her place was a charming and professional, confident and articulate executive from Cam-Field Oil & Mineral. And it struck him right then and there that he'd vastly underestimated Emily Hollings on the professional front. If he didn't know better, he would think he'd been good and thoroughly snowed. Bering felt a shift in his entire being; a knot formed in his stomach as Tag's words of warning came back to him. For the first time since meeting her, he wondered if he really might be in trouble after all.

As she wrapped up the last of her speech, which had come off like more of a fireside chat, Bering knew without a doubt that Emily was a great deal more than good at her job. He was watching men and women he'd known all his life eating out of her hand like ponies at the petting zoo. She was charming and witty and, worst of all, full of statistics and dollar signs and promises of high-paying jobs and "community improvements." And she'd pulled the hospital card. Rankins was in desperate need of updated medical facilities, and she'd basically just promised a few million of Cam-Field's pocket change to the cause if the permitting process was successful.

And while Bering was relieved and, he grudgingly admitted to himself, impressed, he was also terrified. It was as if he'd been deluged by a bucket of ice-cold water. What was wrong with him? What had he been thinking?

Tag was right—Emily was Cam-Field in the flesh, and in spite of whatever personal concerns he may have had for her as a woman, the executive was going to have to be stopped. Cam-Field still had to be stopped. As the crowd began dispersing, Bering stood up and slipped silently from the room.

He looked from one end of the empty hallway to the other and quickly walked to the receptionist's station, which currently stood empty. He plucked the telephone off the desk and rapidly tapped out a long-distance call.

"Jack? Hey, it's me, Bering. Listen, I'm calling about the situation here in Rankins.... Uh-huh, yeah, I think we may have vastly underestimated the, uh, threat here...."

CHAPTER FIVE

THE MEETING WITH the Chamber of Commerce had gone unbelievably well. It had resulted in several appointments with community members and invitations to numerous social events. She'd scored an invitation from the mayor himself to attend the Rotary Club fund-raiser, which she'd learned was unequivocally the social event of the year in Rankins.

Even as she stood shivering on the sidewalk the next morning, Emily realized that for the first time since arriving in Rankins, she felt heartened. She could do this job. Amanda was right—it wasn't going to be any more difficult than any other of the numerous challenges they'd faced. She was going to get it done however she needed to do it.

But exactly how did one go about securing posts in the frozen ground? The sign she'd requested from the graphics department had been delivered that morning (cementing the fact that it really was Jeremy who was the problem at home). They'd done an amazing job of conveying her ideas for the community center onto a large sign. She wanted to hang it right next to the sidewalk in front of her building so people walking by or coming in to meet with her would see it. She'd purchased a shovel and two wooden posts from the building-supply store and now she just needed to figure out how to get the thing put up in this frozen ground....

After what seemed like hours, she was still ineffectually chipping away at the snow with a shovel when the sound of a motor revving caught her attention. She turned and saw that Bering had pulled up next to the curb in his black pickup. He shut off the engine and got out.

"Need a hand?"

"No, I'm just hanging up a sign." This was exactly what she needed right now, she thought with a surge of frustration, Bering happening upon her in another weak moment.

"Well, I drove by earlier and thought that might be what you were doing. How's it going?" He placed a hand on one hip and peered down at the pitiful indentation she'd managed to carve in the snow.

"I'm getting there."

"Really?" he asked doubtfully, not bothering to mask his amusement.

"Really, what?" she snapped. She was cold and yet sweaty underneath her jacket and winded from hacking at the icy snow and getting nowhere. She was irritable and in no mood for him to poke fun at her some more.

He looked at the sign leaning against the side of the building. "Well, isn't this just the niftiest thing?"

"Yeah, I think it turned out well. The center's going to be a great addition to your town."

"Really? How so?"

She stared at him, wondering if he was toying with her again. How could anyone not see the benefit of something like this? "Well, for starters…it will give people a place to get together."

He snorted ungracefully. "We have those places already."

She looked around. "You do? Where?"

"Around here we call them homes and churches. And of course we have the VFW hall, the school, the inn, two restaurants, the café—"

"But there will be things to do here."

"What kinds of things?"

"There will be a gym, with tennis and racquetball courts and a rock-climbing wall. You know, things for kids to do…"

"Look around you, Emily."

She did. Then she looked at him and shrugged. "What are you—"

"Emily, we don't need those things." His tone sounded overly patient, patronizing. "We have things for kids to do. We have things for everyone to do. We have nature. We have ice hockey, skating, fishing, snowshoeing, snow-machining and skiing. We have hiking, biking, hunting and just your general scenery-gazing. For Pete's sake, we don't need a rock-climbing wall—we have actual rocks for people to climb on."

"Bering, Cam-Field doesn't want to take those things away. We want to add to them—"

He barked out a laugh that held no humor. "Emily, just…save it. I don't want to hear your…propaganda."

She bristled and faced him head-on. "Propaganda? Well, by all means, don't let me keep you, then. What are you doing here anyway? Don't you have a job?"

He exhaled slowly and Emily thought he might be trying to gather his patience. "I'm sorry. All I meant was that you don't have to waste your time by trying to convince me—it's never going to happen. But look, I got the impression from watching you scratch away at this snow that maybe you could use a hand.

So I went home and grabbed a few tools. And yes, I have a job. I own a guide service."

She remembered that, but she didn't know exactly what such an enterprise entailed. "What do you guide?"

"People."

She tipped her chin down and raised her eyes up toward his. "People—that's clever. What types of outings do you guide these people on?"

He grinned and said, "Fishing trips, hunting trips, rafting, wildlife viewings and glacier excursions up the coast—things like that."

"What kind of wildlife?"

"All kinds—moose, caribou, bear, wolves…"

"Grizzly bears?"

"They seem to be the most popular critter that people want to see."

"Huh."

"Huh, what?"

She shook her head. "I just can't imagine what kind of life that must be.…"

"It's a great life. I'm happy for the most part—or I was anyway, until very, very recently when I discovered it was all in serious danger of being taken from me."

She dismissed the insinuation. "You actually choose to go out and muck around in this snow-covered nightmare?"

Bering was staring at her as if she'd suddenly sprouted some kind of strange growth on her brow. His voice was incredulous when he asked, "You don't think it's beautiful here?"

The tone actually caused Emily to break into laughter. "Beautiful?" She thought about the fact that Sally had used the same word to describe the town. She ignored that—and the fact that she had drawn a postcard pretty version of it herself. Because that was just it—it was a picture. It didn't reflect the reality—not really. "Bering, are you kidding me? This is the most godforsaken, desolate and bleak, not to mention cold and unfriendly, place that I've ever had the misfortune to encounter. And I've traveled to many, many parts of this country, but you know what my first thought was when I stepped off the plane here?" She answered without bothering to give him time to respond, "That I'd died and been sent to hell, which had quite literally frozen over along the way. I honestly don't know, and cannot even imagine, how you people survive."

His eyes bored into hers as he said, "Okay, first of all, it's not always covered with snow.

And second, we like the remoteness that you so disparagingly refer to as 'desolation,' which is exactly the point. We survive on what we have—and happily. We don't need help. We don't need Cam-Field or any other company coming here and exploiting us or our resources. We're fine just the way we are."

He turned and strode over to his pickup. He removed some tools and went to work. In a matter of minutes he had the sign up. He returned the tools to his pickup and walked back to her.

"Thank you," she said a bit grudgingly. "You didn't have to do this when I know how you feel about me—about Cam-Field."

"Emily, I've told you this doesn't have to be personal. My dislike for Cam-Field doesn't automatically extend to you. And besides, you would have figured out a way—eventually. I have the tools. I have the skills. And I find I rather enjoy helping a certain lady when she's in distress…." He shrugged, an arrogant grin splashed across his face; it was a gesture that Emily was already familiar with. It rankled her and she suspected that he was doing it on purpose.

"Do you think it's possible that you over-estimate the value of your skills where said lady is concerned? You just said yourself I would have found a way eventually."

"Nah, it doesn't matter if I do. I know you secretly like the help."

She rolled her eyes. "You are conceited, do you know that?"

"No, I'm not. I just have a realistic grasp of my value and importance. Now I have to go. I'm late for breakfast with your new pal, Mayor Calder."

"Breakfast?"

"Yes, it's the traditional morning meal."

"Strategy discussion, huh? Tell the mayor I said hi."

He raised his brows but didn't respond to that comment. "Nice job last night, by the way," he said.

"Thank you. You kind of disappeared after the meeting. I have to admit, I didn't expect you to be so...silent." Truth be known, it had made Emily nervous. She'd expected a fierce and direct rebuttal to her presentation, but instead she'd encountered nothing but his looming and scowling presence on the fringe, and immediately after the meeting he'd disappeared. It was nice, of course, as it had made her job that much easier, but it only made her curious about what he was up to.

"I had something to do. But I have to admit that I was surprised."

Emily furrowed her brow. "You were? Why's that?"

"I don't know. I guess I wasn't expecting you to be so…"

Emily's lips turned up at the corners. "Coherent?" she offered helpfully.

"No, no, um…" He paused, searching for the right word.

She tried again. "Prepared?"

"No…"

"Dressed?" she suggested brightly.

Bering laughed. "I'm glad you finally see the humor there. But no, it's just that you're obviously really good at your job."

"Good at my job?"

"Yes," he said firmly, and Emily was surprised at how much the compliment pleased her, and frankly a little annoyed that he seemed surprised. Did he think he was the only one who had skills?

"Thank you. I am good at my job."

"So, is that what this is to you? A job?"

Emily thought about the question. A few weeks ago she wouldn't have hesitated to answer with an immediate yes, because her job was her life and the two were inextricably tied. Now she realized that the answer was the same, but for a much different reason. Amanda was right—she did need to be successful up here in Rankins. desperately so, but she realized now it was because something else was at stake. At this point it seemed to be the key to fully regaining her confidence and self-worth. And so she answered with an honest, but quite different, "Yes."

"Ok, good. After your performance at the meeting yesterday, I understood that—"

Emily felt her hackles rising. "My performance?" she interrupted sharply.

His lips turned up at one corner into a kind of mocking half smile. "You know what I mean—getting friendly with the townsfolk and all, dinner with the mayor, getting invited to the Rotary fund-raiser. I know how Cam-Field operates, Emily. It's important for you to form these relationships—friendships, even—with the locals. You've said yourself that it's all part of the business to you."

Emily pressed her tongue against her cheek, trying to suppress her irritation. He was right, of course, but for some reason it grated on her that he was pointing it out so blatantly. As if what she was doing was wrong or dishonest or something. She'd met some really wonderful people in her work with Cam-Field throughout the years, and just because she was good at her job didn't mean she should have to apologize for it.

"Look, Bering—"

"Take it easy," Bering interrupted her. "All I'm trying to say is that I think we both know that it's going to get…intense here and I…"

"Well, this kind of thing usually does impact a community pretty strongly."

He stared at her and Emily felt her heart kick up a notch. "I'm not talking about the community now, Emily. Now I'm talking about us."

"Us?"

"Yes, I, uh…I feel like we're sort of becoming…friends. And I wouldn't like it if things got, you know, ugly between us."

She shrugged and tried to look casual even as her pulse began to race. "Bering, this is what I do. The only way that would happen is if you're not professional enough to handle it."

"So you're saying that you are?"

She cocked her head and felt confident that her look said it all.

"Good." He went to his truck again and quickly retrieved something. He walked back and handed her a newspaper. "Here you go."

Emily then watched him climb into his pickup and drive off down the street.

EMILY HURRIED INTO the office. She was freezing, so she tossed the newspaper on top of the pile on her desk and fixed herself a cup of coffee. She sipped it and thought about her conversation with Bering.

He didn't want things to get ugly between them? Huh. Well, she didn't, either, if she was honest with herself. Did that mean they were friends? She didn't really know and wasn't even sure what he meant by that exactly. One minute he seemed to take an inordinate amount of joy in irritating her and the next he was helping her out.

She absently opened the newspaper and the first article to catch her eye was titled Looming Disaster to Our Sacred Way of Life. Emily sat up straighter as she saw the author's name—Bering James. So, all that talk about things not getting ugly even as he was launching his own attack? Interesting strategy...

She quickly read the article and then read it again more carefully. It certainly didn't contain anything that surprised her. It accurately outlined Cam-Field's intentions, but with a decided emphasis on the negative impact its development would have on the community. It was very well-done: accurate, well-written and dramatic, but not over-the-top. Just the tools she'd use herself if she were on the opposite side of the issue.

She especially liked the quote about "Cam-Field swallowing our little community like the whale swallowed Jonah, although Jonah undoubtedly enjoyed a better view of a whale's bowel than would the citizens of Rankins gazing out at the monstrous and hideous oil platform on their horizon."

"Morning, Em," Amanda said. "How are you feeling?"

"Okay. Great actually," she said and meant it. She was enjoying the familiar sensation of good old-fashioned competition revving in her blood, but there was something else. She looked around and it dawned on her. "Amanda, it feels like heaven in here. Please tell me that someone finally came in and fixed the heat?"

Amanda nodded. "Mmm-hmm, you have your new friend Bering James to thank for that."

Emily looked up curiously at Amanda's use of the word *friend* and felt a new sensation bubbling up from inside her. Was this his method of softening the blow from the article? Or drawing the battle lines? Either way, it was really nice of him and rather ambitious, too. Fixing the heat in her office and writing a scathing commentary for the paper in the same night? When did he sleep? She felt a prickle of guilt as she remembered that she'd essentially accused him of being lazy that very morning.

But could he really be this naive? Or more to the point, did he really think she was this naive? Emily had had plenty of competitors in business that she respected, and even saw socially on occasion, but she wouldn't call any of them friends. Every gesture, every handshake, every compliment, every party invitation—it was all business to her. So she had a difficult time believing that Bering James would do something like this without the exact same motivation. Of course it was related, she assured herself. It was a direct result of it. Just as Bering had said, they both knew how the game was played. She was an expert at it herself. So why was that thought suddenly rather distressing where he was concerned?

"Huh."

"Yeah, he got someone in here last night after, like, one phone call, and after my having called all over town every day for the last week. Can you believe this place? Honestly, small towns are the best, and this one is absolutely the greatest. Clearly we were being shut out. Bering as much as admitted it to me."

Emily knew that Amanda actually meant what she said. She loved the social dynamics of the little towns that they traveled to and fancied herself something of an amateur sociologist.

"And speaking of our new hero, what do you think of his little diatribe?"

"Well-done. Very eloquent."

"He's definitely going to be a problem." She handed Emily another stack of papers. "Messages and emails from concerned community members—all came in this morning—after the paper came out."

"No surprise there. We'll deal with them shortly." Then she tapped the newspaper still lying on her desk. "There's another interesting article in the paper here."

"Oh?"

"Yes, it seems there is a winter festival coming up this weekend right here in Rankins. Apparently people come from all over the state for it."

"Sounds lovely."

"Doesn't it? And it also says that there are still a few spaces available for vendors. You know what that says to me, Amanda?"

Amanda grinned slyly. "Hot dogs?"

"We've never served them with a side of snow before. Are you up for it?"

"You know I am."

She and Amanda had often joked that more hearts had been won with hot dogs than with any other technique in their arsenal. No matter what information you were passing out, people would almost always take it if you handed it over with free food. "Okay, get on the phone—but not here in Rankins. Call Glacier Town or Polarbearville or wherever the closest thing to a city is and see if you can get us what we need."

"I'm on it."

"And don't forget to find out how we keep everything hot in these frigid temperatures. I'll start on a brochure to pass out and we'll do a raffle of some sort, too, with really cool prizes. People love raffles, and then we can talk to them and answer questions while they fill out the tickets. That will keep them around long enough to give them information…."

SHE AND AMANDA then spent the bulk of the day working, fielding phone calls and answering emails from concerned citizens, most of whom had seen, and were liberally quoting from, Bering's article. They answered countless questions and recommended that people stop by the office to make an appointment or to pick up a more detailed hard copy of Cam-Field's plans for development and improvement. They also encouraged them to come to the town-hall meeting in a few weeks, where the plan would be outlined in greater detail.

Almost ten hours later, Emily was thinking about wrapping it up for the day when Amanda popped her head in the door, wearing an apologetic look.

"Hey, Em? Franklin is on line one."

Emily grimaced and reached for the receiver.

"This is Emily," she said in her most professional tone.

"Emily, dear, it's Franklin."

"Hello, Franklin." She'd always called her stepfather by his name, rather than by any reference to his parental status.

"How are things going up there, dear?" And that was about as close as he ever came to expressing any kind of emotional attachment to her—dear.

"Fine. Very well." Emily didn't dare mention her brief hospital excursion. She knew he would probably send someone to replace her immediately if he thought there was even a possibility the job could be in jeopardy. This was Cam-Field's first effort to tap into the richness of Alaska, and she knew that Franklin Campbell would never let anything prevent him from doing this deal.

It wasn't exactly that he didn't care about her, she knew; it was just that his company had always been his number one love, even above her mother, whom Emily would rank a distant second. Emily thought she herself probably came in somewhere around seventh or eighth, after his sailboat, *Maureen's Mist;* his retired racing stallion, Brighton; his wine collection; his tailor, Johann' and his highly exalted nephew and her ex-boyfriend, Jeremy.

"Emily, progress report."

Emily gritted her teeth. Lately his clipped demands had really been getting on her nerves. Probably because they reminded her of Jeremy, who shared the annoying habit. Even when they'd been involved, he'd say things like "Emily, drive" and "Emily, lunch," and she was supposed to translate these short codelike phrases into some kind of invitation or demand for her compliance. It was bad enough coming from her boss/stepfather, but it was nearly unbearable coming from her co-worker/boyfriend—if that was what he'd even been. She'd spent the better part of a year trying to figure it out.

She forced herself to answer in a level tone, "I've been meeting one-on-one with some of the prominent members of the community. I had a presentation before the Chamber of Commerce last night, which went very well. And we've scheduled the first community forum, which we're marketing as a town-hall meeting, and we've got plans for several other events...."

She continued filling him in and finished by informing him that Jeremy had yet to email them the information they needed.

"Jeremy has had a lot on his mind lately. But I'll make a note to talk to him about it again."

Emily boiled with irritation. *Yes,* she thought, *he's had a lot on his mind, like ordering hand-made Italian shoes and printing new gold-embossed business cards....*

"As usual, it sounds like everything is right on track where your work is concerned. I don't think I need to reiterate to you the importance of this particular project?"

Then why are you? Emily wanted to ask, but of course she didn't dare. "Certainly not," she answered.

"I'm counting on you, Emily. And I know that you won't disappoint me—you so rarely do."

"Thank you, Franklin." Emily knew that this was his idea of a compliment.

"Jeremy has been working very hard here at home."

"I'm sure he has." Her temples began to throb.

"With you supporting him, he's going to make a fine CEO someday."

"I'm sure he will," she replied blandly. With her supporting him? What was that supposed to mean?

"Excellent. Your mother would like to speak with you now."

Her stomach dropped. *He's calling from home?* Emily glanced over at the clock, surprised to see that it was indeed well past eight o'clock. It was so difficult to keep track of time up here, with the lack of daylight hours in the winter. Yet another black mark against this town as far as she was concerned.

It was an hour earlier in San Diego, right about the time Franklin would normally be returning home from work. She really wasn't in the mood to talk to her mother, but was she ever, really? It was always exhausting.

"Hello?" Emily said.

"Emily, darling, how are you?"

"Fine, Mother, and you?" Emily put the phone on speaker and listened to her mother prattle on about her upcoming charity event, of which she was the chair, her latest haircut and the pedicure that Chauncey, her beloved bichon frise, had had the day before. Or was it Chauncey's haircut and her mother's pedicure? She couldn't be sure....

Emily had almost tuned her out completely when her mother abruptly changed the subject. "Have you spoken with Jeremy?"

"Not lately." Emily squeezed her eyes shut.

"Well, have you called him?" Irritation oozed from her tone.

"No, I haven't. We've had some issues with our phones here and I'm really, really busy. I don't have a lot of time for social—"

"Now, I know you've had a little spat," she interrupted.

A little spat? Where did she come up with that?

"But, Emily, Jeremy has assured me that you're going to patch things up."

"Mother, that is not—"

"Emily, Jeremy has been working very hard in his new job and he's counting on your support."

Why was she suddenly Jeremy's "support" person? "Mother—"

"You know when you eventually get married, Emily, you're going to have to think about something other than your job and about someone other than yourself. There's not a husband in the world who would want to be less important to his wife than her job. You've got to…"

She continued to harp, and Emily picked up a pen and began making notes for the article she was going to submit to the paper. She wanted Bering's words hanging in the air for the least amount of time as possible.

She had heard her mother's litany so many times before she could probably recite it from memory. According to her mother, she was supposed to do absolutely anything necessary to make a man happy, including giving up her work, her ambition and her sense of self. That was what her mother had done, and Emily was deathly afraid of ending up like her—superficial, pretentious, cold and uninteresting.

Emily was relieved to finally hang up the phone, but her conversation with her parents had managed to suck the remaining wind out of her already tired sails. Her head throbbed and the back of her neck ached. She sighed deeply and stood up from her desk. She walked over to the window and stared out at the cold darkness.

So Jeremy had told her mother that they

were patching things up? What was that all about? She had been very clear to Jeremy that it, whatever *it* had been, was over. She'd known it the second Franklin had given Jeremy the promotion. She'd seen the smug, superior look on Jeremy's face, and it had all suddenly become so clear to her in that instant. She'd helped him, taught him, nurtured his career, and then he'd swooped in and taken hers away. Why hadn't she seen it sooner? And would it have made any difference? Not really, she thought, because the only part that really hurt was that her stepfather had done it. That she never would have predicted.

The experience had crumbled her foundation into tiny bits and pieces, and she had been left wondering if it was even worth the effort to try to put it back together again. Work had always been her life, and as a younger woman she'd been sure that a career would make her happy. And it had for most of her life; at least, it had satisfied her anyway. It had certainly always provided the meaning to her life.

But now she was questioning what the point of it all was, really, working all the time. She'd thought it was going to get her to the top of Cam-Field one day. But it was obvious now that was never going to happen.

And her relationship, or lack thereof, with her family was never going to change—she was coming to accept that, too. Her stepfather treated her as little more than an employee, and obviously not his best one, as she'd always believed. Her certainty in that regard had always sustained her. But that had all changed when he'd given Jeremy her job.

She'd never had time for relationships; work had always been her first priority, even during her involvement with Jeremy. And initially she'd liked that—finding someone who seemed to place as much importance on his career as she placed on hers. She'd believed that they had that in common, but she admitted now that it had not been satisfying in any way—personally or professionally.

So here she was out in the middle of this frozen nowhere and doubting her life choices. Her stomach churned painfully, reminding her that it, too, was empty and hollow—like her life.

But there was something in her—a spark inside her that couldn't be squelched. She knew it was there, even if no one had ever really fanned its flames before. Jeremy had never brought it to life—had he even tried? If she were honest, Emily never really wanted him to anyway.

Bering popped into her mind. Something definitely seemed to flicker every time she was in his presence, and without her really inviting it. It really didn't seem to matter that they were at odds professionally....

"Is it too warm in here again?" Amanda asked, coming into the office and striding purposefully toward Emily. "The heat seems to be working fine, but maybe it will take some time to find the right temperature. Do you want me to turn it down?" Amanda reached out a hand and placed it on Emily's brow. "Are you feeling okay?" Concern knit her pixielike features. "You look flushed."

"I'm fine. What would I do without you, Amanda?"

Amanda put her hands on her hips and a mystified look transformed her face. "I have absolutely no clue. Sell vacuum cleaners door-to-door?"

Emily looked toward the ceiling as if she were considering the suggestion. "You know what? Right now, that doesn't sound too bad...."

The ring of the telephone interrupted Amanda's laugh. She walked toward it, and Emily squeezed her eyes shut tightly, praying that it wasn't her parents calling again.

CHAPTER SIX

"HELLO? OH, HI! How are you?" Amanda chirped brightly and Emily breathed a sigh of relief. Amanda would never talk to Franklin or Maureen Campbell like that. "Oh, you! No! Is that true? That's so funny." Emily watched her friend's animated face. "Yes, yes, as a matter of fact, she is still here. Can you hold a sec and I'll put you through? Okay, same to you." Amanda put a hand over the receiver and regarded Emily with a big, wide grin. "It's Bering."

Emily felt a surge of energy penetrate her tired bones. It took her by surprise.

"Hello?"

"Hi."

"Bering, thank you so much for getting our heat fixed."

"You are welcome. Did someone from Fritz's Computers call about fixing your laptop?"

"They did. Fritz himself is coming in tomorrow. Amanda talked to him last week and he said he wouldn't be able to get to it before June. Last week he was booked solid and now suddenly he has an opening tomorrow."

"Huh, must have had a cancellation."

"Yeah," she returned drily, "that's probably it. And another funny thing happened this afternoon. You know that copy machine that was on back order for six months? It was delivered today, too."

"Wow, more good news."

"Yep, it's almost like a real office in here now."

They both knew that it was only because of Bering that they were now getting any help for the myriad of problems that had plagued them since they'd arrived. "Thank you, Bering, for putting an end to the siege."

"It seemed an unfair and unnecessary approach. However much they might delay, guerrilla tactics will not win this war."

"You're right about that," she replied quickly. "We've faced much worse than faulty equipment, I can assure you."

"I don't doubt it."

"We were firebombed once."

"What?"

Why did she tell him that? She rushed to explain, "It was just a homemade fireball, a Molotov cocktail. We weren't injured or anything. It did almost burn down our house, but we got out. We were fine." Truth be told, it had been terrifying for both her and Amanda.

He muttered something unintelligible but she felt the tension. His voice was low as he said, "I don't know why I didn't realize how dangerous your job must be sometimes."

"No more dangerous than yours, I'm sure."

"My job isn't dangerous." He sounded baffled.

"Grizzly bears and wolves aren't dangerous?"

"Not if you don't irritate them. They only get upset when you invade their territory."

"I can see that, I guess. But it's basically the same with firebombers," she quipped.

"Emily, that's not funny."

"I know. It really wasn't. But sometimes it's either laugh or cry—and I rarely cry. Are you calling for a reason, by the way, or did you just want to harass me again after a very long day?"

Bering chuckled. "Harassing you is surprisingly entertaining, but I was calling to see if you'd like to do something besides work tonight."

"Oh…" Emily felt her pulse kick up a notch. "What did you have in mind?"

"Tag and I were wondering if you and

Amanda would like to meet us at the Cozy Caribou and maybe try that root beer I've been telling you about."

Emily wanted to say yes. But probably not a good idea, she told herself, because in spite of all this friendly banter, she knew they could never really get past this Cam-Field business. Hadn't his letter in the paper this morning proved it? More than likely he was trying to soften her up for another ambush. That flash of sanity caused her to answer, "I'm not sure if that's such a good idea."

"And why is that?"

"Did you happen to see the paper this morning?"

His tone took on a boyish eagerness as he asked, "So, what'd you think?"

Emily smiled. "It's truly a very good article. It's a shame you aren't on our side. But I think you're missing something here, Bering. What I'm trying to do here is illustrate a point about us socializing. I really don't think it's a good idea, but I do want you to know that I am so grateful for everything you've done and—"

"Emily, all I did was make a few phone calls. It's not like I'm expecting you to surrender in return. I had no ulterior motive for doing so other than the fact that like I told you, that kind of stonewalling isn't going to win this for our side. What is right will win. And obviously I'm right, so I will win."

She chortled and said, "We'll see about that."

"Yes, we will, and in the meantime, I don't see any reason why we can't have a drink. You informed me just this morning that you are a professional."

Amusement washed over her as he threw her own words back at her. She was suddenly conscious of the fact that her headache was rapidly subsiding and the knots in her stomach were dissolving. The tightness in her belly was now of a completely different sort.

"All right," she said. "You got me. Hold on, let me ask Amanda." She held a hand over the phone and whispered, "Do you want to go out with Bering and Tag and grab a drink or something before we head home?"

"Absolutely!"

Emily said goodbye and then turned to gather her stuff.

"Wait," Amanda whispered dramatically. She gripped Emily's arm with one hand and placed her other palm flat on her chest. "I think I feel that fake attack of something coming on...."

EMILY AND AMANDA entered through the back door of the Cozy Caribou, which they discovered was also the door to the bar. They walked through to the restaurant but didn't see Bering or Tag, so they seated themselves at a table. A cheerful waitress efficiently took their order—two birch-sweetened root beers—and as they waited for their drinks, Emily took in the surroundings and decided she very much liked the rustic atmosphere of the place. The floor was constructed of light ash-colored planks, and the walls were paneled in an attractive unfinished wood, which had taken on a faded gray hue and brought out complementary tones in the floor. Antique tools, vintage snowshoes, trapping gear, logging equipment and fishing paraphernalia covered the walls and enhanced the outdoorsy feel. Emily figured the owner could probably make a fortune selling the items off piece by piece online.

Classic rock music blared from an old jukebox in the corner and was accented by the sound of slamming billiard balls from one of two tables situated along one side of the room. But it wasn't so loud that she couldn't hear other sounds. Happy sounds, she thought, family sounds. She took in the clink and thud of mugs and the shuffle of heavy-heeled boots on the hardwood floor. Masculine booming laughter, high-pitched feminine voices and kids' giggles flavored the mix.

Their drinks were being served when Emily looked up and felt the breath catch in her throat. She'd seen him that very morning but for some reason that now seemed like a long time ago—too long. There was something so appealing about him; there was a strength and deliberation in his movements that screamed out self-confidence, which she knew he had in droves. But there was kindness there; she knew that now. He also made her laugh, and he made her think—kept her on her toes. She liked that, too…the way he challenged her. She'd never met anyone who'd ever been quite as much of a match for her in that way….

Amanda eventually caught her stare and turned to look. "Oh, they're here."

"Yeah, did I tell you that he really was named after the Bering Sea?"

"Um, no."

Emily quickly explained. "Isn't that sad? Their mom raised Bering and his sister all by herself. Well, according to Bering, she wasn't really by herself—because of all their extended family and friends. But you know what's really awful? His sister lost her husband in a logging accident six months ago, and she's pregnant with twins."

Amanda hesitated and then said, "That's very interesting, Em. What else have you learned about him?"

"Nothing, I mean, I asked and I, um…" Emily trailed off as she watched Bering standing at the bar joking with a man who'd just seated himself at a neighboring stool. Neither he nor Tag had seen them yet, and Emily realized that they probably assumed she and Amanda would be coming in through the front door. She noticed that Bering kept glancing in that direction and the realization that he might be watching for her caused a warm thrill to spike through her.

"He's pretty intense, Em."

"He is, but it's because he's so passionate about what he believes in, and I like that. I wish I had that kind of passion for something. I admire how he…" Her voice trailed off as she noticed him stand and reach across the bar to pick up a napkin. The ridged muscles of his arms tensed and bulged as he moved, the sleeves of his T-shirt hugging every inch. He swiveled on the stool and picked up his glass.

"You admire how he—what?" Amanda asked with a teasing grin as she watched Emily watching Bering.

"Um…"

"Looks, moves, talks, licks your earlobe, bites your toes, what?"

"Amanda, no, jeez. It's not like that. It's just that he's really—"

"Gorgeous, I know," she finished for her. "Emily, it's okay to admit you're attracted to him, you know?"

"Don't be ridiculous, Amanda. I'm not… He's… I mean, obviously he's a great guy, but I could never…"

"You could never what?" Amanda asked. "Spend some time with a decent guy who really liked you?"

"It could never work. This thing is too much. We're just…friends, I guess. If that's even possible. I don't know."

"Fine, if you so insist. But I encourage you to have some fun with your new friend, though you might want to wipe that look off your face because he is bound to get other ideas."

Emily threw a startled glance at Amanda. "What?"

"I've never seen you like this before."

"Well, that's just…" She started to say *ridiculous* but then caught on that Amanda was in fact doing her a favor. "I'll work on it," she said drily.

She would like to have some fun, she decided as she focused on Bering taking a long pull from his frosty glass. Suddenly he turned and met her eyes, and Emily knew she'd been caught. And the look on his face had her wondering if he was thinking about something more than friendship, too.

ACROSS THE ROOM, Bering felt as if an invisible arrow had pierced his midsection. But it was a pleasant sensation, like a warm explosion in the pit of his stomach. He knew he'd been looking forward to seeing her, but now that she was here in the flesh and smiling at him with that guileless face that he now knew was completely at odds with who she was professionally...

It took his breath away, and it almost made him forget again what she'd been sent here to do, and what he had to do in return. But he didn't want to think about that right now, because she was smiling at him and it just felt too good.

Bering had reached the conclusion that Emily was too serious about, and too fixated on, her work. And while he admired that kind of ethic and he definitely admired the courage that doing her job obviously required, he suspected she was missing the most fundamental rewards of all that hard work. What was the point of working hard if you didn't ever take the time to enjoy what was important in life? If anything positive could be taken from the tragic deaths of his dad and his brother-in-law, it was that. Life was short.

His eyes met hers and held, and then he took a long second to smile back. There was definitely something there, he decided as a rush of satisfaction flooded through him. She felt it, too.

"Tag," he said, trying to get his cousin's attention.

But Tag was deep into one of Mac's yarns that, unbelievably, he'd apparently never heard before. Bering had, several times, and according to his calculations, he was about midway through the hilarious incident, which involved one of their mutual friends, a record-book salmon catch and an angry moose. But he didn't have time to hear it again right now.

He stood and nudged his cousin in the ribs with his elbow. "Tag, they're here. I'm going to go sit down."

"Ouch! What the—" Tag glared, rubbing his side.

"I'm going to sit." Bering gestured across the room.

"What is wrong with you? Sit down, then.

There are empty seats right here at the bar and… Oh," he said, catching the direction of Bering's gaze and quickly getting on board. "I'll get our refills and meet you there."

Bering was already walking away.

EMILY FELT HER PULSE begin to race as Bering approached the table.

"Hi," he said softly and lowered his large frame into one of the two vacant chairs. Emily was struck once again by how incredibly agile he seemed for such a big guy.

His gaze grabbed hers and held on tight. "I am so glad you decided to show up."

Emily smiled and tried not to read something into such an innocuous comment.

He looked over at Amanda. "Hey, Amanda, how are you?"

Amanda grinned and they all chatted until Tag sat down.

Then Bering looked back at her. "So, what did you do with the rest of your day?"

Emily raised her brows and gave him a look that told him how silly the question was.

"Ah, work, of course," he said. He dipped his chin toward his chest as if waiting for more. "And that's it?"

"Yep, that's it." *That's always it,* she added in silent disappointment.

"Hmm, sounds kind of boring."

"It was," she found herself admitting, "but I'm not bored now."

His mouth held a satisfied smirk. "That's good. I see you ordered the root beer."

"I did. A friend recommended it, but I haven't tasted it yet."

The curve of his lips widened into a smile. "That's good, too, because now I can see your face when you try it."

"Bering, what could possibly be so special about it? It's root beer."

He lifted a brow.

Emily gripped the mug and took a sip... and felt her taste buds celebrate. "Wow," she said as she looked down at the mug and then back up at Bering. "What the...?"

The look of pleasure that flashed across his face made Emily smile in return.

"It's the syrup," he explained. "It's from birch trees unique to Alaska."

"Ah, were you worried I wouldn't like it?" she asked.

"No, I wasn't worried. There's sugar in it," he teased.

AMANDA AND TAG wandered off to play a game of pool, and Bering and Emily were soon completely oblivious to the blatant speculation of the other patrons, or to anything else going on around them, for that matter.

"I hope you haven't eaten, because I ordered dinner and I went ahead and ordered something for you, too. I would have asked but I didn't think you were here yet."

"Oh, thank you. That's nice. No, I haven't eaten, and I am hungry. We were really busy today, what with the response to that letter in the paper."

"I think you might work too hard."

"That's impossible," she countered. "There's no such thing as working too hard—there's only working inefficiently."

"But what do you do for fun?"

"Work is fun to me."

He rolled his eyes. "Okay, work is fun to me, too—mostly. But life is full of other fun things—more important things—obviously, than work. I like to fish, believe it or not, in my spare time, even though I do that for work, too. I snowshoe, cross-country ski in the winter. I like kayaking and hiking and backpacking in the summer. I like to read. I spend as much time as I can with my family. My nephews mean the world to me and just spending time with them makes me happy." He gestured at her as if she should continue the thread of conversation.

Emily felt cornered. When she wasn't working, she was thinking about work or reading about work—mining, drilling, fracking techniques... That was who she was, so why she was suddenly embarrassed by this lack of depth, she wasn't sure. Probably because Bering's life seemed so much more multifaceted than hers, more interesting, and the idea of having a relationship with her family like he so obviously had with his made her heart twist in an uncomfortable way. She opted for a subject change.

"Hmm, I'm trying to picture what this place looks like in the summer. I'm imagining it is probably somewhat more palatable?"

His searching look had her suspecting that he'd picked up on her tactic. She was grateful when he let it go. He leaned back and proceeded to tell her how beautiful Rankins was in the summer. How enduring the cold winter was all worthwhile if you could just experience one warm and wild Alaskan summer. Much like the bears, he explained, Alaskans needed the slower pace of winter to recover from the indulgences of the summer. Even Mother Nature cooperated, he pointed out, by giving them so many daylight hours in the summer to enjoy her bounty.

Emily snorted inelegantly and opened her

mouth to voice her doubts, but the waitress showed up with a steaming tray held high above her head. She lowered it, and as heavenly odors besieged Emily's senses, she realized she was absolutely famished. But as she examined the meal set in front of her, she felt her heart sink.

Emily politely waited until the waitress was well away before scowling down at the heaping plate. She leaned over and sniffed. Then she glared up at him. "What is this?" she hissed. "I may not eat fish, Bering, but I certainly know it when I see it."

"That is halibut."

"You say that like that makes it okay. But a fish by any other name is still a fish."

He grinned. "I know, I know, I remember that you don't like seafood. But it's been my experience that most people who say they don't like fish have never had halibut. I just want you to try it, and if you don't like it, then I'll order you something else. Anything you want. The house sirloin is great. We'll have that next time—with the grilled prawns."

She tapped her fingertips on the table and eyed the plate warily. She nibbled on her lower lip. Her stomach was rumbling now and it smelled so good that her mouth had begun to water. She hadn't actually tasted fish since she'd been a small girl, so she supposed it wouldn't hurt to try it. The potatoes looked delicious, and so did the soft fluffy bun next to it—thankfully, there didn't appear to be any nuts or seeds in it. There was also a pile of roasted vegetables she was pretty sure she could stomach. That was more than enough there to fill her up right....

"Emily, it's not going to hurt you. I promise."

"I know that," she said stiffly and picked up her fork. She cut off a generous bite, shoveled it onto her fork, lifted it toward her mouth and then abruptly stopped. She curled her lips inward and studied the morsel on the end of her fork. She waffled for a split second until she noticed the look of challenge on Bering's face.

"You know what? It smells delicious." She confidently kept her eyes locked with Bering's as she carried the fork the rest of the way. And then her mouth exploded with flavor. She tried to keep her face composed.

"Well?" he said.

The knowing look in his eyes had a part of her wanting to deny its tastiness, but her stomach overruled her. She scooped another bite onto her fork and into her mouth. She shrugged a shoulder. "It's edible, I suppose."

Bering shook his head and chuckled. Then he picked up his fork and began eating his own meal.

EMILY QUICKLY READ the notes she had prepared. Laurel Davidson owned the local newspaper as well as the entire city block in which the *Rankins Press* was housed. She'd never been married, had no children, although she did have a younger sister for whom she was the legal guardian. She was generally considered to have very open-minded views for the small town of Rankins, but this seemed to be forgiven due to her fair editorial practices, her gift for diplomacy and her likable nature.

Emily stepped into the office and was surprised by how modern-looking it was. She'd imagined the sounds of clacking typewriters and envisioned a gargantuan antique-looking printing press with an ink-stained white-haired man in a bow tie hovering over it. But instead what she found was a smattering of state-of-the-art computers at several very modern-looking workstations complete with flat-screen computer monitors and ergonomic chairs. Her eyes darted around and she saw no sign of an actual press at all. And there was only one person in evidence, one very young woman, and she was working the reception desk. So much for assumptions, she thought as the girl flashed a friendly smile in her direction.

"Hi, you must be Emily," she said, standing and reaching out a hand to greet her. "I'm Piper Davidson, Laurel's sister. She said I'd know you when you came in and she was right." Emily thought that was an odd statement considering that she and Laurel hadn't even met yet.

"Nice to meet you, Piper."

"So, I heard you were coming to the Rotary Club fund-raising dinner."

"Word travels fast around here, huh?"

"Emily, honey, you have no idea. The whole town has been talking about you and Bering James having dinner together at the Caribou last night."

Emily raised her brows and feigned a look of surprise. She really shouldn't be surprised; she'd worked in enough small towns to believe that what Piper said was true. "Oh?"

"Are you two dating?"

Emily laughed at her directness and decided that she liked this girl. "Let me guess— you do the gossip section for the paper?"

"Now, see, I've been trying to convince my sister that the *Press* is in dire need of exactly such a thing. You wouldn't mind mentioning it to her, would you?"

"Not at all," she said.

"In case you didn't already know, the Rotary Club fund-raiser is a really big deal around here. I bet you have a fabulous dress. Did you donate anything? Are you and Bering going together?"

"You know what, Piper? Forget about my talking to your sister about a column. I think you should bypass this small-town stuff and apply directly to those celebrity magazines."

"Piper, are you pestering Ms. Hollings?"

Emily turned at the sound of the voice that obviously belonged to Laurel Davidson. Dressed in jeans and a snuggly turtleneck, she wore no makeup and her dark, silky hair was pulled back into a sleek ponytail. With her olive skin and high cheekbones, she looked vaguely exotic, yet something about her suggested wholesomeness at the same time. Beauty and trustworthiness—beneficial traits, Emily knew, in a reporter.

"No way," replied Piper. "But she did say that I would be fabulous for a 'noteworthy people' type of column, didn't you, Ms. Hollings?" She looked at her sister. "Did you hear that part?"

"Don't you have work to do?"

She grinned slyly. "I'm doing it."

Laurel gave her a withering look. She put her hand out toward Emily. "It's nice to finally meet you in person, Ms. Hollings."

"Please, call me Emily," she said as she shook Laurel's hand.

"And I'm Laurel. So, are you ready for this?"

"Yes, absolutely."

"Good, let's move to my office, where we're out of earshot of some of my more nosy employees."

"Hey," Piper retorted, "I don't make up the gossip—I just report it."

Emily and Laurel made small talk as they got some coffee and then settled into Laurel's office.

"I'm afraid Piper is right about you being the talk of the town," Laurel said.

Emily grinned crookedly and shrugged a shoulder. "That's good. That means I'm doing my job."

"Yes, and fortunately a good share of the chatter is due to the real reason that you're here—and not because you were seen with Bering last night. Cam-Field's presence here is causing quite a stir. I heard you knocked it out of the park at the Chamber of Commerce meeting. I'm sorry I missed it, but I read the minutes."

"I think it went well. Better than I expected, although I thought I would be hearing a rebuttal from the opposing faction."

"That surprised me, too, initially. But the more I thought about it, the more it made sense. Bering isn't one to waste his energy. He's aware that a lot of this community counts on him and other members of the James family for their livelihoods—and most of those Chamber members know it, too."

Emily furrowed her brow. "How do you mean?"

"You know what Bering does for a living, right?"

"Yes, but suddenly I'm getting the sense that maybe I didn't realize the, uh, scope of his business?"

"I don't know how many employees he has. But he has to have at least ten other guides besides himself in the summer and fall. And he has employees to haul and maintain equipment. He has a secretary who makes travel arrangements. He orders supplies from the businesses in town. The outdoor store alone must get half of their business from Bering and his clients. The bed-and-breakfast and the Faraway Inn basically exist because of his business. His cousin Shay owns the inn and I don't know how many people she employs. Do you see where I'm going here? The clientele that he has are worth serious money and they have important connections. I'm talking about businesspeople and politicians, even some professional athletes, musicians and movie stars.

"They come to Rankins—sometimes with their families and friends—and they drop big bucks here. I don't know the numbers but it has to be a significant industry for this town."

Emily was annoyed with herself. How could she have not seen this sooner? The circumstances that had impulsively brought her here were no longer a viable excuse. She prided herself on being good at her job, had even bragged to Bering about it. She hadn't done her usual meticulous homework and it was clearly catching up with her, certainly where Bering was concerned.

Laurel continued, "The James family is one of the oldest and the largest in the community. By and large, they are wealthy, educated and close-knit. They are also down-to-earth, unpretentious and extremely generous—with their time and money. As I'm sure you can imagine, all of these things add up to make them very popular around here."

Emily thought fast. She may be slightly behind the curve, but it wasn't anything she hadn't faced before. A healthy industry wasn't anything compared to the millions that Cam-Field would bring into this community. In her experience, money talked, and as long as folks were willing to compromise, it usually spoke the loudest.

"I can see I've caught you off guard. So, why don't you give me an interview? Something personal—let the community get to know you, too?"

"Probably," Emily answered with a slow nod. "We'll see how it goes."

"You mean you want to wait to see how badly I'm going to skew things?" Laurel's expression took on a shrewd look as she added, "I have a master's degree in journalism from Columbia, Emily. I can assure you that I know how to be objective."

"You know, I have to ask, what in the world are you doing here in Rankins, Alaska?"

Laurel grinned at that and said, "I take it you're not exactly enamored of our quaint village yet?"

Emily didn't respond.

"You know…it's not as small as it seems."

"What do you mean?"

"The town of Rankins seems small, but the

outlying area contains a pretty healthy number of people. There are ten members on our town council for a reason. And unlike a lot of places, they listen to their constituents. With few exceptions, the vote will go the way of the people."

That much Emily did know from the standard basic research Cam-Field staff had done prior to her arrival. It seemed Rankins was the hot spot for miles in any one direction.

"I've gathered that much," Emily said.

Laurel nodded. "And even though the area is large geographically, Rankins is the only town supporting this entire area. That's why we have as many businesses as we do. We also have our own airport, post office and police department, and other entities that you would only find in larger cities. They might be small, but we have them. That makes us both self-sufficient and reliant on one another."

Bering had relayed some of the same information, albeit in a less...academic tone.

"There is a surprising amount of diversity among the people, too. And people here— they just have their priorities straight, you know what I mean? I'm warning you, Emily, it will grow on you if you're not careful."

"I can see what you mean," she lied smoothly.

In spite of her gradual thawing toward Bering, she felt no warmth toward the town.

Laurel grinned and Emily suspected she could see right through her. "You're certainly diplomatic, aren't you?"

"I have to be, to be successful at this job."

"I get that. So before you do agree to an interview with me, I should warn you that I am even closer to the James family than most."

"Oh?"

"I've known Bering James my entire life, and his sister, Janie, is one of my best friends. She actually works here part-time."

Emily nodded, not having a clue where this conversation was now headed. "You went to school together?"

"Yes, we did. But it goes much deeper than that. Our families have been friends since our grandparents' days. We are tied together in complex ways. So I'm just going to offer one piece of advice, if that's okay?"

"Certainly," she said.

"He's not as…simple as he appears."

Emily thought that was an odd statement. She already knew Bering was about as far from simple as a man could get. She supposed she meant that he was educated like she was and more sophisticated than his provincial appearance. And the priority thing definitely seemed true where Bering was concerned. You couldn't have a conversation with him without him voicing his love and appreciation for his family.

"Bering is a good friend and a good man. His family has been wonderful to Piper and me. If it hadn't been for the James family, I would have lost her."

"Lost her? What do you mean?"

"To shorten a very long story…I was only sixteen when our mom left us. We never knew our dad. The state wanted to put Piper in foster care, but some very strategic strings were pulled and I got to keep her. I'm not giving you a sob story, because it worked out great for us. I'm only telling you this because I don't want you to underestimate them."

"But if you're that close to them, it seems like you would want me to underestimate them," Emily countered.

"I won't lie—I considered that, but the simple truth is that I would like to see some development in this town. The fishing industry isn't what it used to be, and while I'm not entirely sure Cam-Field is the answer that we need, I am willing to hear your proposal before I decide one way or another."

Emily considered her words. "Thank you, I appreciate that. I could really use the cooperation of the media. I certainly haven't gotten a lot of cooperation anywhere else."

Laurel chuckled. "This is a town overflowing with community pride and cohesiveness. To anyone who has lived anywhere else, it might seem over-the-top, but to the people here it's a way of life."

"I've seen a bit of that already."

Laurel grinned knowingly. Then she leaned forward and cradled her chin in the palm of her hand. "Now, when do I get that interview?"

"You've got it," Emily promised, "but not quite yet, if that's okay. Right now I'd like to submit a response letter to the one you published yesterday. I'm sure you can guess which one I'm referring to." Emily handed it over and Laurel took it and read it quickly, going back, Emily noticed, to a couple key paragraphs.

She finally looked up and studied Emily carefully. "Are you sure about this?"

"I am."

She tipped her head and smiled at Emily. "Maybe Bering and his coalition are the ones I should be warning."

CHAPTER SEVEN

"'AND SO I ASK YOU, Mr. James,'" Amanda read aloud from Emily's article in the next morning's paper, "'just what exactly is it that you're afraid of? Is it the scary influx of much-needed money into the economy? Is it the threatening number of high-paying jobs that will help prevent the young people of Rankins from moving out of this community like they've been doing for the last decade at an ever-increasing rate? Or is it the terrifying fact that Rankins may get an updated hospital with state-of-the-art equipment and skilled doctors who know how to use such high-tech lifesaving machines?'"

She whistled through her teeth. "Wow. Okay. Em, this is really good." Amanda had come over from next door to have coffee with Emily before they headed to work together. Now she walked into the kitchen to pour herself another cup. "This is definitely going to stir the pot, so to speak."

Emily called the office and checked the

messages. They'd been bombarded with calls from supporters, and she knew that when she checked the email it would undoubtedly be the same. There'd been quite a few in opposition also, but not nearly as many as she'd feared.

"Twenty-nine messages," she said, pacing back and forth in front of Amanda, "eighteen in support, nine against and two incoherent, but which I'm pretty sure from the tone are against."

Progress, she decided; it was definitely progress. And that was what she wanted. She should be happy, so why did she feel so fidgety and anxious?

"Emily, this is brilliant." Amanda sat on the sofa and continued reading. "Seriously, this is some of your best work. I mean, pushing the tender buttons of patriotism, which, I've noticed, are running rampant here in Rankins?"

"You don't think that's overdoing it? Making it too political?"

"Absolutely not, and there are a surprising number of intellectuals in this community, and I think they're going to appreciate that you're not being condescending to them."

Emily was silent.

"Emily," Amanda said, obviously sensing

her unease, "you just listened to the messages. You're already turning things around."

"I know, and that's great, but..."

"This wouldn't have anything to do with Bering, would it?"

Emily sank down onto the sofa. "Is it that obvious?"

"Well, you did eat fish, Emily."

"Do you think he's going to hate me now?" She covered her face with one hand and groaned. "Now I sound like a fifteen-year-old. What is wrong with me?"

Amanda took a second to laugh. "You didn't hate him after his article. He's not stupid. He had to be expecting some kind of rebuttal."

And that was exactly it. Now Emily was going to be expecting something in return. The thought was both nerve-racking and kind of exciting at the same time. And how was she supposed to act now? The idea that they could carry on a friendship or whatever in the midst of this turmoil with Cam-Field suddenly seemed even more ridiculous than it already had. The ringing doorbell startled her out of her reverie.

Amanda jumped up. "I'll get it." She opened the door to find an envelope sitting on the step. "I hope it's nothing gruesome," she said. She bent and picked it up by one corner and carried it toward Emily. She stopped in front of the sofa and lifted it to her ear. "It's not ticking, so that's a good sign."

She set it down on the coffee table in front of them. They stared at it for a few seconds and then, in unison, sat back on the soft cushions. Emily knew they were both thinking about the time they'd received the dead bird. While on a job in Oklahoma, some sicko had broken its neck, tied a noose around it and sent it to them as some kind of warning.

Emily picked up the envelope. She opened it and saw what looked like a brochure tucked inside. She pulled it out and began reading aloud, "'Stop by and get the real story. Please join the Save Rankins Coalition at their free halibut fish-and-chips booth this Saturday at the winter festival. Information will be available about the true and terrible impact that Cam-Field Oil & Mineral will have on our town. A raffle to benefit our cause will also be held with prizes, including…'" Emily's voice trailed off and she turned toward Amanda, whose stunned look had to match her own.

"What the…?"

Emily shifted the paper and saw that there was a handwritten note: "'Emily, please stop by and I'll treat you to some more halibut, un-less of course hot dogs are more your thing? Hope to see you there, Bering.'"

"Amanda, you didn't say anything to Tag about our hot-dog booth, right?"

"Emily, no, absolutely not. I only made calls to Glacier City. I arranged for every-thing to be delivered early Saturday morn-ing, so it's not even like someone could have seen something…"

For the first time since this battle had begun, Emily felt her temper stir in earnest. How in the world had he discovered this? She was going to look like an idiot passing out hot dogs next to his fish-and-chips. She tamped down her angst and tried to think. It was very well played; she had to give him that. Ex-cept for this little dose of braggadocio that he hadn't been able to resist… Because, as Franklin had taught her, and any good general knew, you never revealed your battle strategy before the battle was fought.

THE DAY OF THE FESTIVAL turned out to be a stunning display of winter—cold but clear and sunny. And as Bering strolled down the street that headed toward the waterfront, he took his time enjoying the view. A fresh skiff of snow blanketed the landscape and made the blue of the sky even more vibrant than usual.

The winter festival was an annual event that had started a few years back by a group of local businesses, clubs and artisans. Vendors sold food, local crafts and artwork, and merchants offered free samples or handed out information advertising their products or services. The event had grown tremendously the past few years due to the ice-carving competition, which had begun to increase in popularity and now drew people from all over the state. This year was looking to be the best turnout ever. It was a great way to bring in some revenue during the winter, which was traditionally a slower time for Rankins.

Vendors had been setting up since early that morning, and as Bering neared the spot where he knew Cam-Field's booth was supposed to be, he was surprised to see no activity there. There was a trailer in its place, so he figured someone must be busy in there boiling hot dogs.

He grinned as he thought about how he'd managed this coup. His cousin Shay, who ran the Faraway Inn, had called him a couple days ago. She was going to be operating a booth promoting both the Faraway Inn and Bering's guide business. They'd been chatting about it and she'd mentioned that her friend Susan, who was a teacher at the high school, was helping with the booth for the PTA. They'd planned on selling hot dogs to raise money but were thinking of changing to donuts because they were having a hard time finding enough buns. Shay had called her supplier in Glacier City, who was also the supplier for both the Cozy Caribou and Top Rock Café in town. Nobody, it seemed, could get hot-dog buns until Monday or Tuesday—after the festival.

Shay had thought that was odd and had mentioned it to her friend Darlene, who was in charge of the placement of the booths at the fair, where she'd learned exactly who had purchased every hot-dog bun in Glacier City.

Bering admired Emily's creativity. He had to admit it was a good idea to insert herself into the community in this way—and with free food no less. He and Shay had quickly called a meeting of the Save Rankins Coalition. Shay had reserved a spot for their use and drawn up the brochure. Then members of the coalition had begun distributing them around town. It was perfect—who would want to eat a hot dog when they could have fish-and-chips? But even better than that, it would look as if Emily had stolen the free-food idea from them.

He hadn't been able to help himself—he'd just had to send Emily a brochure. Bering imagined how annoyed she must have been when she'd opened the envelope and read his invitation. He nearly laughed aloud at the thought. But how upset could she get? She was the one who had assured him of her professionalism.

He loved this town. In spite of the fact that people often knew your business (or thought they did) and the rumor mill ground strong, it was worth it. And, as proven by today's victory, often those close connections came in quite handy.

The ice carvers had already started, so Bering slowly wound his way toward the water's edge, where they had set up that morning. He figured that was why there was such a crowd down there already. But as he neared the location, he could see that a throng of people were gathered around something else. It looked like…flames?

A fire pit?

He glimpsed a female figure bustling around the tables that had been placed around its perimeter. Emily? What was she doing? Serving something…but it didn't look like hot dogs, unless she was serving them out of cups. As he continued studying the scene, the crowd parted enough for him to spot a brightly painted banner that read Brats and Brew Courtesy of Cam-Field Oil & Mineral.

All he could do was gape as he took in the scene: cozy-looking flames burning in a huge rock-encased fire pit, delectable smells wafting from its direction, people crowded around talking and laughing, eating and drinking, courtesy of Cam-Field. And with a smiling and charming and witty Emily mingling with them all.

He heard a rustle and looked down to see that his cousin Shay was standing beside him. She crossed her arms over her chest and didn't say a word. They watched in silence for a few moments.

"Free beer?" Bering finally asked. "She's giving away free beer?"

"No. Not free beer, Bering—free Grizzly Quake microbrew. You know how long the line was to get into Grizzly Quake Pub the last time I was in Glacier City?" She quickly answered her own question, "Three hours. And now here it is, right here in Rankins—and free no less. And bratwurst from Cowen and Co.—your choice of moose, caribou or good old-fashioned pork. They come already cooked but you can get them served with these cool metal roasting sticks—made by Kella Jakobs."

Bering knew Kella Jakobs. She was a local artist who specialized in metal sculpture. Her work was in very high demand. He owned some of her pieces himself. He imagined that by the look of things, she was probably doing a booming business at her booth today.

Shay continued, "So you can crisp your dog if you want to—over the fire pit. The roasting sticks are for sale if you want to keep one, which everyone does, so they can roast their giant-size handmade marshmallows, too. That's what's in those bins over there." She pointed toward yet another crowd off to one side.

Bering looked over but didn't say a word.

"We've been beaten at our own game, Bering."

"I see that, Shay."

"How did they put this together so quickly?"

Bering had to hand it to Emily. He never would have believed she could counter this well and so quickly. Not only was she obviously resourceful, she was also extremely creative—and downright industrious. And he had to own the fact that it was due partly to his own mistake, too. He'd underestimated his opponent yet again and tipped his hand. He should never have sent her that invitation…. But how could he possibly have imagined that she would throw this…this…neighborhood bonfire party in response?

Bering glanced down at Shay. "How are we doing with the fish-and-chips?"

"Pfft," she scoffed. She pointed at the ground. "I'm standing here, aren't I? I told two of the girls they could go home already. I caught Tag eating over here about an hour ago, and when I asked him what he thought he was doing, he said that he can have fish-and-chips anytime he wants at the Caribou, but Cowen's moose brats he can only get in Glacier City."

Bering shook his head, his appreciation for Emily's ingenious scheme growing by the second. "Not to mention the Grizzly Quake…"

"Oh, yeah, the first one is free, then you have to pay. But you should see the cool souvenir pub glass it comes in. I was thinking of buying one myself."

"What are people saying about Cam-Field?"

"They're not saying anything, Bering. That's the problem. What are we going to do?"

Bering's gaze landed on Emily once again.

She looked cold, he thought, as he watched her clench the collar of her jacket tightly together with one hand. She looked up then and their gazes collided. Hers held an unmistakable look of triumph. He tipped his head in acknowledgment and hoped his expression didn't make him out to be a sore loser.

Then she held up a beer. Was that a toast or an invitation? He immediately decided to accept defeat gracefully and take it as the latter.

Bering shrugged a shoulder and answered Shay, "Go have a beer, I guess."

IT WAS SOON CLEAR to Emily that Bering wasn't going to let one defeat, no matter how crushing, decide the war. The Save Rankins Coalition countered with a rally, which Emily had to admit scored him a moderate victory. They marched from one end of town to the other with signs and banners. They handed out anti-Cam-Field literature. They picketed the mayor's office, the homes of the town-council members and, for some reason she didn't quite understand—Emily's office.

She had hot chocolate and coffee from The Top Rock Café and baked goods from the Donut Den delivered to the entire crowd. That quieted their chants of "Cam-Field can't!" and "We don't need your corporate greed!" only long enough for the crowd to scarf down a few maple bars and apple fritters.

Opposition calls, letters and emails came pouring in, although Emily had to laugh at the three who had added thank-you notes for the refreshments Cam-Field had provided during the rally. This town was something else, she thought, politeness and consideration even in the throes of combat.

Emily considered that little show of town devotion as a win on Bering's part, and obviously he did, too, as the coalition scheduled another rally for the following Friday. But Emily had managed to make a few allies of her own and was alerted to the plan.

"Friday night," Emily said to Amanda as she hung up the phone. "That was Piper Davidson from the newspaper."

"Why is Piper on our side?"

"That girl has got aspirations." Emily pointed at herself and added, "She's making connections, and wisely so."

"And it's not just a rally—he's got a guest speaker. Evan Cobb. He's scheduled to give a speech at the high-school gym and then they're going to rally afterward, by candlelight down on the waterfront, to remind everyone of the incredible view of Rankins without Cam-Field's oil platform desecrating the horizon—or some nonsense like that."

"Evan Cobb?" Amanda looked alarmed. They knew Evan Cobb very well. He was a renowned environmentalist and Cam-Field protestor.

"Mmm."

"By candlelight?" she asked.

"Yep, they've got, like, a thousand biodegradable floating-candle things. They're going to float them out into the bay or something. Ugh."

"Yikes."

"He's not even a real scientist," Emily said with annoyance.

"But he's an amazing speaker," Amanda countered. "And we both know that how you say it is almost as important as what you say. And imagine how beautiful all those candles floating out into the bay will be...."

Emily felt the apprehension sink into her along with the silence. She allowed it to take hold—welcomed it. She did some of her best thinking this way—keyed up, wheels spinning...

"We can't let this happen," Amanda finally said.

Emily tapped a finger to her pursed lips in thought. "I know, but we can't counter-picket, because we don't have the numbers. And even a lot of the people who are with us secretly wouldn't support us publicly at this point. And how pathetic would we look down there while they had their pretty candle moment? We can't compete with that."

"Too bad we couldn't call in a snowstorm," Amanda joked. "It would keep Cobb from getting up here and it would smother all those candles."

Emily's eyes darted up to meet hers. "Amanda, that's a great idea."

"Emily, I have the utmost faith in you, but even you have no pull with Mother Nature. You do know that, right?"

"SHAY, CALM DOWN," Bering said into the phone. "She did what?"

"She booked Rushing Tide to perform on Friday at the Cozy Caribou."

"Clark and Ezra Mayfield's band?"

"Yep, and at the Caribou. Why would Tess say yes to that?"

In spite of his annoyance, Bering was impressed. Clark and Ezra Mayfield were Rankins's two most famous hometown-boys-done-well. He had gone to school with the brothers and considered them friends even though they had moved away right after high school to pursue their music careers. They were wildly popular in Alaska, and growing more so around the rest of the country every day. Short of booking two NFL teams to skirmish at the Rankins High School stadium, he couldn't think of anything better to draw attention away from his rally.

"Tess probably didn't know who was behind it. Emily Hollings obviously has connections that reach beyond the oil industry."

"There's no way to counter this one, Bering. We're going to have to call off the rally."

"Yep, that's okay, Shay. We'll reschedule."

"But not with Evan Cobb. That's the only date he had available for months. We only got him by absolute luck—and even then I had to practically promise my firstborn."

"We'll schedule something else. She can't book a band every night for the next month."

"Are you sure about that, Bering? This woman is clearly a force to be reckoned with."

Bering was quickly realizing just how accurate that assessment was. "I'll figure something out," he said, secretly glad to have another opportunity to spend some time with her....

EMILY TOLD HERSELF that her attendance at the concert had nothing to do with the fact that Bering would be there. Laurel, who had alerted her to the fact that the Mayfield boys were going to be in town, had also informed her that they were friends and classmates of hers—and Bering's.

She decided to go, briefly, just to make sure that it was going smoothly. She knew it wouldn't be the best venue for campaigning—not only would people not be in the mood to discuss business, but it would be extremely difficult to do so in the noisy atmosphere anyway.

The music was in full swing when she slipped into the crowd at the Cozy Caribou. She was impressed by the turnout and by the Caribou's transformation. The wall that normally separated the restaurant from the bar had been removed. A stage was set up in the back and tables were scattered around an opening in the middle, which was serving as a dance floor. Twinkle lights had been strategically strung around. It almost looked like a real club one might find in any city, albeit with much more casually attired patrons.

She knew Amanda was already in the middle somewhere with Tag. She spotted Laurel, who had told her she would meet her, near one side of the bar.

"Hey, you made it," Laurel said as she finally managed to wend her way through the crowd.

Emily gestured around her. "This is fantastic."

Laurel nodded knowingly and said, "Tess knows how to throw a party. She owned a nightclub in Seattle years ago. She sold it and moved up here like fifteen years ago. She transforms it like this for special events like parties, or even an occasional wedding."

Emily pointed at the stage. "And these guys are great."

"They are. They are going to be famous someday. I'm sure of it. They are the nicest guys, too—haven't lost that hometown decency that I love about most of our guys."

Someone grabbed Laurel's attention, so Emily turned toward the bar to order a drink and found herself face to chest with Bering.

"Hey," he said.

"Hi." She grinned up at him. "I'm surprised to see you here. Aren't you supposed to be swimming in the bay tonight or something like that?"

He was clearly trying not to smile, though doing a poor job of it. "Our rally was canceled."

"Really? That's too bad. Why?"

"You are something else, do you know that?"

She grinned at him warmly and didn't know what to think. There were sparks of attraction—maybe—in his eyes. "What does that mean?"

"You, I have discovered, are downright clever. And…" His voice trailed off as he folded his arms over his chest and thrummed the fingers of one hand against his biceps.

"Thank you—I think."

"I'm not finished. You might not thank me when I'm done."

"Uh-oh."

"You are also sneaky and sly and under-handed, and clearly you are getting help from one or more traitorous townsfolk."

"I like sneaky and sly. They both imply intelligence and ingenuity."

"Both of which you obviously possess—in excess."

His look was appreciative and Emily felt herself warm at the compliment, even though she still wasn't sure if it was supposed to be such. "As to underhanded, how is this different than what you did to me—or attempted to do to me—at the winter festival?"

"Well…I have righteousness on my side."

She scoffed. "I have economic growth on my side."

"Which is fine in and of itself, but at what cost?"

He suddenly looked way too serious and Emily didn't want to spoil the mood by engaging in a fruitless conversation. She skirted the subject. "You obviously have spies, too."

"Emily, the whole town is on my side. This place is full of spies. Look around you."

She did, but she didn't see anything that hinted at overt surveillance. "Looks like everyone is having a really good time to me."

"That they are—thanks to you."

She cocked her head and looked up at him. "Even you?"

He bent his head until his lips were nearly even with her ear. Emily inhaled sharply as his warm breath caused a shiver to erupt along her skin.

"Yes, Emily, especially me..."

THE NEXT WEEK was more of the same. The Save Rankins Coalition held a meeting on Tuesday, which they opened to the public, and signed up new members. The rally was rescheduled and held on Wednesday evening, but it didn't pack the same punch without the prominent guest speaker. And they took a double hit as the candle thing didn't work out, either, because as Amanda had initially wished for, an unexpected snow flurry blew in. Bering told Emily that his cousin Shay had accused her of paying for some kind of a satellite snow machine to ruin the event. She told Bering to tell his cousin to be careful about giving her ideas....

Shay held a cheese-and-wine tasting at the Faraway Inn on Thursday, where, according to Piper Davidson, Bering, several other local businessmen, prominent citizens and a state representative mingled with the crowd and bashed Cam-Field's environmental record.

But Emily packed her schedule even tighter than the Save Rankins Coalition. She did a presentation for the Women's Club on Monday, one at the VFW meeting on Tuesday and a Q-and-A at the electric co-op on Wednesday. She and Amanda went around town dropping off stacks of new informational brochures on Thursday. And in between them all, she had appointments with citizens, lunch with the mayor and the planning commissioners, and dinner with the president of the Chamber of Commerce and two board members from the local Building Contractors Association.

Neither side planned anything for Friday

because they both knew the Rotary Club dinner was scheduled for Saturday, and that tended to take up a lot of the town's time and attention. Emily called that day an open house and invited townspeople to wander in at their leisure and look over the photos and literature. They were surprisingly busy and Emily felt as if the mood in the town was finally shifting solidly—in her favor.

CHAPTER EIGHT

EMILY AND AMANDA spent most of the day on Saturday, the day of the Rotary fund-raising, dinner at the office. The phones were eerily quiet, though, and email was nearly nonexistent. The whole town seemed to be abuzz with excitement. Emily had intended to run a few errands on her way home only to find signs on the grocery store, the drugstore and the bakery informing patrons that they'd closed early because of the event. The parking lot of the beauty shop, however, was overflowing.

Emily and Amanda went home to change and freshen up, and then arrived at the VFW hall a few minutes early, but it already appeared as if the whole town had indeed turned out for the event. The highlight of the night, she soon learned, was the fund-raising auction. A long series of tables running along one side of the room contained all the items and/or a description of the item to be auctioned. Community members, clubs and local businesses from all over the borough, and even the state, had made donations. Emily was impressed by the number and variety of goods and services on the roster: everything from exotic vacations and expensive excursions, to fishing and hunting equipment, Native crafts, a brand-new ATV and a gorgeous cedar-strip canoe, which to Emily looked more like a work of art than a boat.

Emily noted that some of the most enthusiastic pre-auction buzz seemed to be over two guided outings generously donated by James Guide and Outfitter Service. She moseyed over toward the display and picked up a brochure. Her brows raised in surprise as she looked at the retail price of one of his trips. Laurel hadn't been exaggerating Bering's success or his likely impact on the community. She had to admit that the wildlife excursions sounded kind of fun....

"Thinking of taking a boat ride?" the man beside her asked as he gestured toward the photo display.

Emily looked up and into the prettiest pair of green eyes that she'd ever seen on a man. A quick glance revealed that the rest of him was equally as attractive. "It sounds like a lot of fun," she said. "Have you ever been?"

"Absolutely, it's a blast."

"Is it worth the price?"

"Totally. Bering is the best. The only thing better would be a sightseeing tour in my Cessna 185." He handed her a brochure.

Emily introduced herself with an outstretched hand. "I'm Emily Hollings."

"I know," he said, gripping her offered hand. His face held an enigmatic grin. " Jiminy Blackburn."

Jiminy? She repeated silently. *You've got to be kidding me.* It was a good thing the guy was so incredibly good-looking. "Nice to meet you, Jiminy."

He chuckled and said, "I know you're thinking about the cartoon cricket."

"Well, I certainly wouldn't have been crass enough to mention it," Emily said with a grin, appreciating his candor.

"Please call me Jim—or Cricket. Most of my friends call me Cricket, and I definitely think we should be friends. Nice article in the paper the other day," he said, before she could comment. "I bet that got Bering all riled up." He added a bark of laughter and looked absolutely delighted with the prospect.

"Thank you. Except that it wasn't my intention to get Mr. James riled up—what I was trying to do is illustrate to the entire community the benefits of Cam-Field's proposed presence here."

"Hey, you're preaching to the choir." He placed one palm flat on his chest. "I'm on your side. And even better," he said, lowering his voice to a conspiratorial whisper that to Emily felt a little flirtatious, "I'm on the tourism board *and* the town council. And seriously, I'd be happy to take you up anytime." He gestured at the brochure she was still holding.

"Thank you," she said. "I just may take you up on that one of these days. What are you going to be bidding on tonight, Cricket?"

"Emily—" he looked aghast "—I most certainly cannot reveal that information."

"Oh? And why is that?"

"Because then you'll bid it up."

"Ah, I see," she said with a chuckle. "Is that how this works, then?"

"It is indeed. Just wait and see how cutthroat this thing can be. People end up paying three, four, five—ten times—what these items are worth just to beat out someone else. Two years ago Mayor Calder was bidding on a two-week condo stay in Cancun when…"

BERING WATCHED THE EXCHANGE between Emily and Cricket Blackburn from across the room and heard the warning bell go off in his head. The biggest womanizer in the entire state of

Alaska was standing way too close to Emily and undoubtedly plying her with his best lines. Bering felt an unfamiliar pang jab him as he watched Cricket reach out and touch her shoulder. And when he leaned over and whispered in her ear, Bering was overcome with the urge to walk over and scoop Emily up in his arms, and carry her out the door.

What in the world was wrong with him? He knew very well that she was more than capable of taking care of herself, so why did he feel the need to look out for her at the same time? Emily was tough; he knew that. He only had to think about how she'd bounced back after their first meeting as proof of that. She was also brave, taking on this town like she was—taking on him like she was. She was also clever and funny, and he liked how she constantly kept him guessing what she'd come up with next. She seemed to be making friends right and left if her socializing here tonight was any indication, not to mention the connections that had somehow enabled her to ferret out many of the coalition's plans.

All of this combined made him wonder why she couldn't see this situation in the way that he did. Was her job really that important to her? So much so that it blinded her to what was really important in life? Maybe that was the answer: maybe he needed to show her what really mattered....

He tensed as he watched his friend slide his hand around Emily's elbow and guide her over to the next auction table.

EMILY COULD SEE right through the charming and handsome Cricket Blackburn. Although she found him witty and engaging, she deftly sidestepped his invitation to dinner. Even though she had no professional complications with this man, she just wasn't interested. And from a business standpoint, a quick time-versus-benefit analysis said it would be pointless—he'd already revealed that he was on her side.

But if she were completely honest with herself, Bering was the real reason for her hesitation. If she was going to spend some time with someone in a manner unrelated to work, she realized, she wanted it to be him. She managed to untangle herself from Cricket's attentions and was ready to head over to the bar to get a cold drink when she sensed a presence behind her.

"Having a good time?" A voice tickled the back of her neck as an arm reached around her holding a crystal flute of sparkling liquid.

Emily smiled and turned toward him, enjoying the pleasant tingle that his presence evoked.

"Wine?" he offered.

"Thank you. Bering, I was…" She started to say that she'd been looking for him, but as her eyes swept over him, it was like being blasted by a wave of icy wind. She inhaled a sharp breath. In his tailored slacks and button-down shirt, he looked much closer to the type of businessman she was used to dealing with. And she was suddenly struck by the unsettling notion that maybe he was more like that than she'd realized.

His hair was still long but he'd somehow managed to tame it, and his face was cleanly shaven. Emily wasn't all that surprised to see that flinty hardness in his eyes that she'd become familiar with. In her experience, it meant that he was annoyed. Had she finally managed to get to him? Why did that notion cause her concern? It should make her happy, because if that was the case, it meant that he was worried about the progress she was making.

"See anything you can't live without?" There was an edge in his tone that made her uneasy.

He tipped down the brochure clutched in her hands. She swallowed nervously and tried to muster a playful tone. "There is some really great stuff here. I'm interested in quite a few things, but you certainly seem to be the popular item here tonight."

"Is that so?" he answered flatly. "I think I could make the same claim about you."

She looked at him quizzically.

"Be careful with Cricket Blackburn, Emily."

"What?"

"He's a cad and a womanizer."

It wasn't what she'd been expecting. Emily felt herself grinning with both amusement and relief. "A cad?"

"Emily, I'm not joking. The man has very little respect for women. Look, if you don't believe me, ask around." He gestured around him as if the VFW hall was a courtroom full of witnesses.

"I'm afraid it's too late," she returned soberly.

Bering scowled down at her. "What do you mean?"

She shrugged and hoped it looked nonchalant.

"Emily…" Bering drawled with the same steely tone. "You're not going out with him."

"I'm not? But he invited me on an airplane ride and I already agreed to—"

"An airplane ride?" he interrupted tightly. "I just bet he did. Well, un-agree."

"Bering, I can't do that. It would be rude. Besides, as I'm sure you already know, he's president of the tourism board, and if I can swing the favor of the tourism board…"

"Emily, this isn't about Cam-Field. This is about you and—" He stopped in midsentence and Emily couldn't help but wonder if he'd been about to add *me* to the end of that statement. That thought caused warmth to bloom from somewhere deep inside her.

"—and I want you to be careful."

"Careful? You think he'd hurt me?"

"No, not exactly," he said irritably. "We're getting off the point here."

"What is the point exactly? Is he a bad pilot?"

"No, he's an excellent pilot. He actually flies clients for me sometimes. But he's also a womanizer—that's my point."

"You mentioned that already."

"Then listen to what I'm telling you."

"I'm trying, Bering. But all I've heard is that he's a womanizing cad, which I think is redundant."

Bering huffed out an exasperated breath. "Emily—"

"He said you were a friend of his."

"I am."

"Can't wait to meet the rest of your friends."

"Emily, he is a good friend of mine. That's a fact. But it's also a fact that he's known for his callous disregard for women's feelings."

"Callous disregard?" Emily snickered through her hand.

"Emily," he said again with obvious and forced patience, "I can see that you're not taking me seriously here, but all I'm trying to do is look out for your best interests…."

"Is that what you're doing?" A spike of happiness shot through her as she realized that if he was looking out for her then he wasn't letting this business get to him like she'd feared.

He shrugged. "Yes, I'm warning you about him and—"

"Bering," she interrupted and to her surprise he stopped talking. She looked around them to make sure no one was listening. She crooked her finger so he'd bend toward her. "What I was going to say before you interrupted me is that all I agreed to do was to give a presentation to the tourism board."

Was that a blush she saw rising up his neck? Hmm.

"Oh," he said.

"But thank you for trying to watch out for me. I really do appreciate it."

"Um, yeah, I..."

"Bering, I'm so glad that we can be civil in the midst of all this—"

"Civil? Emily, I want—"

The look on his face, the tone of his voice, had Emily holding her breath....

The sound of Amanda calling out to her took the place of whatever he was going to say. She turned her head and waved, held up a finger to let her know she'd be right there. But when she turned back, his face was a mask of steely composure. She wanted to ask him what he wanted, but she knew the moment had passed.

"Let me walk you to your seat. The auction is about to start."

A COUPLE HOURS later, Emily had purchased a haircut (for herself), five swing-dance lessons (for Amanda) and a five-course fish dinner for two from the Cozy Caribou (she was thinking of inviting Bering). And now she was seriously considering bidding on one of Bering's wildlife excursions. It would make a perfect birthday gift for her brother, Aidan.

Aidan would like Bering, she decided as her mind wandered toward her half brother, and he'd love it here in Rankins, too. She hadn't spoken to him in weeks, and she'd only received a few emails, which wasn't all that unusual for him when he was on one of his research expeditions. But she always missed the contact, and she would have loved to have had him to talk to while she'd been going through this whole ordeal with Jeremy and Franklin.

Aidan was her only family member that she felt even remotely close to. And they hadn't even grown up together. He had been raised by his bohemian mother on the southern coast of Oregon. His mother had seen to it that he visited often, for Christmas, two weeks every summer and for the occasional long weekend. Emily had been allowed to visit him in Oregon, too, and one time when she'd been in high school on her spring break. He'd been in college in Hawaii at the time, studying plant life on the Big Island. It had been one of the greatest times of her life: hanging out on the beach with her cool big brother, hiking, snorkeling and playing in the surf.

She wondered if Bering had ever been to Hawaii....

He would like it, she decided. With his curiosity about wildlife and his appreciation for nature, it would be intriguing to explore the exotic locale with him. He was sitting at the next table and she tried not to stare when he removed his jacket and placed it on the back of his chair. She recalled him talking about all the things he liked to do in his spare time. She hadn't even been able to name one thing. How pathetic was that? It made her long to find something she liked to do in her spare time, which would be easier if she ever had any. She did like to draw. That was something. Although…why didn't she ever have any spare time? Bering obviously juggled a successful business and family and…spare-time-fun activities. Even her stepfather had hobbies. Suddenly Emily felt cheated….

"Em, are you paying attention?" Amanda was saying in a low voice.

"I'm sorry, what?"

"Are you watching this?"

"No, I'm, uh—I was just, um, thinking… What's going on?" She tuned back into her surroundings and noticed the heightened murmur of the crowd.

Amanda whispered, "There appears to be a bidding war going on."

"Oh, that's nice."

"Yeah, and it's over your sketch."

"My sketch?" Emily asked, her voice rising several decibels. "Not, the one of the town—"

"Shh," Amanda said and then began whispering quickly. "Don't be mad—promise you won't be mad?"

"Amanda!"

"Okay, okay, someone from the Rotary Club came by last week, right? To solicit donations for the auction. And we, uh, I didn't even know about it, so I didn't have anything prepared, but the woman saw it sitting on my desk and, well, she loved it, so I…"

"Amanda," she gritted out through clenched teeth. "How could you? It's not good enough for something like this. I mean—"

"It is too good enough, Emily. The bidding is going crazy. You should be flattered."

"Amanda, I'm going to kill you—"

"Shh, Emily, shut it. I can't hear what's going on."

Emily sat back to watch the action unfold. As it turned out, the item was indeed a hot ticket. But she was relieved to learn that Amanda hadn't donated it in her name, but in Cam-Field's, and she hadn't signed the drawing. So she calmed down as she realized that no one would know that she'd done it.

The bidding continued until the only two remaining bidders were Bering and an older gentleman sitting at a table near the front of the room. Finally the other man raised his paddle for the last time. Bering lifted his hand to acknowledge the cheers and applause. His eyes locked on Emily's and his face broke into an enigmatic smile. Did he somehow know that she'd drawn it? Emily tried to quell her nervousness and smiled in return.

Later, after the conclusion of the auction, Emily had gathered her winnings, including her coupon for the wildlife excursion she'd won, and was scanning the room for Amanda when she saw Bering sauntering toward her.

A hitch of anxiety tightened her chest as she noticed he had the framed drawing tucked under his arm.

"Did you have a good time tonight?" he asked.

"I really did," she said enthusiastically. "It's been a lot of fun. And wow—what a turnout."

"It's always like this. Rankins has always had a strong sense of community spirit."

"What a wonderful way to live," Emily commented and was startled to recognize how true it was. Her words were similar to ones she'd uttered hundreds of times over the years, but now she felt different as she said them. The magic of the evening had somehow enabled her to really imagine living in a close-knit community like this.

Because, she realized with a start, for the first time in her life, she'd begun to consider a life outside Cam-Field. Was this honestly something she would like? Community fund-raisers, long hours spent sketching the local scenery and spending time with the most incredible man to be found within a few thousand miles? She almost laughed aloud at the thought. But it couldn't be any more drastic than the cruise-ship idea she'd been mulling around in her brain. Emily wondered if she was possibly experiencing some type of precursor to a full-blown nervous breakdown. Maybe this was what all the trade magazines were warning about when they referred to executive burnout.

"This," Bering said softly, turning the sketch for her to see, "this is what I'm trying to save. Emily, think about how this is all going to change if Cam-Field gets its claws in here. You're doing a great job of making people think about how much better their lives could be if they only had more. But what about this?" He pointed at her drawing. "What about what they already have, and what about the ways Rankins would suffer in the process of Cam-Field's so-called improvements?"

"Bering, I..." Emily opened her mouth to tell him that she was the one who'd drawn it, but as she looked into his face, the sincerity and raw emotion she saw halted her words. She realized that he was trying to appeal to her emotions, which had been attempted plenty of times over the years and was usually the most effective tactic the opposition employed—more effective even than economics. It never worked with her, though, so why did she feel a lump the size of Rhode Island gathering in her throat?

"I'd like you to have this, Emily,"

She squeaked out the words, "What? Why?"

"So that no matter what happens, you can always see Rankins through my eyes—through the eyes of the people here who love this place like I do—just like it is."

"It's… I'm touched, Bering. Thank you. But…"

"But what?"

"But you know that things can't stay the same forever, right? The world changes and it evolves and usually it gets better. Wouldn't you like to see that for Rankins?"

Hardness settled over his features. "Emily, your speeches are wasted on me and you know it. Change is not always for the better. Think about the natural world and how Mother Nature usually takes her sweet time as she evokes major changes. Evolution is a slow process filled with minor adjustments that are a reaction to a creature's immediate environment."

Emily's lifelong Cam-Field training kicked in instinctively as she fired back. "Progress is the advancement of human society, Bering. It's forward movement, it's the betterment of civilization, it's improvement."

He looked away for a second and then met her eyes with a searching look. "Do you believe that? Do you genuinely, in your heart, believe that Rankins will ultimately be better off if Cam-Field comes here and digs it up and paves it over?"

"It doesn't matter what my heart feels, Bering. If Cam-Field doesn't do it, someone else will, and at least Cam-Field will bring good along with the change."

His voice was charged with the same emotion that was reflected in his eyes. "It absolutely does matter what your heart feels, Emily."

She had no idea how to respond to that. It seemed superfluous to point out that this exchange only illustrated the gulf separating them. She felt her hope deflating. She'd been right after all—there was no way for them to manipulate around this situation. They both had too much riding on its outcome. Silence stretched long and heavy between them. Anxiety gnawed at her and she wondered how to make a graceful retreat.

He shook his head and muttered something under his breath. He looked up for a few seconds and then back down at her. "You know what I'm thinking?"

"I couldn't possibly begin to imagine," she said. In fact, what she imagined was that he, too, was finally realizing how impossible this was and he was going to tell her to take a hike. The thought of having Bering as a full-blown enemy instead of the frenemy that he was now filled her with something close to despair. She would miss this—she would miss him....

"A cease-fire."

"Hmm?" Her heart leaped in response to what she thought she'd heard....

"I would like to call a cease-fire—a one-day reprieve from this...craziness." He gestured toward the coupon she'd won. "Take a ride with me tomorrow and cash that in. I'd like to show you some of what I love about this place. Things you can't see by just walking around town. Things that are even more amazing than what this sketch captures ."

"Bering, that sounds lovely, but I can't. I have to work. I have too much to do—"

She stopped herself as it occurred to her that only minutes ago she'd been pondering the notion of taking some time to discover what she liked outside her job. Why couldn't she learn to manage both work and play like other people did? Bering seemed to be pretty good at it. And she liked that about him—envied it. How better to learn such a concept than from someone who had seemingly mastered it? The idea was too tempting to resist.

"You know what? I will," she said happily, "but this had better be some excursion. Did you see how much I had to pay for this?"

CHAPTER NINE

EMILY WAS READY and waiting when Bering arrived the next morning, and inwardly unsettled by how much she was looking forward to their outing. She tried to tell herself that she needed to maintain her distance, stay detached, hold on to her objectivity…but another part of her wanted to wholeheartedly embrace this cease-fire and let her feelings guide her. It was not a concept she was familiar with.

She opened the door before he had a chance to knock. He'd told her to dress warmly, so she'd donned silk leggings under her fine-gauge wool slacks, and a snug turtleneck beneath a thick peacoat. Her feet were encased in expensive and fashionable ankle-high boots. Bering stopped when he was about three feet from her. He had the cutest scowl on his face. Emily wondered what was wrong at the same time that she hoped he wasn't going to cancel.

He placed his gloved hands on his hips as

his eyes traveled up and down the length of her, and then back up and down again. "I thought I told you to dress warmly," he finally said.

"I did." She glanced down at her outfit and then shifted her gaze back up to meet his. "I am."

"It's five degrees out here."

"Yeah, I know, it's really cold." She stood outside the doorway shivering.

Bering looked up at the star-studded sky and muttered a stream of mostly incoherent words, although Emily made out *ridiculous* and *city girl*. Then he looked at her. "Emily," he drawled, "would you step out here with me for a second?"

"Sure, let me grab my bag and we can get going."

"No, no, we're not leaving yet. Shut the door and come over here for a minute."

Emily obliged, walking with careful steps across the icy sidewalk. For some inexplicable reason, the pathway to her front door seemed to constantly be frozen into a solid sheet of ice. She'd noticed that other places she went they didn't have this problem. She made a mental note to ask Bering about it. Unfortunately, her shoes always seemed to make matters worse. She was wearing boots now, so that should be helpful, but they didn't seem to be doing much good on the—

"Woo!" she shrieked as she slipped and nearly fell—would have fallen if Bering hadn't reached out and held on to her.

"Whoa," he said.

"Whoa," she echoed, gripping his hard shoulders for balance. "Hi," she said and grinned up at him. Her heart picked up its pace as he held her firmly until she was steady.

"Okay," he said, keeping his hands resting lightly on her upper arms. "Now, are you cold?"

Emily looked around as if deciding how to correctly answer the obvious question. "Uh, yes, of course I am. It's freezing out here. I thought we'd already been over that."

Bering looked down at her. "You've been outside for a total of what, thirty seconds? And you're already cold. So, tell me, exactly how does this," he said and nodded at her, "constitute dressing warmly?"

Emily frowned at him. "Hey, this stuff is supposed to be top quality. I ordered it online before I came up here."

"I'm sure it's fine for a stroll down the block on a chilly night in Southern California, but it's not appropriate for the outdoors of Alaska. I should have thought of this. Do you have anything else?"

Emily thought for a second. She shook her head. "Uh-uh. This is all my warmest stuff."

"Okay, come on." Bering grabbed her hand and pulled her toward the house. Emily's feet slipped completely out from underneath her this time. He caught her and scooped her up in his arms as if she weighed nothing more than a sack of flour. He carried her into the house, barely pausing in his stride to open the door. He set her down and shut the door behind them.

He strode purposefully toward the kitchen, picked up the phone and dialed. *My sister,* he mouthed and pointed at the receiver. "Janie! Hi! No, no, I'm not calling to cancel. I'll be there. Of course not. Yeah, that sounds fine." He was silent for a second before he spoke. "Can I say something? I'm calling for a reason here." He listened again for a second. "Hey, now, that's a little harsh, isn't it? Are you busy? Right now. Okay, I'm coming over. I need to borrow some things. Did you finish the...uh? You did? Great, okay, see you in a few."

He turned toward Emily. "We are going to make a quick stop on the way."

Bering's sister lived in a large gray-and-white painted two-story home just a few miles from Emily's rented duplex. Bering informed her that it was on the way to his place anyway, where his business was based and where they would ultimately be departing from.

Janie opened the door and Emily saw instantly that she was a smaller, red-haired version of her brother. She had the same engaging smile that Bering had, and although there wasn't quite the same spark about her, Emily felt immediately drawn to her. She was obviously pregnan,t and Emily could see the tension on her face and the purple tinge beneath her eyes. Bering had mentioned on the short drive over that grief and a difficult pregnancy were taking their toll. Emily found herself wanting to offer comfort in some small way.

"It's nice to meet you finally, Emily. Bering has talked about you a lot."

"You, too, Janie. And I'd be willing to bet that what I've heard about you is far better than what you have heard about me."

Janie opened her mouth, then shut it and laughed. "You have been causing a bit of a stir around here. I'm not gonna lie."

"Well, we are trying to put that aside for the day while I collect on the trip that I won at the auction last night. In fact, I'm glad we stopped by here. Now there's a witness in case I fly off the back of this snow-machine thing and Bering changes his mind and leaves me in a snowbank."

BERING WATCHED THE INTERACTION between Emily and his sister with both relief and satisfaction. It was good to see Janie laugh. She didn't do it enough these days. She tried to stay strong for the boys, but he knew how much she struggled. At first, Bering had been so worried about her that he'd sought professional advice. He'd learned that the grieving process had to run its course. But still, he worried. He tried to spend as much time with her and his nephews as he could.

As Janie gave Emily pieces of winter gear to try on, they talked and laughed as if they'd known each other for years. Janie cracked up when Emily made a joke about how unattractive the fluffy winter clothing was. "It's like marshmallow puff and overstuffed comforter conspired together…"

Emily had a way with people, Bering thought, and with her intelligence and easy charm, he suspected that she could have been successful at nearly any profession she chose. And why the oil and gas industry? He imagined that she could be so much happier in a position where her job entailed making people happy rather than trying to smooth over their anger. It was obvious to him that she wasn't really happy—not deep down where it counted. He'd seen it when she had been in the hospital, and although she had been adept at hiding it since, he knew it was there. He wondered if she even realized it.

When Emily was suitably outfitted, Janie bundled all the gear into a duffel bag. As they were leaving, Janie handed him a small gift bag. "Don't forget this," she said.

"Thank you," Bering said and then they made arrangements for his upcoming baby-sitting session.

"Tuesday night?" Emily asked as they solidified the details. "Can I help?"

"You don't have to do that," Janie said. "Bering is used to it. He does it all the time."

"I know, but I'd really like to pay you back in some way for letting me borrow these things."

Something stirred within him when Emily made the offer. He sensed that Emily wanted to do something to help his sister, and that meant a lot on one level, but even more on another because he knew that there wasn't anything she could gain for Cam-Field by helping him babysit.

Janie looked questioningly at Bering.

He shrugged. "Hey, if she wants to help…"

After Bering had arrived home the night before, he'd spent a good part of the evening thinking about the conversation they'd had after he'd given Emily the drawing. The brief interchange had left them both tense. Two weeks of campaigning had proven that they were miles apart professionally, but things seemed to be completely different on a personal level.

Was he a fool to believe that they could somehow keep this campaign from interfering in their relationship? For the day, yes, he believed they could, but what if he wanted more than this one day? And something was telling him that this one day with Emily would never be enough.

As they drove out of town, Bering talked about his family and how devastating the loss of Janie's husband, Cal, had been. They had married the year after Janie had graduated from high school and within the next three years they'd had Gareth and Reagan. She had been a married mother of two by the time she was twenty-one, but Janie had made it look easy. Everything had always come easy to her, Bering explained. She was beautiful, outgoing and one of those people who seemed to be good at everything she attempted.

He recalled how Janie had often mentioned how happy she was that Cal wasn't a fisherman like their father had been. How his work as a logger, while dangerous, didn't fill her with dread like the thought of him fishing did. And then he'd been killed when the road beneath him gave way, sending the log loader he'd been operating tumbling down a mountainside.

It was obvious to Emily that Bering would do anything for his family. And clearly they needed him. She would do anything for Aidan, but that was different because he didn't need her—not on a daily basis anyway. She thought about her mother and stepfather. Her mother seemed too shallow to need anything but money. Franklin had always seemed to need her—at Cam-Field anyway. At least, she'd always felt that way until the promotion. Even that seemed unimportant, though, compared with the role Bering played within his family.

Daylight was arriving as they turned onto a snowplowed tree-lined gravel drive. At the entrance, a huge slab of rock had been carved with the words *James Guide & Outfitter Service*. The property was heavily wooded but they soon drove into a sizable clearing. There was a large attractive building and several smaller outbuildings. One was obviously an office as it was marked as such.

"It's really beautiful here," Emily remarked. "Does the river run through your property?"

"It does," Bering said, "all one hundred and sixty-four acres of it. I'd like to build a house right back there someday." He pointed off in the distance.

"What's in all the buildings?" she asked as they pulled up in front of the largest. It was tall with unpainted but attractive wood siding.

"Boats, vehicles, equipment," he said as he hit a switch on the visor. A door opened and he efficiently turned the pickup around and backed into the open bay. "If it's okay with you, I'm not going to take you on my usual guided tour. This one will be better and I promise you'll get your money's worth."

She agreed and hopped out of the vehicle. The building was full of more sporting equipment than Emily had ever seen outside a store. There were two more pickups, ATVs, snow machines, boats and inflatable rafts. Tools, equipment and fishing poles hung on the walls. The place appeared neat and tidy, though—full but organized. Emily didn't doubt that Bering could find whatever he needed in an instant.

They removed the outerwear that they'd packed earlier and began putting it on, Bering instructing her on some of the finer points, like making sure her gloves were pulled over her sleeves and that her socks weren't bunched into the bottom of her boots.

"Oh, I almost forgot," he said. He walked back to the pickup and retrieved something from the backseat. She recognized the bag as the one Janie had given him just before they'd left her house.

"Here," he said, handing it to her. "This is for you to keep. Janie made it. She knits things—hats and scarves and mittens and stuff. She doesn't have any red hats right now but she said she'd make you one if you like this."

Emily reached in and removed the fluffy softness. She pulled it through her fingers. "Like it? I love it." She felt something at one end and looked down to find a small ivory-colored button had been sewn onto it. She examined it closely and discovered it had a wolf drawn on it. It was like a tiny work of art. She assumed it must be Janie's signature of some sort.

"Bering, thank you." She wrapped it around her neck and pulled it snugly into place. "Hmm, is it possible? Have I finally discovered the secret to staying warm here? I doubt I'll ever take it off again." Emily grinned at him but he was staring back at her with a weird look on his face.

"What? Is something wrong?"

"Nope. You, uh, you look nice in red."

"Thank you. It's my favorite."

"I remember."

He'd remembered…? Emily felt a rush of pleasure as she recalled that she had indeed told him her favorite color. "I never get a chance to wear it, though."

"What do you mean? Why?"

"I read one time about this study that was done on how bright colors offend some people and that just wearing a certain color can cause a person to unconsciously dislike or distrust you," she rattled off. "And that, as you can imagine, would be very bad in my business."

She met his baffled stare for a few long seconds.

He shook his head as if he couldn't quite believe it. "That is one of most ridiculous things I've ever heard. Seriously, Emily—top five on the most-ridiculous-of-all-time list."

She opened her mouth to argue and then shut it. Right then it did seem pretty clear to her that it probably was near the top of the over-the-top list of extreme habits she'd adopted in her quest for corporate perfection.

"Yeah, okay, you might be right about that," she conceded. She tugged on the ends of the scarf. "I'm scratching that one starting right now...."

EMILY HAD NEVER ridden on a snow machine before. She stood still as Bering helped her put on a helmet and some goggles. Then he strapped a pack onto the back of the vehicle and climbed on.

"Okay, come on," he said, waving her over.

"Um, what do I do?"

He looked over his shoulder and patted the seat behind him. "Hop on and hold on."

She stepped closer, hoisted her leg over the side and settled on the seat behind him. She wrapped her arms around his waist and Bering started the engine. They took off across the snowy landscape. The wind felt like liquid ice where it swirled under her chin, so she pulled the scarf up higher. Bering's large form blocked most of the wind, and surprisingly, she soon realized she wasn't cold. And the ride was sheer exhilaration.

She loved every minute of it, and after about forty-five minutes, Bering slowed and turned onto a narrow path between the trees. They traveled for several more minutes and then stopped as they neared what appeared to be the edge of a cliff. A tidy-looking cedar-planked cabin sat off to one side. A set of stairs led up to a deck that wound around it, all of which appeared to have been recently shoveled of snow.

"Okay, here we are," Bering said and cut the engine. Emily climbed off. Bering did the same and removed his helmet and then hers. He grabbed her hand and began trudging across the crusty snow.

He stopped suddenly. "There, look." He pointed at the river below, and Emily immediately saw what he was pointing out. A moose, no—she saw two moose. Emily squinted toward them and realized that one of them was actually on the opposite side of the ice-encrusted river. Neither animal bothered to lift a head to even glance their way.

"Doesn't the sound of the snow-thingy bother them?"

"Nah, they're used to it. I come by here quite often on animal surveys."

"Really?" she said.

"Yeah, it's part of my work with the Department of Fish and Game."

"To watch moose?"

Bering nodded and added, "And other critters that frequent these parts."

"Like what?"

"Like caribou and bears and wolves and foxes and various kinds of birds."

"Grizzly bears? Of course there are grizzly bears out here. Why didn't I think of that? They're on your brochure...."

Bering grinned at her obvious discomfort. "Don't worry, they're hibernating right now. They won't be out for another month at least, not till the spring. The sows come out with their cubs and I tell you, you've never seen anything cuter than a bear cub. Have you ever seen one?"

"Um, no," she said and silently hoped that she never did.

"Man, are they cute," he repeated. "And you've never seen anything meaner than a mama bear protecting her cub—except maybe a moose."

"A moose? You're kidding, right?"

Bering shook his head. "Absolutely not. They're vicious when it comes to protecting their calves. Remind me to tell you some stories. Come on." He motioned forward and headed toward the cabin. He produced a key and unlocked the door.

They went inside and Emily looked around the cozy interior. Off to the right there was a small kitchen with a breakfast bar that separated it from the dining area. She saw two doorways, and Bering pointed to one and told her it was the bathroom and the other a bedroom. Straight ahead there was an overstuffed couch and two easy chairs. There was also a telescope on a tripod, which angled down toward the river below.

"I'll be right back," Bering said and exited out the door.

A few minutes later he came back in with a load of firewood piled high in his arms. He dropped down to one knee and placed it next to the woodstove, and before long he'd produced a roaring blaze. Emily was amazed at how quickly it began to warm the interior of the small cabin.

She commented on it as she peeled off her jacket and laid it on one of the chairs. Bering did the same.

She looked out the window to see if she could still see the moose. "Hey, what's that?"

Bering walked to the window and peered over her shoulder. "Ah, I was hoping they'd be back today. That's a wolf. I love wolves. To me, they symbolize so much about Alaska—wild and tough, imposing and beautiful…"

She thought about the button on her scarf. She started to ask him about it but he had leaned over and was adjusting the lens of a spotting scope that was mounted on a tripod in front of the window. "Here," he said, "take a look."

Emily looked through the lens. It seemed so close…almost as though she could reach out and touch it. She could see its frosty breath as it sniffed around the base of a tree. She could pick out the gray-and-brown colors in its fur and was spellbound by the way they swirled and blended together. In an instant, she was completely lost in the sight, and her fingers itched for her sketch pad.

"Where are the rest of them? I thought wolves liked to run around together."

"They do. But they also run around solo sometimes. I recognize that one, and the rest of his pack is down there somewhere. They had moose for lunch yesterday, so if we're patient, we'll probably see more of them coming in for leftovers."

"You recognize him?" she asked.

"Yep, that's CL-42—*Canis lupus* 42 or, as I refer to him, Bob."

"Bob?" she repeated. She studied Bob for

a moment and then asked, "How can you tell for sure it's Bob?"

Bering quickly explained the characteristics that made him unique.

"What do they eat besides moose?"

"Caribou, birds, voles, squirrels, hare, beaver and around here they eat salmon, too."

"Of course," she remarked drily, "even the wolves like seafood in Rankins."

He laughed. "Wolves are actually a lot more opportunistic than most people realize. They hunt, but they also scavenge a lot. Because we have so many salmon spawning in the rivers around here, they will munch on them just like the bears and the birds do— easy pickings for growing puppies."

As they talked, several more wolves did indeed appear, and in only a few minutes Emily could easily identify one individual from another.

Bering then began regaling her with stories about the protective nature of the mother moose. And by the time he finished telling her about the mom who treed the bow hunter and then proceeded to stand vigil for ten hours until help finally arrived, Emily had a new respect for the awkward-looking animal.

Then she became totally absorbed in wolf-watching while Bering prepared a simple meal.

"Hey," he said sometime later.

Emily started and turned toward him. "Sorry. I've got my very own 4-D animal documentary going on here. This is amazing. You actually get paid for this?"

"Yep," Bering said. "There's a little more to it than this, but yes."

"Amazing," she repeated. "And don't make fun of me for being a city slicker, but the wolves are so cute it's difficult to imagine how vicious they can be."

"Cute, huh? Are you actually admitting then that there is more to our enclave than ice and snow?"

"Hmm, I suppose," she teased.

Bering leaned over and tilted the scope, turning it away from her. "In that case, you probably don't need this anymore, then?"

Emily reached over and placed her hand on top of his. "No, wait, wait, wait. That's okay. It's not really that bad. I mean, I can suffer through it. It's not like there's anything else to do...."

"No, I'm sorry I forced this on you. First the fish and now the wolves... I can only imagine how boring it must be to a cultured sophisticate such as yourself. I'll just—let me just get this out of your way."

"All right, all right, you win. I admit it. I'm

enthralled. With wolves. And moose. And in the snow no less. There, are you happy?"

Bering smiled. "Yes, I am—especially because I know how difficult it was for you to admit it. Just wait until this evening."

Emily's eyes widened with surprise. "What?" she asked, slightly breathless. "We're going to be here tonight?"

"Yes, is that a problem? Don't tell me you have more campaigning to do? We're in the midst of a cease-fire, remember? I get the whole day."

"I remember, Bering," she retorted playfully, "and there's always campaigning to be done. But no, it's not a problem."

The whole day? Emily liked that. There was such an easiness about being with him. Even when they were seemingly at odds, it was usually fun—teasing and exciting and yet somehow comfortable.

She was so used to being in work mode, but Bering somehow shifted her out of that effortlessly. Probably because there was so much depth to him—he loved his work, obviously, but he was so much more than his job. That was all Emily felt she had ever been, and she was coming to realize that it wasn't what she had thought it would be. She wanted to be more than her job, too.

"Good," he said with a long, slow grin. "Lunch is ready."

"Good," she returned and added her own smile. "I'm starving. What are we having?"

"Clam chowder, ham sandwiches, smoked salmon and apples. How does that sound?"

"Well," she replied wryly, "I like ham."

He chuckled and shook his head. "Are you going to argue with me about lunch?"

"I don't know," she said. "Are you going to make me eat something weird?"

"Have I forced you to eat anything weird yet?"

"Yes," she said. "You have. I saw a picture hanging on the wall at the Caribou yesterday and Crab Johnson informed me that it was a halibut. I never would have taken a bite of that fish, Bering, if I'd seen how ugly it was first."

CHAPTER TEN

NOW BERING WAS TELLING her about the college internship he'd done in Alaska's far north studying polar-bear genetics. Emily found it fascinating. Or she would have, she was sure, if she could actually concentrate on what he was saying for any length of time. She couldn't stop thinking about how good she felt—relaxed and stress-free—and how long it had been since she'd felt this way. She couldn't recall. The entire day so far had been great—the snow-machine ride, the cabin, the wildlife. But she knew it was Bering who really made the difference. It wouldn't have mattered what they'd done, she suspected; it would have been like this.

"…and that's how we tag the polar bears," he said, finishing his story.

She took another sip of her coffee, which Bering had made on the woodstove top with a percolator. She had watched in fascination as the pot had hissed and bubbled and a mouth-watering aroma had quickly filled the cabin.

It was piping hot and Emily thought it was the most delicious coffee she'd ever had. It seemed ridiculous that she often spent five dollars for a cup of coffee back at home—coffee that didn't even compare to the richness of this frontier-style home brew. The thought made her smile. Almost everything seemed different here, she was coming to realize, in a good way.

"Bering, thank you again for bringing me out here. It really is… It's incredible."

"I'm glad you like it."

"I suppose this is part of the job for you, though, huh? Showing tourists like me around?"

Bering smiled and turned toward her, sliding one arm along the back of the couch. "Sort of, but you are much more fun than most of the clients I cart around, I can assure you."

Emily raised a skeptical brow. "Really? Laurel told me you have some pretty interesting and, uh, high-profile clientele."

"Laurel exaggerates."

"No, she doesn't. She's an excellent reporter."

"That's true. She is. We've had a few celebrity types, I guess."

"You don't seem too impressed."

"Clients are all the same to me. I mean, I treat them all the same. I try to give each and every one the absolute best wilderness experience that they ask for. And every guest gets the same amount of respect and privacy. I really don't think about what they do for a living while they're here."

"I believe that about you." And she did. She couldn't imagine there was much superficial about a person that would impress Bering.

"Good. It's true. So I should also tell you that this really isn't part of the job."

"What's that?"

He pointed back and forth between them. "Coming out to my cabin—I don't bring clients out here. It's only for family and friends. I have other cabins for clients."

"Oh." Her heart picked up its pace. "So…" She felt as if something was melting inside her as he stared into her eyes. Her blood seemed to warm and a tightness swirled in her stomach. Attraction, yes—she'd felt that almost since the beginning—but it was so much more than that. She felt content, yet edgy and excited at the same time. She couldn't believe how addictive the sensation was becoming. She wished she could feel it all the time. Was that even possible?

What would it be like to spend every day

with a man like this? No, not a man like this, she corrected herself, but this man in particular.

BERING WANTED TO kiss her. He'd been thinking about it since she slipped that scarf around her neck. Who was he kidding? He'd thought about it long before that. Had resisted for so many good reasons…but suddenly all those reasons why he hadn't, why he shouldn't, flew right out of his mind…. The way she was staring at him couldn't be anything but an invitation. And after all, they were in the middle of a truce….

He found himself leaning toward her, studying her face, trying to read her emotions, which seemed, incredibly, to be mirroring his own. She wanted this, too; he was sure of it. He watched her eyelids fall as his lips neared hers.

"Cease-fire," he whispered as he slowly closed the rest of the distance.

He slipped the fingers of one hand around the back of her neck, entwining them in her silky hair. The other curved around her shoulder. She scooted closer and wrapped her arms around him. He groaned quietly and lost himself in the kiss, in the feel of her soft lips against his, in her eager response.

Bering wasn't prepared for the flood of emotions that were overtaking him. It wasn't just his body telling him he wanted her; it was his heart telling him he needed her. And that was something he'd never felt for any woman. This was what he'd been waiting for...this was why he'd never invited any other woman into his cabin, into his life. But along with this realization came another: Emily was not the woman he should be having these feelings for. She was not the woman he could have these kinds of feelings for.

He pulled away and took a deep breath, trying to get a grip. He sat back and brushed a hand over his mouth, but it only made him recall the sensation of her lips pressing eagerly against his.

"Bering, this feels like more than a cease-fire. Maybe we should—"

He ruffled a hand through his hair in frustration. "Emily, I'm so sorry. I shouldn't have done that. I know this is just confusing things even more...." And all he wanted to do as he looked into her wide, questioning eyes was kiss her again. What kind of an idiot fell for the one woman he cuoldn't possibly have?

EMILY STARED AT BERING as he tried to explain why kissing her had been such a huge mistake. She watched his lips moving, but she couldn't make sense of it—not in any meaningful way. She had reacted to his kiss without thinking and she hadn't recognized herself. One kiss from this man had made her feel more alive than she ever had in her entire life.

Pleasure like she'd never imagined in a simple kiss. It had been as if something that she hadn't even known was missing was suddenly there, like the combination to some secret lock had finally clicked into place. And it had opened the door to reveal feelings she hadn't even known existed within her. How could she not have known that she needed something so vital?

It was just proof that where Bering was concerned she really had no control over her emotions and apparently very little over her actions, as well. Out-of-work-mode Emily seemed to enjoy a lot more of life than work-mode Emily had even anticipated. That partly alarmed her, she thought, but strangely that also comforted her. Because for the first time in her life, she didn't have to think about something, plan something or organize something—she just knew it was right.

And now Bering was telling her that it was all wrong?

How could that be? He was the one who had told her that this Cam-Field business didn't matter. He had done a fine job of proving that concept was, in fact, possible. So why couldn't they be more?

She liked the cease-fire. Couldn't they just extend that for…like…indefinitely? Of course, she knew that wasn't possible, but she also would never have believed that the feelings she had for him were possible, either. Wasn't love supposed to conquer all or at least lessen the obstacles along the path to romance? Not that they were in love, but… Clearly she needed to rein in her feelings, but she didn't think she could stop them now if she tried. It would be like trying to stop a freight train with her bare hands.

She stared at him as he looked back at her and she thought for a moment that the truce would hold and he would kiss her again.…

He stood abruptly. "Come on," he said, "let's take a hike. We'll be out of daylight soon."

Emily blinked in surprise. "A hike? What? How? The snow is three feet deep."

"I'll show you."

A SHORT TIME later, Emily decided that snowshoeing with Bering, while fun and exhilarating, was not in the same league as kissing Bering. It was really hard work. Bering obviously slowed his pace for her sake. She wanted to remind him that she wasn't supposed to be working today, although she had the feeling that this didn't seem like work to him. They took a trail that followed the bluff along the river. The scenery was spectacular and it almost made her forget how difficult the hike was.

After what felt like miles, but wasn't as she could still see the cabin when she looked behind them, they stopped briefly to enjoy the view and, Emily suspected, to allow her to rest.

"Are we in any danger of being wolf-packed?" she asked.

His lips turned up into a crooked grin. "Wolf-packed?" He repeated the term.

"Yes," she said, "you know, packed off by hungry wolves—wolf-packed. It's a technical term specific to the wolf-watching industry. I'm surprised you're not familiar with it."

"So am I, and here I thought I knew a lot about wolves."

"Clearly you don't know as much as you thought," she replied knowingly. "And now I'm not sure I trust you to answer my question."

"No," he said, grinning. "We're not in any immediate danger of being wolf-packed."

"Immediate danger?" she repeated skeptically.

"They are a good ways away, they've just eaten and they generally don't hunt people."

"Generally," she repeated wryly. "I really don't like that word, either, *generally*. Because the implication is that there are exceptions to whatever generalization you are making."

An amused Bering reassured her that she was safe from the wolves, and as she could see the wide expanse the animals would have to cross in order to even get close, she began to relax. And the scenery soon distracted her again from how physically demanding the hike was.

But by the time they got back to the cabin, Emily was wiped out. She removed her boots and peeled off her outer layers. She downed an entire bottle of water and then sank down into the soft cushions of the sofa.

BERING WENT INTO the kitchen to prepare another pot of coffee, and by the time he came back, Emily was snoring softly, her body curled into the corner of the sofa.

Two hours later, he was concerned his

level of adoration had reached stalker levels. He'd never watched a woman sleep before. There was a warm knot in his chest that he was entirely unfamiliar with as he studied her. He was relieved that her skin seemed to have achieved a healthier glow. He recalled the grayish pallor and the bags she'd had under her eyes for the first few days he'd known her. And the utter despair he'd seen in her eyes. He didn't ever want her to look like that again. He wasn't sure if she would ever talk to him about it or if he should ask her outright what had happened before she'd come to Rankins. Would that be outside the bounds of friendship he was trying to maintain? He wasn't sure and he feared that those lines were already irreparably blurred anyway. *Kissing someone will do that,* he silently berated himself.

He looked out the window and then back at her sleeping form. He hated the idea of waking her, but he didn't want her to miss the show. He dropped to one knee before the sofa. He couldn't resist pressing his lips softly against her brow first. Then he stroked the soft skin of her cheek with his knuckles. "Em? Emily?" he whispered close to her ear. "Wake up."

Emily sighed and opened her eyes. "Bering?" She murmured his name and blinked a couple of times. Then she sat up quickly. "What...?"

"Hey," he said. "You fell asleep."

She ran her hands over her hair, tucking pieces behind her ears as she did so. "Oh... now I'm embarrassed. I never do this."

"Why would you be embarrassed? Naps are good for you."

"If you're three years old," she countered. She stretched and looked around languidly. Then she gasped and stood. She walked toward the window. The night was black but stars and shafts of glowing colors were lighting the sky.

"Northern lights." She whispered the words, clearly awestruck by the glistening, swirling colors sweeping and dancing across the sky and seemingly right in through the cabin's window.

"I thought you should get a good look from up here on the mountain while you are in Alaska."

A breathless "Wow" escaped her lips.

"I know we aren't supposed to discuss this today and I know I'm the one who called for this cease-fire, but this is just one of the many, many reasons why I love it here."

"Bering, if this is your idea of sneaking in

a little campaigning, I'm okay with it," she joked softly. "I've never seen anything so incredible in my entire life."

They watched silently for a long time. Bering wanted to take her hand, to touch her, to kiss her. He wanted…her. He squeezed his eyes shut and willed himself to get ahold of his emotions. It was too late. He was owned, he realized with both resignation and despair. He was owned by Emily Hollings, a city girl who worked for his archenemy. Was there some possible way they could make this work? He wasn't sure, but he knew he couldn't touch her again until he had an answer to that question.

"WELL," BERING SAID a short while later as he came in from the cold. "I've got good news and bad news."

"Bad news first—always," Emily said.

"The snow machine won't start. The battery is dead."

"What's the good news?"

"This machine comes with a pull mechanism so if an imbecile like me lets the battery go dead, it can still be started."

"Oh, cool."

"Yeah, except there's more bad news."

"What?"

He held his hand out then and Emily could see a broken, frayed nylon cord dangling from his grasp.

"Uh-oh, what are we going to do?"

"We'll be fine here for the night. Tag is working this evening, but I can radio him and he can bring me a new battery after his shift in the morning. I usually have a spare one here but I used it and didn't replace it. So that's my own fault."

Emily swallowed and looked around, suddenly nervous at the idea of spending the entire night alone with him.

"Emily," he said, mistaking the cause of her anxiety, "we'll be fine, I promise. I spend days at a time out here. I know you're not used to roughing it like this, but I promise we have everything we need. Please don't worry—wolves rarely break into cabins," he quipped.

"I'm not worried," she said with a grin. "I trust you. And it doesn't seem all that rough really."

"It doesn't?" Bering asked. "You're not going to freak out without a phone, or a TV, or your computer?"

"Nah," she said. "I always enjoy a break from the phone, Amanda will be checking my email and I rarely watch TV. We didn't even have one when I was growing up."

"Really?" he asked. "How is that possible? Were you really poor?"

She laughed. "Really, and no—not poor, my stepfather thinks it's unproductive for children to watch television.

"He might be right about that on some level. He couldn't stop me from watching it when I went away to school, but by that time I was so used to not watching it that it didn't really interest me that much."

"How old were you when you went away to school?"

"Twelve."

His face took on a look of concern. "That seems so young. My nephew is going to be twelve next year, and I can't imagine him going to the store alone, much less away to school somewhere. Weren't you homesick?"

"Not really," she said and added silently, *Homesick would imply a family-type environment healthy enough to miss.* Lonely at times, yes, but not homesick. Bering looked as if he wanted to ask her more questions, so she quickly changed the subject. "Do you have any games or cards?"

"I do," he said. "What's your pleasure? Rummy, cribbage, chess?"

"Cribbage," she returned confidently.

Cribbage was one of the few games Franklin had taught her and encouraged her to play as a child. He'd thought the strategy involved would somehow translate to the business world. Emily hadn't seen how, but she'd enjoyed it, so she hadn't complained. She'd also gotten very good at it—or so she thought.

With Bering she had clearly found a rival. They wound up tied three games each, and in keeping with the spirit of the current cease-fire, and a mutual promise of a future tie-breaker, they decided to call it a night.

Bering really did have everything they needed for a comfortable stay. He had a spare toothbrush and he gave her one of his T-shirts to sleep in. She took only a few minutes in the tiny bathroom. She quickly washed her face, brushed her teeth and slipped the T-shirt on. She was swimming in it, but paired with her comfy borrowed long johns, she was set. Bering traded places after she came out.

He emerged quickly. Emily was already sprawled out on the sofa. He insisted that she take the bedroom. She refused. He sat in the chair next to her.

"You are a stubborn woman."

"You've accused me of that before, and I thought I'd adequately dissuaded you of that notion." She grinned sweetly up at him. "I am determined, yes, but not stubborn."

His look was skeptical.

She ignored it. "You know what you are?"

"What's that?"

"You're spoiled."

Laughter erupted from between his lips. "I am not spoiled."

"Yep, you are. You are used to having your own way. And when you don't, it really gets to you. That's spoiled."

He leaned forward and rested his forearms on his legs. His eyes traveled over her face for several silent seconds and Emily wondered if he would throw his mistake speech out the window and kiss her again. He looked as if he wanted to. She definitely wanted him to. She hoped she was making that clear. Her breath caught as he reached out and tucked a stray tendril of hair behind her ear.

"That's probably true," he acknowledged, his voice low and soft. "In fact, it's becoming painfully clear that that is exactly the case where you are concerned. You definitely get to me…."

He leaned back and Emily was disappointed even as her heart sang at his mischievous grin.

"Good night, then, determined Emily."
"Good night, spoiled Bering."

AFTER AN INORDINATE amount of time speculating about what was happening between them and if it would all go back to campaign-as-normal when they returned to town, Emily finally fell into a deep and restful sleep. The next morning she figured her peaceful slumber was due to the amount of exercise she'd gotten as she woke to discover that her limbs were stiff from the hike. She really did need to get more exercise, she supposed, and made a silent vow to do so.

Tag showed up early with a new battery for the snow machine and they had it installed in what seemed to Emily like a matter of minutes. Then Bering took Emily home. He walked her to the porch, lingered way too briefly, made her laugh and then said goodbye.

She stepped through the door, turned and placed her back against it and slowly slid to the floor. She tried to analyze her feelings. It was odd to be so happy and yet disappointed at the same time. She sat with her eyes closed for a few seconds, opened them on a sigh and then screamed.

"Amanda! You scared me to death."

"Sooo...I guess I don't need to ask how your date went?" Amanda was lounging comfortably on the sofa with a magazine resting in her lap and a smirk planted on her face.

"What are you doing here?"

"I was worried about you. I couldn't get ahold of you last night, so I called Tag and he told me you were with Bering. I came over here early this morning to find out how your little excursion went, and imagine my surprise when I found you not yet at home. You guys run out of gas?"

"Funny. But for your information, it was a dead battery."

"Good one," Amanda said, "very original. Emily, what is going on?"

"Amanda," Emily said helplessly, "I have absolutely no idea."

"You like him, don't you?"

"I really don't think—"

"Oh, come on, Em, I always tell you all the details of my love life."

"That's true, yes, but the difference is that I never ask."

"Ouch." She added a chuckle. "But now I know the answer is yes, because if it was no, you would have denied it right off."

Emily tried to look dubious. "Really?"

Amanda countered with a knowing glance.

"Emily, how long have I known you? Now, tell me everything."

Emily couldn't help but smile. "It was good, Amanda. Really good," she repeated. "I had no idea just hanging out with a man could be like that. He's smart and interesting and…attentive…but…"

"But…? Come here and have a seat and I'll get us some coffee, and then you're going to tell me everything, including what 'attentive' means to you." She stood up and hustled into the kitchen.

She came back with two steaming mugs of coffee. She handed one to Emily and then took a seat next to her.

"So he kissed you?" Amanda asked when Emily was through telling her about their outing.

"He did. But then he took it back."

"Emily, he didn't want to take it back. He was trying to get your permission. He was trying to be a gentleman. Trust me—you give him the green light, he'll kiss you again."

"What if he doesn't?"

"He will."

Emily silently hoped she was right, even as she considered the wisdom of it all. Maybe Bering was right.… "I don't know what to do now."

"What do you mean?"

"I mean, maybe I shouldn't give him the green light or whatever. What would be the point? I know this can't work out—long-term, I mean. It's impossible."

"Emily, you don't know that. Seemingly impossible situations have a way of working themselves out all the time."

"But how could I possibly stay away from him now?"

Amanda stared at her dumbly. "Why would you want to?"

"I don't."

"Then don't," she answered quickly. "For once in your life, Emily, just go with it. Don't overthink it—just enjoy it."

That was funny, she thought, and seemed telling, because it was the not thinking that had got her to this point in the first place.

"HI," EMILY SAID a couple evenings later when Bering answered the door to Janie's house.

"Are you sure you want to do this?" he asked.

"Sure. Why wouldn't I?" Emily asked as she came into the house to meet Bering's nephews.

Emily didn't have much experience with

kids but she was great with people, so she figured it couldn't be that much different....

A short time later she decided it was much, much different and way more difficult. Bering's nephews were nine and eleven years old and Emily was sure the younger one, Reagan, had not stopped talking for longer than a thirty-second stretch. Bering had mentioned that he was really smart, but she was pretty sure the kid was literally some kind of genius. He lost her somewhere in the middle of a story involving genomes and RNA and a deadly virus that was spreading like wildfire in some African jungle. He wrapped it up by informing her that should she ever start bleeding out of her eyeballs, she should get to a hospital immediately. She tried not to laugh as she assured him that she would not hesitate to seek medical attention under those circumstances.

"Do you like video games?" Gareth, the older one, asked her when he could finally get a word in.

"Um, I don't know," she said. "I've never played any."

"You've never played a video game?" he repeated incredulously. "Were you raised in a cave or something?"

She shook her head and smiled. "Not a

cave, but my stepfather did not allow any video games in our house."

"Wow, that's rough, and we complain about our screen time."

"I didn't know what I was missing, so it wasn't so bad. I wasn't allowed to watch television, either."

"No television?" The look on his face made Emily laugh, as if she'd just revealed that she'd been hung from her toenails and beaten with a bamboo pole.

"Is your dad like a communist or something?"

"Was it a religious cult?" Reagan asked.

Emily laughed. "No, he's not a religious extremist, nor is he a communist—he's about as opposite of that as you can get, actually."

"A capitalist," Reagan shot back confidently. "Awesome. Like the first Reagan."

Emily looked quizzically at Bering, who explained, "His father named him after Ronald Reagan, and thus our Reagan has taken the responsibility of being the namesake of a famous and important person very seriously. He's researched the former president extensively."

"Ah…well, then, Reagan, you will be happy to know that you are in the presence of a fellow devotee."

Reagan looked skeptical, but then again, so did Bering. Gareth looked mortified.

"Reagan, maybe we should—"

"What was his middle name?" Reagan interrupted his uncle.

"Wilson," Emily answered immediately.

"That's an easy one, though," Reagan said. "You had probably even been born when he was still president."

Emily gestured at him to bring it on.

"Birthday?"

"February 6, 1911," she responded promptly. "Born in Tampico, Illinois."

"Nickname?"

"That depends. He had quite a few. A lot of people would say his most famous nickname was the Gipper, which he earned from a character he played in the movie *Knute Rockne, All American*. The character's name was George Gipp. There are a couple others worth mentioning, but the one I would go with is Dutch because he received it from his father in childhood, so it was with him the longest."

"Hmm, that's not bad," Reagan said, a dose of respect seeping into his tone.

Emily smiled, but apparently the young trivia king was only warming up.

"Name one thing he was the only U.S. President to ever have done."

"Ooh, that's a tough one but I'm going to have to go with the fact that he was divorced."

"Good answer," Reagan acknowledged. "What state was he governor of?"

"California—twice—1967 and again in 1971."

"So, you know he was a lifelong Republican, then?"

Emily crossed her arms over her chest. "You're trying to trick me, right? Any self-respecting Ronald Reagan fan knows that he was originally a Democrat. He switched parties in 1962."

"Congratulations," Reagan said and stuck his hand out. "It's really great to meet you, Emily."

Emily chuckled and shook his hand. "You, as well, Reagan. So, I am here for the entire evening. What would you guys like to do?"

"We're not watching a Reagan movie," Gareth said quickly before Reagan could answer.

Reagan shrugged, acknowledging that it had been an option he was going to suggest.

Gareth asked, "Do you want to try playing a video game, Emily? I can teach you."

"Sounds good," she said.

Emily soon discovered she was completely inept at virtual soldiering. An hour later she had failed to save planet Earth no less than twelve times. Twice she had single-handedly, albeit accidentally, annihilated it and the entire human race along with it. Gareth was a very sweet and patient teacher. He reminded her very much of his uncle, who, thankfully, took over her remote and fought much better on the endangered planet's battle front than she had.

She spent the next hour playing a trivia game with Reagan, and although she lost, he informed her that she had fared better than anyone else he'd ever played. She graciously accepted the compliment.

After that they made pizza and French fries and watched an action movie that she'd never seen. It was nearing ten o'clock by the time Bering announced to the boys that it was time for bed. She thanked them both for an awesome evening and said goodbye. They shuffled off to brush their teeth and Bering walked her to the door.

"So," he said, "I have to go out of town for a couple days for work. I'll call you when I get back."

"Oh," she said. A wave of disappointment washed over her at the thought of not seeing or talking to him for even that long. "Where are you going?"

"Washington, D.C. It's an annual thing. Every year I go with our state biologists to attend a presentation of wolf data to the Department of the Interior. Every state with a wolf population is represented."

She nodded and smiled in his direction, hoping she could pull off the nonchalance that she was striving for. "Okay, well, good luck. Be safe."

He looked as though he wanted to say something else and Emily wished that he would. She was disappointed at the turn their relationship had taken. They'd seen each other every day since they'd returned from the cabin, and even though they were back in campaign mode, things were good between them. But that was all, just good—cordial and…friendly.

It was becoming increasingly clear to her that friendship was indeed as far as Bering wanted to go. Apparently he'd meant it when he said that kiss had been a mistake. Even though there were moments that felt flirtatious and even a couple times when he'd looked at her with what she would swear was longing. But she was beginning to think she had been imagining it.

Was she imagining that right now? Emily

didn't know how she could make her light any greener....

He stepped toward her and reached for her hand. "Emily, I—"

Suddenly, Reagan shouted his uncle's name from somewhere down the hall and they heard footsteps coming toward them. He flashed her an apologetic smile and gave her fingers a gentle squeeze before releasing them. They said their goodbyes and Emily slipped quietly out the door.

As she drove home, melancholy once again took hold of her. She thought about the relationships in her life and how different they were from the relationships that Bering had. For the first time in a long time, she ached for the family she'd never had. For the first time ever, she longed for a family of her own. She missed Bering and he wasn't even gone yet. She missed him and he wasn't even hers.

CHAPTER ELEVEN

"HELLO? YES, GOOD morning, sir. I'm looking forward to that, as well." Bering kept the
cell phone pressed closely to his ear as he
climbed into the airplane. Bering glanced at
his watch. "I'm on my way. Tag is flying me
to Anchorage and then I leave from there in
three hours. Sounds great. I appreciate it."

Bering clicked off the phone and quickly
buckled his seat belt. He knew Tag wouldn't
go anywhere until he did. He watched silently
as Tag began the preflight maneuvers. In all
the years they'd been flying together, he'd
never known him to skip even a single step,
which was probably the reason they were both
still alive—that, and his cousin's phenomenal
ability to stay calm in virtually any situation.
It was a trait that helped to make him both an
excellent paramedic and an expert pilot. Flying could be extremely dangerous amid the
temperamental Alaskan weather; between the
mountains and the coast, there was always
something exciting brewing in the skies. But

Bering had only seen him really rattled a couple times, and they'd had their share of close calls together. Bering supposed it was just one part of what kept them so close.

Tag finished up, but instead of taking off, he turned and looked at Bering. "So, what are you going to do now?"

Bering glanced over at him, but didn't quite meet his eyes. "About what?"

"About what?" Tag mimicked with a roll of his eyes. "You know what 'what' I'm talking about, but if you want to play that way then I'll give you a hint—she's thin, blonde, pretty, blue eyes. She also happens to have a giant Cam-Field brand on her back. And, in spite of whatever it is that's going on between the two of you, it is still her job to strip this little town that we love of everything that we hold dear."

"What are you trying to say, Tag?"

Tag shrugged. "I think I just said it. This can't end well, Bering."

Bering stared at his cousin. "Why do you have it ending before it's really even begun?"

"Aside from the fact that I'm assuming that she doesn't know exactly what connections you have, there are two things that can happen here—either she wins and our town is destroyed, or you win and she pulls up shop and leaves right along with Cam-Field."

"So I shouldn't get involved with her? Or I should, but I should also tell her everything about myself so that she can then use that information to ruin Rankins? And her eyes are gray."

"I think you've just proven my point."

Bering sighed tiredly. "It doesn't have to matter, Tag."

"But it does matter, Bering. I know you and you're not going to be able to live with yourself after using someone in the sense that you are here. And I'm not criticizing you for your motive. It's just the means—"

"I'm not using her," Bering interrupted. "I don't need her to accomplish this."

"Then what are you doing?"

He flashed his cousin an irritated look. "Saving Rankins."

Tag let out an exasperated breath. "What are you doing with Emily?"

Bering shrugged. "I like her."

"But you realize she's not going to like you, right? After she finds out what you're up to?"

He didn't want to think about that possibility. He didn't want to believe that it could even be likely, not after the time they'd spent together. He'd never felt this way about anyone before, and the reason he hadn't taken it any further was because of the very possibility that Tag was now throwing in his face.

"I'm well aware of that, and I'm hoping to find a path around it. Our relationship is—"

"Relationship?" Tag repeated the word. "Is that what it is?"

"I don't know."

Tag shook his head. "Well, you better figure it out, Bering. I'm afraid you could do some real damage here. Amanda has said some things—"

"She's not as vulnerable as she appears, Tag. Trust me. And I seem to recall that it was you who not long ago told me she was trouble."

"That was before."

"Before what?" Bering stared hard at his cousin for several seconds as the meaning behind his statement sank in. "You think I planned this?"

"I don't know, Bering. I do know that you've been pretty worked up about this whole Cam-Field thing for months now and it does seem rather, uh, propitious that Emily came along and now you two are…"

"Are what?" Bering said.

Tag lifted a shoulder as if to say he didn't know, but the look on his face spoke volumes.

"I know you spent the night at your cabin with her, so why don't you tell me?"

"It wasn't like that. You know I had a dead battery."

"Okay, Bering, come on. It's me, Tag. You and I both know you could have managed to get that snow machine started. Or you could have come up with some other means to get out of there if you had really wanted to."

Bering was shocked at his cousin, who knew him too well. There was no point in arguing. "That's undoubtedly true. But, Tag, do you really think that I would sleep with a woman in order to undermine her business plans? And we're not just talking about some woman here—we're talking about Emily. That's insulting. We're friends, maybe more. I would like more, I'll be honest. Am I sure how to achieve that? No, I'm not. Do I believe it's even possible? I don't know. But I thought you were on my side anyway."

"It's not a matter of undermining her business plans. It's a lot more than a business plan to you and to me and to the majority of this town, for that matter. And what I'm saying is that I think it means more than that to Emily, too. I'm not sure why exactly, but I've gotten the impression from Amanda that there's a lot riding on this job for Emily, too."

"What do you mean?" Bering said as a rush of uncertainty coursed through him. It was the same thought he'd had himself—something that went beyond her obsession with her career. Something more that she wasn't telling him. But to be fair, there was quite a bit he wasn't telling her, too. He had only told Emily part of the reason he was traveling to Washington, D.C.

"I don't know. Amanda has said some things that indicate she's got a lot invested here. I haven't asked directly because I don't want her to think I'm spying for you or anything."

Bering rubbed a hand over his jaw as he turned to look out the window into the darkness. Tag had a point—he'd specifically asked Emily if this was just a job for her and she'd said yes. He'd been relieved by that answer, but what if there were things she was deliberately keeping from him, as he was from her? The thought was unsettling.

"You know I'm on your side, Bering," Tag added. "I've always been on your side and I always will be. But it's not like you to cheat to win. Or to step all over someone to get what you want. That's what Cam-Field does, Bering, not us." He finally turned his attention to the airplane and Bering was glad for both the noise and the distraction.

In spite of what Tag was insinuating, he hadn't intended to get so involved with Emily. A wave of guilt washed over him. Who was he kidding? He'd been drawn to her almost immediately. At first he'd wanted to help her, then he'd been worried about her and now he just wanted to be with her. How could he have possibly foreseen these feelings he had somehow developed along the way?

And along with this came the realization that what he'd admitted to Tag was true—he wanted more than friendship. But did he want that more than he wanted to save this town? More than he wanted to preserve his way of life? He wanted both. What lengths would he go to in order to have them both?

He wanted Emily, yes, but he wanted her on his terms. That notion was troubling. Emily was right—he was spoiled. He was used to having his own way. And for the first time in his life, he wanted something he truly could not have. He would have to choose, and he couldn't be the only one he thought of when he did.

BERING HATED WASHINGTON—D.C., not the state. The state, he loved; it was the nation's capital that he couldn't abide. He couldn't imagine how Senator Marsh could bear it. The man was an avid outdoorsman and usually spent a few weeks every year camped out in one of Bering's cabins. He would come up in the summer for the salmon fishing and then again in the fall to hunt moose. And occasionally he would make the trip in the winter to enjoy the solace and the snowshoeing. Over the years he had become a friend, and although today it was a different type of business that brought them together, he was still genuinely glad to see him.

"Bering, welcome. How was the wolf conference?"

"Good, Senator. It's always nice to see old friends." Bering reached out and shook his hand. "Thank you for taking the time to meet with me."

They made small talk for a few minutes before the senator got down to business. "Now, bring me up-to-date on what's currently happening in Rankins."

"You know the basics already. Cam-Field has a team in place and they've begun their pitch—in earnest. They've scheduled a town-hall meeting in a couple weeks and the town-council vote is a couple days after that."

Bering filled him in on what had gone

down in Rankins over the past weeks. He felt himself missing Emily even as he relayed details of the conflict between them.

"And while they are doing their best to get the entire community behind the project, the fact is they only need the votes from the town council. The town council usually votes the way of the town, and so Cam-Field wants the support of the community. And things will go far more smoothly for them, development-wise, if they have that support, but they don't have to have it. And the truth is, Jack, I'm worried."

Senator Marsh nodded his head. "We've been doing some research out of my office. Unfortunately, Cam-Field has some very deep pockets. Very little debt, some prime real-estate properties and huge profits in the last five years—astronomical profits, actually, what with this oil situation and how it's been."

The senator went on, "And this Franklin Campbell is one shrewd character, I can tell you that. Whip-smart and a heck of a busi-nessman. He has resisted every temptation to overextend himself and has focused solely on this company of his, which explains the mil-lions of dollars."

Bering grimaced. "How many millions?"

"More like a billion, but you know what,

Bering? I honestly don't think it matters. The environmental lobby is all abuzz about this. Thanks to you, Evan Cobb and others have been blogging about it. And, if it reaches the point where we need legislation, I will get the votes. I love my hunting trips, Bering. You know that better than anyone."

The conversation gave Bering a measure of relief and it must have been evident on his face. Senator Marsh reached over and clapped him on the shoulder. "Rest assured, son, I will do everything in my power to shut this project down, or delay it indefinitely. There are other, albeit more costly, routes for Cam-Field to access this oil lease without involving Rankins or the surrounding area at all."

Bering nodded. "Thank you, Senator."

"I should also mention that there is some other interesting stuff we are looking into. I'm not quite sure what to make of it yet. What's the name of the guy in charge up there for Cam-Field?"

Bering cleared his throat and regretted the words even as he knew he had to say them. "Emily Hollings."

The senator's brows shot upward. "A woman, huh?"

Bering resisted the urge to add that she was so much more than that. "Yes."

"Boy, I would not have guessed that. From what I've learned about Franklin Campbell, I would have predicted that he was old-school through and through. What do you think of her so far?"

"Smart, tough, articulate, good at her job," he replied.

"I'll get someone researching her right away. Now, I hope you like roasted lamb…"

"EMILY, I WOULD LIKE you to meet my mother, Claire James." He placed a hand on her shoulder. "And this is Emily."

Bering's mother smiled and held her hand out to Emily. "Hello, Emily, I'm so glad you could come. It's wonderful to meet you—finally." She cast a chastising look up at her son.

Emily noticed, pondering the meaning there, but he only chuckled as he leaned over and kissed his mother on the cheek. "It's nice to see you, too, Mom."

"How was your trip?"

"Short," Bering said.

"Successful?"

"Yes, very."

Emily saw Bering's jaw tighten as he looked down at his mom. Was it her imagination or had there been some kind of message in the look that passed between them? She hoped that everything had gone okay for him.

He'd only returned the previous evening and Emily hadn't had a chance to ask him any details about his trip. The conversation had been brief, consisting mainly of Bering's invitation to Sunday brunch at his mother's house.

Janie appeared in the doorway and Bering stepped into the kitchen with his mother.

"Emily, I'm so glad you're here," Janie said. "Thank you for helping Bering the other night. The boys could not stop talking about you. I hope they didn't wear you out too much."

"No, I enjoyed every minute of it. They are great kids. Bering talks about them all the time. He talks about all of you, actually."

"I don't know what they would do without their uncle," she said with a warm smile. "Then again, I don't know what I would do without him, either."

Emily was becoming familiar with that feeling herself. "Thank you so much for the scarf, Janie. I wear it all the time. Is the wolf button the signature on all your work?" She gestured toward the rack behind her, where she'd hung it along with her coat.

Surprise flashed briefly across Janie's face

before it transformed with an engaging smile. "Well, you're welcome. But all I did was fill a special order. And the wolf button is unique to your scarf."

Emily tilted her head and stared at Janie, processing this information. "A special order?" she repeated.

"Yes, I was kind of surprised because Bering's never actually requested anything so specific before, but I'm glad you like it."

Bering hadn't mentioned that he had asked Janie to make it special for her. And she suspected, from the look on Janie's face, that she knew that, and might be trying to tell her that, too. She smiled conspiratorially and said, "I really, really do. You know, you could start a business."

"I've always liked to knit, but after Cal died, I found that it was one of the few things that just…made time pass. That probably sounds weird, huh?"

"Not at all," she said. Drawing did that for her, she explained to Janie, and although the circumstances were obviously different, she thought she could understand at least a little. She recalled how she'd filled many lonely hours when she was young and had first gone away to school. She would draw for hours, just turn her brain off and get lost in it. It made perfect sense to her that Janie would need something like that.

Their conversation was temporarily put on hold as Bering's relatives began filing into the house. She was promptly introduced to a variety of aunts, uncles, cousins and too many little ones to count or to even keep track of. Some she'd already met at the office, or during one community event or another, but no one seemed to hold her connection with Cam-Field against her—not outright anyway. Emily watched and listened with fascination as hugs, kisses, scowls, jabs, teasing and plenty of laughter gradually filled nearly every square inch.

It seemed to Emily that she was a source of curiosity to them all. And she thought keeping up with a boardroom full of keyed-up executives was a challenge. She was subjected to several subtle questions, many thorough perusals and a couple outright interrogations, but she had expected as much and all in all she thought she handled herself fairly well.

The atmosphere seemed to mellow considerably after dinner. And how could it not? Emily was absolutely stuffed full of some of the best food she'd ever eaten in her entire life.

The children disappeared into the basement, although stomps, shouts and giggles could be heard drifting up the stairway. Adults gathered in the living room and kitchen with steaming mugs of coffee or tea. Emily wandered into the wide hallway to discover it contained two walls of photographs, spreading from nearly floor to ceiling. She quickly spotted Bering in several photos.

There was a whole story laid out on the walls and Emily had no idea how much time passed as she eagerly perused the contents, her imagination churning with images of Bering as a child, and then as a teenager, and throughout it all his interaction with this crew of loving family members.

"Hey," Bering said a while later, coming up behind her. "Here you are. I thought maybe you'd bolted."

"No way." She gestured at the walls. "I'm enthralled by your family."

"Enthralled," he said with a nod. "That sounds so much better than the terrified or horrified that you could be."

She turned toward him. "You know how lucky you are, right?"

"I do. But thank you for saying so."

He leaned over her shoulder to peer at a photo. His nose brushed against her neck and

Emily inhaled sharply as a warm thrill spiked through her.

"Mmm," he said, "you smell good."

"I do, huh?"

"Yeah, like lavender and—" he sniffed loudly and ungracefully "—ham."

"Ham?" she repeated with a giggle. "It's actually bacon," she whispered. "I dabbed bacon grease on my wrists and behind my ears this morning."

"Really?" His tone was infused with amusement.

"I just wanted to try to fit in here."

"Then next time use bear grease," he said with a chuckle. He pointed at a photo. "This is my dad."

"I figured," she said. "You look just like him."

Bering raised an eyebrow. "You know, some people say he was a very good-looking guy."

She squinted at the photo. "Uh, he's okay."

He laughed and then stepped closer. "I missed you. I haven't had anyone to keep my ego in check for three whole days."

His look felt flirtatious, like the pre-kiss-and-speech Bering. The cease-fire Bering?

"Did you miss me?"

She tipped her head and studied him with narrowed eyes. "I don't know…I barely remember you. Give me a second…Bernie? Baird? Wait—is it Barry?"

He reached up and ran a thumb lightly down the side of her cheek and across her lower lip. Emily let out a soft gasp. He cupped his hand along her jaw, dipped his head and kissed her. His lips were warm and insistent, and though much too short, the kiss was thorough and full of heat. It took a second for her to catch her breath.

"Does that help you remember at all?"

Emily blinked up at him. "Maybe," she whispered dazedly.

"Good."

"I didn't think you wanted to… You said…"

He ran a hand through his hair. His voice sounded strained. "Emily, it wasn't because I didn't want to."

"Why, then?"

"Because I was doubting my own assertion that we can remain…um, friends in spite of your job."

"I don't normally kiss my friends," she returned softly.

"I don't, either."

"Bering, what are we doing?"

He reached out and wrapped one hand around the back of her neck and the other around her waist. He pulled her to him and held her in his arms. "I don't know, but I do know that I don't want to not do it anymore. I tried that. I told myself I wasn't going to kiss you again after that first time, and I won't anymore if you don't want me to. But I had a lot of time to think while I was gone and I know it's going to be complicated but, Emily, I—"

"It is," she said anxiously. "It is complicated, but you're the one who keeps saying that we can… You've actually made me believe it."

He closed his eyes for a few seconds. He opened them and asked, "Is that what you want?"

"Yes."

"Me, too," he said and grinned down at her.

He kissed her again and took his time doing so.

They were both breathless when they parted. "Emily, I think we should go. There are some things we need to talk about and—"

"I hope I'm interrupting?" a voice called cheerily from just a few feet away.

Emily jumped. Bering didn't flinch but muttered something under his breath and then said, "You are." He didn't take his eyes off Emily.

"Bering," Emily returned in a chastising tone, "she wasn't trying to—"

"Trust me, she was." Finally he looked at Janie. "What are you doing skulking around here anyway?"

"Chaperoning, and obviously it's needed," she quipped. "Actually, I was using Mom's bathroom. The other ones were occupied and you know how it is when you're this far along…"

"You've mentioned it often enough," Bering said drily.

"Just wait till you have a pregnant wife," Janie answered matter-of-factly. "Then you'll be singing a more respectful tune. Do you want kids, Emily?"

"Um…" Emily said. She was flustered— flushed from the close contact with Bering and also embarrassed at being caught at it. "I do." As she managed to get the words out, she realized in that moment how much she did. Janie seemed happy with her answer if the look on her face was any indication. But it wasn't something she felt like discussing right now. It felt too intimate—too intermingled with these new and confusing feelings for Bering.

"Bering, um," Emily muttered, overtaken

by the urge to change the subject and the course of her thoughts. "Maybe we should—"

"Go? Yes, we should definitely go. Mom," he halfheartedly shouted down the hall. "Thanks for the delicious meal. We're gonna go."

There was no way he could be heard over the cacophony of noise still radiating throughout the house, but he took Emily's hand and started down the hallway.

"Bering, stop!" Emily chastised. "I was going to say move into the other room with Janie. But if we are leaving, then we will thank your mom properly and say goodbye to every single one of your relatives."

"Really, Bering, how rude," Janie added, a pleased look on her face.

"Oh, Emily, no," he said with a groan. "That will take forever. We can slip out and no one will even notice. I promise they won't mind."

"Hey, it'll only take a minute." She turned to walk toward the chaos.

Bering snaked a hand out and nabbed her wrist before she could get far. She yelped in surprise as he tugged her back toward him. "Emily, think about this. It'll be at least an hour before we get can out of here. If we go out the back—"

"It's not going to work," she said as he tried halfheartedly to pull her along. "Nothing will stop me from properly thanking your mom and your aunts and saying goodbye to your relatives. What in the world is that? I didn't know you had spiders that big in Alaska." She pointed up at the ceiling and then darted down the hallway as Bering fell for it completely.

Janie called out, "Oh, wait, Emily, you know what? You guys can't leave yet anyway. You haven't had dessert."

"Dessert?" Emily stopped and turned immediately when she heard the word.

"Yep, there's pie."

"Pie?" Emily cast an accusing look at Bering, hands on her hips. "There's pie, Bering."

"I—" Bering said.

Janie clarified, "There's huckleberry, apple and coconut cream. Have you tried our huckleberries yet?"

"In your mom's scones," Emily replied.

"Those are good, but they don't compare to pie."

"Huckleberry pie? Bering, you know I'm not leaving here without trying that pie."

Bering groaned. "Of course you're not," he muttered, and then he looked at Janie. "I've created a monster. First, I couldn't get her to eat—now I can't get her to stop."

Emily laughed and continued through the doorway, waving over her shoulder.

BERING TURNED AND LOOKED at his sister with narrowed eyes. "I will get even with you. You know that, right?"

Janie grinned at him. "I do, but you know what? It's worth it. And besides, I still have two months to go before these kids are born, and I know it won't be anything too severe before then."

"That just gives me more time to plot."

"She's a doll," Janie said, abruptly changing the subject. "I thought she'd be so uptight. You know...corporate executive and all? But she's so not. I like her, Bering."

"Me, too," he replied.

"I know." She nodded and added a knowing grin.

"What do you mean?" Bering returned skeptically.

"Bering, you're my brother. I know you. You've got this—" gestured up at him "—look plastered all over your face, and you can't take your eyes off her. You've never asked me to knit a scarf for anybody before. In fact, you have never asked me to knit anything for anybody ever—until now."

He knew it was all true. He didn't care.

Janie placed one hand on her stomach and the other flat against her chest and grimaced.

"What's the matter?" Bering asked quickly. "Are you okay?"

She took a deep breath, blew it out slowly and finally answered, "Yes, it's just heartburn. Babies didn't like those pork chops. I'll be fine."

Bering watched her closely for a second. "Are you sure you're okay?"

Her voice was quiet and sober when she spoke. "Yes, I'm fine. But what are you going to do?"

"About what?"

"About being in love with your archenemy? About being in love with a woman who's going to leave you?"

"Janie, I'm not—" He couldn't bring himself to deny it, but he couldn't quite admit it, either. Because what would that say about him as a person if he could fall in love with someone and yet not be totally honest with her at the same time? But would he even be willing to try to make this work with her if he wasn't? Being away from her for the past few days had made him see things differently.

He had missed her. It had made him want to take advantage of whatever time they had, regardless of the outcome. It had prompted him to kiss her again, and this time he knew he could never take it back....

He leaned against the wall. But along with that, he realized he couldn't avoid things much longer, either. What was she going to do when she found out the truth? And what was he going to do when she left him? He wasn't sure which would come first, but both were inevitable, and both filled him with dread.

CHAPTER TWELVE

BERING WAS QUIET when, almost two hours later with Emily stuffed full of pie and carrying a take-home container full of more pie, they finally left. It was as if admitting—by not denying—his feelings to his sister, he had brought emotions that had been only simmering beneath the surface to a full rolling boil. He'd never been in love before, so along with the joy of that emotion, there was also fear. He was scared of loving her because he was afraid of losing her and he couldn't see any scenario now where that wouldn't happen.

The drive to his house was quiet, both of them seemingly absorbed in thought. Bering opened the door for Emily, and they walked in and removed their coats and boots.

Emily turned toward him. "Bering, are you okay?"

He had intended to talk to her about everything—about their relationship and this situation with Cam-Field. He had wanted to reassure her, and himself, that they could work something out. But now as he stared down at her, he realized that his silent admission of love had changed everything. Suddenly it seemed as if so much more was at stake. How could this have happened? All he'd wanted to do for months was to save Rankins from the evil grip of Cam-Field, but now it seemed that in order to do that he had to surrender his own chance at love.

He stared at her for a long moment and then reached out and wrapped a hand around the back of her neck, entwining his fingers in her hair. "Emily, I—" he began, but he knew that he couldn't say the words to her. He couldn't complicate things any more than he already had. For all his bold talk, he knew that by doing what he was doing with regard to Cam-Field she would never forgive him. And if he told her he loved her first, it would only make it worse. As Tag had suggested, it would all seem like part of some ploy. He was overwhelmed with the thoughts and feelings that were colliding within him.

"Did something happen on your trip?" she asked, her eyes wide and questioning.

A strangled sound emerged from the back of his throat. "I missed you," he whispered, skimming his fingers lightly over her shoulders and down her arms. He bent and covered her lips with his own. He poured every bit of himself into the kiss and into his touch. He loved her, and he wanted her to love him back. And if he couldn't say it, then he was going to show it. Even though he knew it was irrational and impossible, he wanted her to love him back so that when it was all said and done none of it would matter because they'd still have each other.

"Okay," he finally said against her lips. "I'm going to stop kissing you now."

"Why?" she said. "You just started again."

He took a deep breath and looked into her eyes. "Emily, first of all—I've never not wanted to kiss you."

She smiled tentatively. "Really?"

"Yes," he said shakily. "And this means yes." He kissed her again. And again, and then his mouth began to travel slowly toward her ear....

"Bering," she gasped as his teeth nipped at the creamy skin of her neck.

His hands slid up from her waist and encased her rib cage, and he was struck by how tiny she really was. She seemed so much bigger when she was talking—larger than life, actually, and the thought brought a smile to his lips. He kissed her once more and then wrapped his arms around her and held her close.

A SHORT TIME later, they were browsing through Bering's vast movie library and he was voicing his astonishment at how few Emily had actually seen. He set the ones she had seen off to the side and Emily agreed it was a pitifully small pile. Then he started a must-see stack that he insisted they would watch together.

Emily didn't mention that they couldn't possibly watch that many movies if she were to remain in Rankins for another year, much less the few weeks or months of time they had remaining. Their lack of time was way too depressing and one she refused to allow herself to think about.

They agreed on a movie and eventually settled on the sofa.

"I can't believe you guys get together like that every Sunday."

"Not every Sunday, but a lot of them."

"How fun that must be."

"It is," he said. "Tell me more about your family."

She frowned. "There's not much to tell."

He dipped his head down and kissed her. "Please," he urged.

Emily sighed. "Bering—"

"Please."

"What do you want to know?"

He had one arm curled around her shoulders and he slowly began to trail a finger up and down her arm. "What's your dad like?"

"My biological dad died when I was a year old. He already had Aidan with Aidan's mom, Stephanie. Then he married my mom and had me. He died a year later—Aidan was four. We both look like him from the photos that I've seen."

"Your mom remarried?

"She did. When I was three, so the only dad I've ever known is my stepfather."

"So…a mom, a stepdad and a half brother—if I remember correctly?"

"Yep, that's it."

"What's your brother like?"

"He's great—supersmart, like Reagan. He's very easygoing and laid-back—not like me. He's a scientist, a botanist."

"And you said he lives in Oregon?"

"Well, when he's not traveling he's usually there. He goes all over the world to study plants. He's passionate about endangered plant species."

"Wow, that's really cool."

"It is," she said with a proud smile. "I'd love for you to meet him."

"What about your parents?"

"What about them?" she asked soberly.

"Why don't you want to talk about them?"

It felt strange hearing that spoken aloud. Why didn't she like to talk about them or her relationship with them? "Um…"

He reached over and picked up her hand. He began to gently rub the palm. The contact was incredibly soothing and for some reason she decided to tell him. He was so easy to talk to. She inhaled and then blew out a long breath. "We're not close. I love my mom, but we're very different. She has these really specific ideas about what being a woman means—staying home and taking care of her husband. She's very dependent on my stepfather for everything and I don't like it. I don't understand it. She doesn't think my career is going to find me a husband. She doesn't understand my choices. It's a source of tension between us."

"So what does she do with her time?"

"She gets lots of facials, laser procedures and plastic surgeries. She shops and gets her nails done. She does do some charity work but honestly I think she does it more to socialize than anything else. We don't have anything in common and we don't have much to talk about."

Bering pressed a kiss to her temple. "What about your stepdad?"

Emily thought for a minute about how to

describe someone she had such complicated feelings for. "My stepfather is a good man. He's a great provider and a good husband to my mom. But he's also a difficult-to-please workaholic. Now that I'm an adult things are better—or they were until recently—because we have this driving work ethic in common. But we don't talk about anything personal. We aren't a family unit in the traditional sense—nothing at all like your family."

BERING LIFTED HER HAND and kissed her fingertips. He felt bad because although she relayed the information impassively, he could tell she was feeling anything but. What Emily described was the polar opposite of his family. He couldn't imagine functioning without the cohesive love and support of his family. He wanted Emily to have that; he wanted her to be a part of a real family—a family like his.

"I'm so sorry," he said.

She shrugged. "It is what it is. I do have Aidan, and his mom is really great to me, too. I think of her like an aunt. She always made sure that Aidan and I had as much of a brother/sister relationship as we could. It's because of her that I saw so much of him growing up."

Bering decided to ask her the question that had been nagging at him since he'd met her, and especially since his conversation with Tag. "Why are you here, Emily?"

"What do you mean?"

"Why did you come to Rankins? I mean, I can deduce that you are obviously pretty high up in the ranks of Cam-Field, so you must have some discretion about the jobs you work on, so why here? I know for a fact Cam-Field is working on projects in Louisiana, Oklahoma, Texas and North Dakota right now—to name a few."

"Someone has done his homework, I see." Bering smiled and squeezed her hand.

"I requested it," she confessed.

"Really?" That was not what he expected her to say.

"Yep," she said. "I, um, I sort of had an issue at work a few months ago."

"An issue?" he prodded.

"I was passed over for a promotion," she said. "I had broken up with this guy." She shook her head as if to convey his unimportance. "He got the promotion instead of me—undeservedly so, but that's another story. I was more upset about the promotion than the guy. And, as this is Cam-Field's first attempt to establish business up here in Alaska, I impulsively jumped at the opportunity to take it on."

He nodded. "Because you thought it would serve the double purpose of showing your boss what you've got that he missed out on and getting away at the same time?"

"Exactly, but unlike you, I did not thoroughly do my homework. I was unprepared for both the hostile environment and the hostile community."

Bering leaned over and kissed her. "I'd be willing to bet it's probably the only time in your entire life that you have neglected to do your homework."

"That's probably true."

"I'm so glad you chose this particular time to become a slacker."

"Me, too," she answered with a grin. She reached out and threaded a hand around the back of his neck, pulling his face close to hers. "Bering?"

"Hmm," he said.

"My turn."

"Oh? Okay. I thought you were going to kiss me."

"I may, but first, thank you, Bering. Thank you very much. Now tell me all about it."

"What?"

"The scarf—I thanked Janie for it tonight, but she let me know that I should really be thanking you. So tell me."

He grinned and sat back, but entwined his fingers with hers. "Oh…well, I kept watching you at all these events—freezing like crazy— and I kept wondering why you didn't dress appropriately. So, I had my sister knit you the scarf. You probably aren't even aware of it, but you go like this a lot." He pulled at the collar of his shirt, bunching it up beneath his chin.

"Bering, that is so sweet. But what about the wolf button? It's absolutely gorgeous—a little work of art."

"That's a piece of whalebone that Kella Jakobs scrimshawed for me. I used to wear it to bring me luck. I love it and I, um, I wanted you to have some small bit of Alaska with you when you went home." He smiled slowly and hoped the feeling in his heart was showing in his eyes. He admitted, "And I liked the idea of you wearing something that had been mine. So I asked Janie to sew it on. I hope you don't mind that I gave you a used button…."

Emily opened her mouth but no sound emerged. She closed it, stared at him for a minute and then leaned toward him again. "Bering?" she whispered.

"Yes?"

"I am going to kiss you now...."

EMILY WAS DEFINITELY warming up to the place, she decided as she stepped out into the frozen morning air. Now that she was dressed for it, she hardly seemed to notice the cold anymore. Even the frigid wind that used to blow down the collar of her jacket had been waylaid by her scarf. She gazed around in wonder; Bering was right, there was a rugged kind of beauty about the place that she was beginning to appreciate, especially when she was out at Bering's cabin watching the wildlife or, even better, out at Bering's cabin watching Bering.

And he'd definitely made it his business to show her the finer points that Rankins had to offer. In addition to sightseeing around his cabin, they'd done more snowshoeing and gone sledding with his nephews. They also went on a double date with Tag and Amanda to the Cozy Caribou for the house sirloin dinner he had promised her. They'd spent more time with his family and she'd met some of his friends.

She had to admit to herself that he had a good life. But she certainly wasn't going to confess these thoughts aloud. She'd already conceded enough to him as it was. Of course, just about anyone's life would be easier if they were as popular in this town as he was. Even the people that she knew were on her side still loved Bering. Laurel had been right about that; it appeared as if the whole James family shared that beloved status, and there had to be close to a hundred of them if you counted up the entire extended family.

And even though she and Bering were clearly waging a battle professionally, they had all treated her with nothing but kindness and respect. So far, Bering had been right— business appeared to be just business where the Jameses were concerned. But Emily still believed that that would all change if— when—Cam-Field won the right to destroy their little town.

Destroy? When exactly she had started to think of this assignment in Bering's terms she wasn't sure, but as the days had passed, she acknowledged that was what she had begun to do. Though she didn't believe it necessarily, she assured herself, she was just getting caught up in the passion and community pride that blazed in the town. It didn't do any good to remind herself that in all her years with Cam-Field, she'd never gotten quite so caught up in it before.

For the most part, she and Bering had managed to avoid discussing the issue beyond a lighthearted teasing about who was winning the public favor. But underlying the new level they had reached in their relationship, the topic still simmered. Emily tried to tell herself that it didn't matter, but the persistent ache in her heart reminded her otherwise.

Laurel had been more than fair in presenting Cam-Field's side in the *Rankins Press*. She was going to be publishing her editorial in favor of Cam-Field's development at the end of the week. Laurel had become a friend and Emily was sure that she was also a big part of the reason that they hadn't been run out of town.

And that was why she had agreed to sit for an interview. Laurel thought it would help her case if people knew more about her as a person. But for some reason Emily was nervous. There wasn't that much to know about her. She was afraid that people would see how uninteresting she really was, because compared to life in Rankins, hers seemed so mundane. Her plan was to try to stick to the issues surrounding Cam-Field's presence in Rankins as much as possible.

"So, now that you have been here for a month or so, how do you like it in Rankins?"

Laurel asked as she pushed a button on her recorder and set it on the desk.

"I do like it," Emily said without hesitation. And she realized with a start that she really meant it. "And in spite of what some people may have you believe, Laurel, I want to preserve all the core aspects that make Rankins such a unique and special place. But let's be honest here. Rankins hasn't seen much growth in recent years. We'd like to change that—to help ensure that Rankins can continue to exist, and not just exist like it has been doing. We'd like to see it grow and thrive."

"That's a pretty strong assertion and the implication within that statement is that Rankins needs Cam-Field. But as I'm sure you're aware, Rankins has existed since the gold-rush days."

"Unfortunately, the gold is gone now, Laurel. But what is here is a wealth of oil deposits," Emily pointed out. "And Rankins only stands to benefit from that. But without utilizing that resource, the projections for the future economic growth of Rankins for the next decade show little to no growth. But with Cam-Field's help, those numbers head in the exact opposite direction."

"The citizens of Rankins will have a

chance to voice for themselves what kind of growth they'd like to see next Sunday at the town-hall meeting, correct?"

"That is absolutely true, and if the community involvement that I've seen since I've been here is any indication, we're going to have a packed house."

"You can count on that. But why is Cam-Field so concerned with what the community thinks? It's really only the town council who votes on the permit approval."

"That's a really great question, Laurel. We, at Cam-Field, believe that what we do is more than just provide jobs and dollars for a community. Our goal is always to collectively improve a way of life. Economic growth doesn't mean much in a town if the people aren't benefiting from it. If Cam-Field intended to come in here and rob Rankins of its valuable resources, as some members of this community have been suggesting, then that would only be benefiting Cam-Field. We believe that business of this kind should be a give-and-take. That's why we've pledged the millions of dollars that we have to improve this community—for the hospital, the school and in the construction of the community center."

"Okay, that is all very important information, but it's also information that's already out there. You have done a great job of letting this community know what Cam-Field can do for it. What I'd like to do now is find out more about the face of Cam-Field, so to speak. You have been here for about a month now and you've met a lot of people and participated in numerous community events. And I've been out there, too, and I have talked to a lot people, and what I've discovered is that the citizens of Rankins are curious about you, as well as Cam-Field. Where does Emily Hollings call home?"

"Well, I travel an awful lot, but when I'm not on location like this, I live in San Diego."

"What do you do with your spare time?"

"What spare time?" Emily joked. "I work pretty much all the time, although I have picked up a new hobby since I've been here in Rankins...."

"Oh, really? What's that?"

"Halibut."

"Fishing?"

"No, eating." She laughed and added, "I've also discovered that I enjoy snowshoeing and..."

It continued on in this manner for another ten minutes, and Emily found that it was easy for her to talk about the things she liked about Rankins. She knew that Bering and others would probably think she was only saying them in an attempt to earn their favor, but she hoped she came across as sincere, because she was.

Emily could sense the interview was wrapping up. Soon Laurel thanked Emily for her time and snapped off the recorder.

"So, how'd I do?" Emily asked.

"Great. It's obvious that you've done this before."

"Is that your way of telling me that I lack a certain amount of candidness? Is that a word? Candidness?"

"No. Well, I suppose it is. And yes, it's a word, but I didn't mean to imply anything negative about you. I just meant that you are very polished."

"Thank you, I think."

"Can we talk off the record for a minute?"

"Of course."

"How's it going with you and Bering?"

Emily decided it couldn't hurt to answer the question—off the record. "We're good, I think. At least from my side, we are. Why? What have you heard? Or maybe I should ask what Piper has heard."

"No, it's nothing like that, and I know this is none of my business. It's just that you guys seem like you're getting rather, um…close and so…how are you guys going to reconcile everything? It's no secret that one of you is going to win this thing and one of you is going to lose."

Emily had no idea how to respond to that concern. She already couldn't imagine her life without Bering. He had taught her so much about how to live. Sure, she'd seen the world and had some adventures, but she knew now that she'd just been going through the motions. She'd eaten the halibut, metaphorically speaking, but she hadn't really savored it. There had always been a motive behind her actions, a means to an end, a job to do.

But Bering seemed to savor everything about life, he was incredibly generous in sharing it with her, and she was loving every minute of it. He didn't have an ulterior motive like she usually did, and she couldn't believe that someone could be so giving of himself without asking or wanting anything in return. Anything beyond her time, that was, which Emily was more than happy to give.

She had no idea how to define their relationship. Although her experience with relationships was dismal, albeit much of that was her fault. She'd never invested the time before—had never wanted to—but the time she spent with Bering was exactly how she'd dreamed things should be, better than she'd dreamed.

Her dreams before had centered almost exclusively on her career. And now, when she thought about it, it seemed crazy that she'd made such a drastic change to her thought processes so quickly. But it had happened without even trying. It wasn't as if she wasn't still working hard at her job. She was and she wanted to be successful; it was just that she thought about other things at the same time. Like people—Bering, Janie and her boys, his mom, his cousins, Tag and Shay, and even the friends she'd made....

She worried about Laurel, and Piper, and the other community members who were solidly in her camp. What would people think of them if they knew how hard they'd been working on Cam-Field's behalf?

Bering had somehow taught her this—this genuine concern for other people. She loved that about him and she was realizing how satisfying it was to allow that kind of empathy to flourish in herself. Bering had done that, too—he was making her a better person.

"I don't know, Laurel. But I do want you to know how sorry I am in advance if any of this makes your life more difficult."

Laurel grinned. "I'm not worried about my

life, Emily. I'm a reporter. I thrive on conflict. I am worried about you, though. I know we haven't known each other that long, but I consider you a friend. And Bering is my friend, too—you know that, but..."

"But what?"

"This is all off the record, and honestly, I really don't know anything concrete, but I can feel it in the air—something's brewing. Haven't you noticed it? This town is essentially in the midst of a civil war and yet things have been so calm the last week or so. Remember what it was like when you first arrived? People were half-crazed and everyone had an opinion. And now it's like, I don't know... People are still worked up, but it's different. And Bering—he seems so blasé about it all lately. I mean he's going through the motions, but I don't see the fire that I did at first. And maybe it's because of your, um, relationship but I don't know..."

Emily felt a gathering of fear in the pit of her stomach. Laurel was right. And she hadn't seen it. She'd believed that people were more at ease and respectful because of her relationship with Bering and other members of the James family. And she'd thought that things had mellowed between her and Bering for the same reason. But what if that wasn't the case?

What if they knew something she didn't? But on the other hand, wasn't it also possible that she'd managed to sway the majority to Cam-Field's side and people were accepting—even embracing—the inevitable? But no, not Bering—he would never accept it. She wouldn't if she were in his place. She needed to think.

"I see what you mean. Like a calm before the storm kind of thing?"

Laurel nodded. "Exactly, and maybe it's the reporter in me—seeing conspiracy everywhere. But I just want you to be careful, Emily. I don't want you to get blindsided or…"

Heartbroken. Emily finished the sentence silently as a cold feeling of dread spread through her. And Bering, she realized suddenly, had definitely acquired the ability to break her heart.

CHAPTER THIRTEEN

JEREMY WAS READY to blow his top. He could feel the veins bulging and pounding in his neck as he scanned the model in front of him. He picked up a tiny stick of fake debris and then set it back down on top of the tiny pile. He'd asked the graphics department for a mock-up of the building that Cam-Field was proposing to have built for the new Argot & Co. headquarters.

Argot had become a veritable cash cow of oil and gas deposits located off the coast of Louisiana before the last hurricane hit. The petroleum deposits were all offshore and thus still in perfect shape, but the platforms had suffered extensive damage and the onshore infrastructure had been blown to bits. The company was hugely in debt and in danger of going under if someone didn't invest in its recovery. Cam-Field intended to be that someone and had made an offer to invest a substantial amount of money in exchange for a share of the company.

It was a simple request, he'd thought, of the graphics department. But what he was looking at now was apparently a replica of the post-hurricane destruction along the coastline of Louisiana.

"Doug? It is Doug, right?" Jeremy asked as calmly as he could manage.

"Uh, yes, sir," Doug said with a wide grin. He stood at attention in front of Jeremy's desk with two other members of his team.

"Fine, yes." Jeremy went on, "Doug, what is this?"

Doug bobbed his head up and down, and answered proudly, "It's Louisiana, sir. And this—" he pointed at a miniature little funnel blob of fake crystals and sequins "—is Hurricane Lula before she hit the coast. We thought it would be a nice touch to show her path across the ocean, too." He trailed his index finger over the bright blue faux ocean.

"Mmm-hmm." Jeremy nodded. "But why?"

"Well…I'm not a meteorologist or anything, but it's my understanding that when a tropical storm hits an already moist weather disturbance, a hurricane is often the result," Doug explained soberly. "And the winds and stuff are a serious bummer."

"I know that," Jeremy managed to utter

through his stiffened jaw. "But why is it sitting on my desk?"

Doug furrowed his brow and looked down at the model. "Did you want it in the conference room, sir?"

"No!" Jeremy nearly shouted. It took all of his effort to lower his voice. "No. What I meant was, why did you make it? And where is the mock-up of the new Argot & Co. headquarters?"

"Whoa," Doug said with wide eyes.

"What do you mean, 'whoa'?" Jeremy barked.

"I'm sorry, dude, er, I mean, sir, but I'm pretty sure that you asked for a muck-up."

"A muck-up?" Jeremy repeated incredulously.

"Yes, sir, you asked for a muck-up of the coastline where the Argot headquarters is located. So I thought you meant you wanted to see the post-hurricane destruction. You know," he said and added finger quotes, "'the wrath of Lula'—that's what we've been calling it. I think that's dope, don't you? And here it is." Doug beamed proudly and gestured at their work. "Boy, that storm really did a number on that building. See?" He pointed at a pile of painted toothpicks. "That's it right there."

Silence gave way to tension as Jeremy stared into the faces of the morons made up Cam-Field's graphics staff and wondered how they could possibly be so stupid. He'd seen their work before and it had always been brilliant. Emily was always bragging about how they had the best graphics staff in the industry. She'd also warned him to tread carefully around the quirky, eccentric, but extremely talented bunch.

You needed to be patient, she had explained, and you had to communicate exactly what you needed, she'd advised, and if you could do that, they'd do anything for you. They could make gold out of yellow construction paper, she'd added proudly. Of course, he hadn't really taken her words to heart. Like the rest of the advice she'd given him, he'd pretty much blown it off. Well, he was paying for that now.

He'd had all he could take. He banged his fist on the desk. "Out! I want you all out of here. Now!" he screamed and pointed at the door. He so badly wanted to fire them all, but knew that he'd not only be looking at a wrongful-termination lawsuit, he'd also have no graphics staff. "And when you come back it had better be with a mock-up! Do you hear me, you imbeciles? I want a mock-up! A mock-UP of the new Argot & Co. headquarters building that we are proposing to build for them. Do you understand? A model—a mock-up."

They scampered out of the room and Jeremy slumped back into his chair. He needed a new game plan and he needed it quickly. Emily.

BERING BROWSED THROUGH his notes in preparation for the impending conference call that would give him the latest update on the halting of Cam-Field's business here in Rankins. He looked at his watch impatiently; just a few more hours and he would be meeting Emily at her house.

Bering was trying not to let his feelings of guilt spoil his time with Emily. It was important, he kept telling himself, to continue to show her what an amazing place Rankins really was. The fact that their relationship had escalated to something beyond friendship was irrelevant. The fact that he felt confident that he would prevail in preventing Cam-Field from taking over the town was also beside the point.

And to all appearances, he and the Save Rankins Coalition were still fighting hard. The two sides had had a busy few days of back-and-forth. First there was Bering's re-scheduled rally. And although Evan Cobb had been unable to attend, one of Bering's former environmental-sciences professors had come instead. He'd given a very compelling speech and an even better Q and A. Bering had been pleased with the turnout, although, as expected, Emily had responded with a successful venture of her own.

She had arranged a book giveaway and signing by Robert Galleon—a scientist who had written a bestseller on the importance of American oil independence. He was the perfect advocate for Cam-Field's cause because he appealed to the energy-independence crowd as well as to the business-minded.

Bering had gone to both events and had counted more town-council members at Emily's event than had been at his. But when he'd learned that neither one of them had anything planned for this evening, he'd suggested they spend it together. Emily had agreed without hesitation. She hadn't even seemed to give work a thought.…

His phone rang; he looked at the number and noted with surprise that it was two hours early. He picked up the receiver.

"Bering, glad I reached you. It's Jack."

"Hello, Senator," Bering said and they exchanged a few pleasantries.

"Look, Bering, I've got some news for you that I think you'll be happy to hear. The conference call is off."

"That's good news?"

He explained, "I think you'll find it so in this case. Not only are we going to be able to shut this thing down, we are now headed in a whole new direction. And we have started an investigation. We've been looking closely at some of the other projects that Cam-Field has been involved with over the last few years. Some shady things appear to be going on. It seems Cam-Field has always been very meticulous with environmental reviews—until the last year or so."

The senator quickly filled Bering in and they said goodbye, but Bering sat gripping the phone for several minutes as he allowed the ramifications of the senator's words to sink in. "Probable fraud…" He should have been thrilled by what he'd heard, but instead the news filled him with unease. A month ago he would have been ecstatic to hear that Cam-Field might be embroiled in legal trouble. But that was all before Emily. *Emily.*

As he gently replaced the phone into the cradle, he worried about how this investigation would affect her. Would she lose her job? Would she blame him? He tried to tell himself that she was a big girl, that she could handle it. She'd been working for Cam-Field forever, and it certainly wouldn't be the first time a roadblock, or even a bomb, had been thrown in her path. He knew it wasn't even the first time that Cam-Field had been investigated for one thing or another. Why didn't that make him feel better? And if she did lose her job, was there any way that she would ever stay with him?

Obviously she wouldn't stay with him—she would probably never speak to him again. And even if, through some kind of miracle, she didn't hold it against him, she was still leaving. She worked for Cam-Field, and she was going to be heading for the next job soon, the next little town like Rankins to come into Cam-Field's crosshairs. But that offered no comfort, because what he really wanted was impossible—he wanted to save Rankins, but he wanted Emily, too.

EMILY TOOK A QUICK SHOWER, dried her hair and then dressed in a pair of yoga pants, a long-sleeved T-shirt and a fleece hoodie. She slipped her feet into a pair of fuzzy slippers and padded into the kitchen. She opened the fridge and began removing ingredients. Cooking seemed so overwhelming to her, although much less so than it had a couple weeks ago, as Bering had succeeded in teaching her how to make omelets, pancakes and grilled cheese.

Certainly she could do dinner, she told herself as she scowled down at the plastic-wrapped chicken lying on the counter. Couldn't she? She had called Janie and asked for some advice on what to fix—something she knew Bering liked, but that wouldn't be too complicated. Janie had been full of ideas and had even offered to come over and help, but Emily had declined, wanting to do this on her own. Now, as she studied the recipe Janie had given her for one of Bering's favorite dishes, she wondered if she should have taken her up on that offer. She glanced over at the clock and hoped the few hours she had would be enough to complete the task.

She had thought about Laurel's warning and decided that it didn't matter. Bering and his Save Rankins Coalition had been fighting hard, and if he had something up his sleeve, then so be it. She reminded herself that it wouldn't be anything different than she had encountered before. She would answer in kind and that would be it. This sort of sparring went with the territory. She smiled to herself. She knew that it really was becoming just a job for her. She was still committed to it; it was only her relationship with Bering that made things feel different.

Besides, she had her own long-term plans now, but she wasn't going to think about the repercussions of those, either. Tonight, she would do her utmost to enjoy an evening with Bering in exactly the manner he'd taught her—putting business aside.

After an exhausting wrestling match with a stubborn naked chicken, Emily felt like the victor. The disagreeable bird was now skinless and drowning in a buttermilk concoction as the recipe outlined and Janie had instructed.

Almost two hours later, she was rethinking her plan to include dessert in her menu. She'd also asked Janie for a dessert to bake. She'd never baked a cake before and now she stared down at the gooey mass she'd removed from the oven. She'd flipped it over onto a platter as per the instructions, but she doubted that was how it was supposed to look. She blew out a breath and wiped the sweat from her brow. The hoodie was long gone, her sleeves were pushed up and her hair was piled messily on top of her head.

Bering—and his sister and his mother and his aunts—made it look so easy, but cooking was difficult. And messy—she was glad she'd started early so she could clean up before Bering saw this catastrophe. He'd never let her hear the end of it. She reached over and poked at the cakelike substance. Maybe she could shape it back together somehow, because it didn't resemble any kind of cake she'd ever seen, and there were chunks still stuck in the bottom of the pan. Probably that wasn't supposed to happen. She chewed on her lip and perused the recipe once more. She flipped the little card over. Oh, dear, there was more on the back? Grease the pan? She'd missed that important detail. And apparently she was supposed to let the cake cool before she inverted it?

"Ugh!" She let out a groan of frustration.

"What are we doing here?"

Emily jumped and turned. Bering was leaning nonchalantly against the doorframe. Her heart thumped heavily in her chest, partially from being startled but mostly because of him. And she definitely didn't want him to see her like this.

"Bering, what are you doing here? You're not supposed to be here for at least another hour."

"I finished early," he said. Something flashed across his face but was gone so quickly she didn't have time to identify it. A look of amusement transformed his features as his eyes darted around the kitchen, taking in the mess of pans, measuring cups, bowls and the pile of flour she'd spilled on the floor but decided to clean up after she got the cake into the oven. But then she'd started making the frosting and she hadn't had time to get the broom. Now as she looked around, too, she wondered how it had managed to travel and spread across nearly every surface of the kitchen.

He sauntered toward her and Emily felt her pulse begin to flutter. He looked on the verge of laughter.

Emily, feeling slightly embarrassed, tried to smile up at him. "I am cooking dinner for you, which includes dessert. I wanted to do something to repay you for everything you've done for me—and with me. But..."

He reached out a finger and trailed it across her cheek, which caused her blood to spike warmly and words to fail her. He withdrew his finger and held it aloft. The tip was white with flour. He blew it off and then draped his arm over her shoulder.

"I see," he drawled slowly and then gestured toward the steaming pile on the counter. "What's that?"

"Cake!"

"Really?" he asked doubtfully.

"Yes," she squeaked.

"That explains the flour, then."

"Yep." Emily could see the humor of the situation. "Does it not look familiar? Janie said it was one of your favorites."

"She did, huh?" He peered at it more closely. "I'm getting old and forgetful, clearly, because I do not recognize it. What kind is it?"

She picked up the recipe card and handed it to him. "Chocolate-cherry something-or-other," she said. She pointed at the plate. "See that? Your sister even gave me the cherries. But I've only recently discovered that there are two sides to this card."

Bering's lips twitched. He flipped it over and then looked back down at the cake. He made a sniffing sound. "It smells delicious, though. I can't wait to try it."

"Bering, look at it."

"I'm sure it will look better after it's frosted."

"I highly doubt it. Why aren't you giving me a hard time about this?"

His brows traveled up onto his forehead.

"Are you kidding me? Emily, I'm thrilled. You're cooking for me. I don't care what it looks like. At the risk of sounding like a perfect chauvinist, I'll admit to liking this attempt at domesticity."

"Bering, this is a disaster. I don't think, uh, domesticity is my thing."

"Maybe not." He chuckled. "But maybe you just need a bit of practice. But either way, I don't care...." He picked up a chunk of the cake and put it in his mouth. "Mmm," he said and added an appreciative moan. "I do recognize it now. It's Aunt Margaret's recipe."

"Yes!" Emily cried triumphantly. "That's what Janie said."

He picked up another piece and offered it to her. "Taste," he said softly.

She opened her mouth and he slid the cake inside. She nodded. "It is pretty good."

"What else have you got?"

"There's chicken soaking over there, but is there any chance you would settle for just cake for dinner?"

Bering looked down at her and grinned. "You would like that, wouldn't you?"

"Yes, I would. I really, really would."

"Not a chance." He walked over to the chicken and lifted off the plastic wrap. "Now, this I recognize. It's one of my favorites."

"Janie said it was." She popped another piece of cake into her mouth.

He stared at her.

"Whafft?" she asked, her mouth now stuffed full of cake. "I'm *frilly hungrfy.*"

He crossed his arms over his chest. "Stop eating the cake, Emily. It's dessert. And as I've been trying to tell you for the last few weeks, dessert comes after the meal."

She stole another quick nibble. "Okay, okay. Man, you are so bossy. Has anyone ever told you that before?"

"I may have heard that a time or two from this junk-food-addicted blonde I know." He shook his head. "You'd think she'd be grateful for all my help and advice, but all she does is complain and sneak unhealthy snacks behind my back. Sometimes she even trashes portions of the healthy meals I prepare for her. Can you believe that?"

"Maybe you should quit trying to feed her toast that's full of dried bugs and wheat germ on the sly. Have you thought of that?"

"If you don't start eating what I feed you, I really am going to sneak some bugs in, and trust me—you'll never even know they're there."

"I don't really think you'd do that," she

said, but couldn't keep the doubt from creeping into her voice. "Would you?"

"Probably not, if you are willing to make a deal here."

She looked at him suspiciously. "What kind of deal?"

"I'll help you cook this meal if you call off the rally on Saturday."

"The rally? Bering, I can't do that." She had two speakers coming, including a lady who was one of Alaska's most popular and well-known businesswomen, and the other, a charismatic state senator. This was to be her last big push before the town-hall meeting on Sunday and the town-council vote was Tuesday. There was no way she could call it off.

"Emily, it's not going to make one bit of difference in the big picture and you know it. Those councilmen and women have already made their minds up. One more public battle between us isn't going to matter."

Laurel's warning flashed through her mind. Why did he seem so unconcerned? Why wasn't he planning something of his own? Was he that confident he would win? Why would he be? She and Amanda felt as though they had secured more council votes. It was close, yes, but when it came down to it, she didn't think the majority of them would turn down what Cam-Field was offering. "Then why call it off?"

"I'd like to spend the day with you on Saturday."

"Oh."

"Emily, your town-hall meeting is on Sunday. Just have Tara Gillsby speak at that event if you think it will make that much of a difference. I'd like to spend another day with you before this whole thing goes down—before whatever happens…"

She stared at him as her stomach tightened with anxiety. It was the first time either one of them had mentioned aloud what they'd both been thinking. After Tuesday, things would never be the same—one way or the other. She was trying desperately to figure out what this meant—on more than one level. But she knew, even as her mind tried to calculate the ramifications what she was going to say.

"Another cease-fire?" he asked softly, and Emily couldn't resist the longing she read on his face. It made her heart soar and it filled her with hope. And no matter how fruitless her head said that hope was, she couldn't stop her heart from deciding this one…

"Okay," she said. "How about this…" She thought for a moment. "I really can't cancel on Tara Gillsby. But I'll let Amanda handle everything on Saturday—and by *everything* I mean I won't even call to check in and see how it's going. I'll spend the day with you. We'll call it a cease-fire compromise?"

Bering nodded slowly. "Okay," he said. "I can live with a compromise."

CHAPTER FOURTEEN

EMILY AND AMANDA were sitting on the sofa in Emily's living room drinking coffee and going over the details for the town-hall meeting that night.

As agreed, she'd spent the previous day with Bering and it had been incredible. They'd gotten an early start the following morning when Bering picked her up and they had watched the sun rise over breakfast at Craven's B and B, then they'd gone boating. He had pointed out landmarks as they cruised along the shore. Then they had traveled up the coastline and into a scenic fjord to get up close and personal with a glacier. Emily had been mesmerized by the sight, and the sound, of the giant mass of ice, which reached all the way to the water's edge. They'd spent the evening at Bering's, and Emily had barely even thought about the rally.

And on the return trip, as she'd viewed the town from out in the water, from nearly the spot where the proposed oil platform would go, she'd decided what she was going to give Bering for his birthday. His birthday was tomorrow—the day before the vote—and he hadn't even told her. Thank goodness Janie had called....

"Do you want to go over your speech one more time?" Amanda asked as she flipped through the last of the pages stacked in front of her.

"Amanda, thank you again for yesterday. It sounds like you did a great job."

"It went well. It was fun. It must have been difficult for you, though, huh?" she teased. "Keeping your nose out of it?"

Emily shook her head as if she couldn't quite believe it herself. "Surprisingly enough, no, it wasn't."

Amanda's brows lifted in mock surprise. "Well, Em, that is great. It's so nice to see you enjoying yourself for a change. Now, how about this speech?"

"Nah, I think I'm ready. Do you think I'm ready?"

"Emily, honey, you were born ready."

"Now, if I only believed it." Emily sighed and laid her head back against the soft cushion of the sofa.

"What?"

"Oh, Amanda, I don't know. Normally I

can convince myself that what I'm saying is true—or that there is at least some truth to it."

"Emily, what you're saying is true." She paused as if thinking about the statement. "It certainly isn't untrue."

"I know. I mean, it's true, but is it right?"

"Is it right?" Amanda repeated. "Um, Emily, what are you talking about? What's going on in that brilliant mind of yours?"

"I don't know, Amanda. Things have changed for me. It's like my drive is gone. These people love this little town, and yes, we are going to bring in more money and jobs and blah, blah, blah. But is it worth it? Really, when it's all said and done? Is it really worth it? This is such a special place, don't you think? I mean, really and truly unique, and I don't know... Should we be the ones to ruin that? All in the name of more money for Cam-Field's already stuffed coffers?"

"Um, Em, I think Franklin would prefer that you say that it's all in the name of 'progress,'" Amanda quipped. They both burst out laughing. It was one of his favorite buzzwords.

"Seriously, though, what are you saying here exactly?"

Emily shrugged. "I guess I'm saying that I don't know what I'm doing it for anymore."

"Well, for starters you're doing it to show your stepfather and that smug jerk Jeremy that they didn't win. Everyone knows that Cam-Field wouldn't be half the company it is without you."

"Thanks, Amanda." Emily felt the tears welling up in her eyes. "And what is with these tears? I've cried more in the last month than I have in the last twenty years. Have you noticed that?"

"Listen, you have every right to cry once in a while. You've been through so much in the last few months, in your entire life, really, if you think about it. You do know that no one else would have put up with what you have?"

"Yeah, I think I'm finally figuring that out." She glanced at her friend, took a deep breath and then exhaled slowly. "I'm not going back, Amanda."

"What do you mean, you're not going back?"

"I don't have a future with Cam-Field anymore. I don't want a future with Cam-Field anymore. I always thought that I would take the reins of this company one day, and that has been my sole focus in life. But I know that's not going to happen now. And I can't work for Jeremy. I don't even want to work with him. I've lost it." She shrugged helplessly. "My ambition, it's gone. I don't care about my job anymore. I don't care about Cam-Field. And I see so clearly now how my feelings for Franklin have been wrapped up in my feelings for Cam-Field. I'm not sure how I feel about him when I separate him from the business. But I think I'd like to find out."

Amanda gaped at her as if she couldn't quite believe what she was hearing. "But what will you do?"

"I'm going to finish this job, and by *this job* I mean I'm done after the vote. I do want this, for me. But I also want it for Franklin because I know how important it is to him. But however it goes, I'm quitting." Emily was stunned to realize how torn she was between wanting to score this victory for her stepfather and by seeing Bering's, and Rankins's, precious way of life preserved.

"Okay, okay…" Amanda was clearly trying to soak it all in. "But what will you do then?" she asked.

"I've got quite a bit of savings." She tilted her head to one side and said, "Maybe take some time off. Maybe go see Aidan in whatever jungle he's camped out in. And then I'm thinking about getting a job on a cruise ship."

"A cruise ship?" Amanda repeated incredulously.

"Yeah, doesn't *cruise director* sound great? You'd—"

"Em, honey, we all would like to be a cruise director, or cupcake taster, or whatever, but you can't just up and quit." Amanda paused and looked skyward for a second. "Can you? Well, heck, maybe you can." She smiled at Emily and then reached over and patted her hand. "I know you've been avoiding this topic, but since we're talking about your future here…um, what about Bering?"

Emily shook her head and tried to keep a fresh bout of tears at bay. "That will all be over soon anyway. He's going to hate me and I know it."

"Why would he hate you?"

"Because Cam-Field is going to get the approval from the town council and Rankins will begin its metamorphosis and then Bering is going to resent me. And eventually it will turn to hate."

"Oh, Emily, you don't know that."

"Yes, I do, Amanda. And you do, too. You've spent enough time with Tag and Bering yourself to know how closely tied their lives are to this place. Cam-Field threatens everything they are and everything they have invested here.

Sure, industry will grow, but what about tourism? Bering and his coalition are right—what tourist is going to want to come here after all this construction is completed? Who is going to want to live here when the entire character of this town is changed?"

She let out a miserable sigh. "It doesn't matter anyway, right? I've seen you do this before, Amanda. The end of a job—the end of the relationship, right? I mean, it's in the nature of this kind of thing for it not to last..."

"You're in love with him."

"What? No. Don't be ridiculous, I'm not..." She couldn't possibly be in love with him, could she? Did she even know what love felt like? No, she didn't, and surely it didn't happen this fast, did it? No, it couldn't.... Right, so why was it that when she thought about leaving him her chest got all tight and constricted as though she had a piano sitting on it? It made it difficult to breathe. Yeah, that was why she kept forcing herself to not think about it—so she could breathe properly. How could she have been so careless as to allow herself to fall in love?

"Are you going to tell him?" Amanda asked.

"No, of course not."

"Emily, he's probably in love with you, too."

"No, Amanda, and even if that were true, it doesn't matter. It can't last. It can't." But she wanted it to, she really did. Now that she thought about it, she'd never wanted anything so much in her entire life—not even the title of CEO of Cam-Field Oil & Mineral. But she couldn't say it out loud, she wouldn't, because then everything would hurt even more than it already did.

She could handle it; she'd been a master at handling her emotions her entire life. Until she'd found herself in Rankins anyway.

Now she executed a one-shoulder shrug and remarked lightly, "You, of all people, know what it's like to fall in love, to get involved in a relationship that you know is going to end. Give me some advice. Tell me what to do."

Amanda shook her head sadly. "Emily, no, I don't. I've only been in love with one of the guys that I met on one of these jobs, and I got engaged to him. I would have left everything to be with him. I had planned to, remember? Sure, it didn't work out. But all the other times—I've had a good time and maybe felt a little tug of sadness, but if I'd really been in love, Em, I would have stayed. Or I would have figured out some way to work it out."

Emily stared at Amanda a long time before

she spoke. "Why haven't we ever talked about this stuff before, Amanda? I mean, you're my best friend."

"We have, Emily. I do talk about it. You've just never heard it before."

Emily knew that what she said was true. She'd always listened as Amanda prattled on about the men in her life. Her chatter had always been amusing and entertaining—like a good gossip magazine—but it hadn't ever really seemed serious to her. The difference between then and now was that she just couldn't relate before. Had she really been that single-minded? That obsessed with work? The answer, she knew, was an unqualified yes.

"Amanda, I'm sorry. I've been like some kind of unemotional robot, haven't I? How have you put up with me all these years?"

"I've always preferred to think of you as more like Sleeping Beauty. I've been patiently waiting for you to wake up. And it's finally happened, but I think we have Bering to thank for that."

She looked at Amanda and didn't try to mask her anguish as she asked, "This is going to be really hard, isn't it?"

EMILY STARED AT THE SKETCH she'd drawn, the one that Bering had won at the Rotary auction and then given to her that same night. She carefully removed the sketch from the frame, signed it and placed it into a different frame—one she thought suited it much better. She wrapped it in red tissue paper and then placed it in a box.

When Janie had called to invite her to Bering's surprise birthday party, she'd been touched. She didn't think she'd ever get used to his family's thoughtfulness. But she'd also been worried. What could she possibly get for him? Where did these people even shop? She'd asked Janie.

"Oh, we do a lot on the internet now. Glacier City is only about three hours away on a good day. It's not exactly a thriving metropolis or anything, but you can get almost anything you need. It used to be that we'd drive, or pay an exorbitant amount to fly, to Anchorage a couple times a year, stay a few nights with my mom's cousin, but now that Tag has his pilot's license, we fly more often than that—and it's a lot faster and cheaper than buying a ticket."

"Wow."

"I know, I know. It seems really backwoods, huh? But you'd be surprised at how good you get at thinking and planning ahead.

And now with the internet…well, it's so much easier."

"Is it casual?"

Janie laughed. "Sweetie, it's always casual here in Rankins—even when it's not. The only time people even attempt to dress up is for weddings, funerals, church and the Rotary fund-raiser. And usually that just means flannel that's been ironed with a spray of starch."

Emily smiled at hearing her previous conjecture spoken aloud. "Okay, so do I bring anything?"

"Nah, it's going to be at the Caribou, so everything's taken care of. Just bring your lovely self and Amanda if she wants to come."

Now, as Emily wrapped the box, she hoped that Bering would understand the symbolism behind it. She wanted it to convey to him that it had worked, his efforts had paid off—he had managed to make her fall in love with Rankins. She was grateful to Bering for "waking her up," as Amanda had suggested, and in spite of what happened, win or lose, she wanted him to know that.

She was going to take the memories of Bering, and of Rankins, and tuck them away and keep them forever. They would see her through the rough patches, and she knew that she'd never be the same again. Because if one good thing could come from it all, it was that she was finally ready to live. To live life the way Bering lived it, the way he'd shown her that she could live. She wiped at the tears that streamed down her face as she wondered how she could possibly do any of that without him.

EMILY WAS NERVOUS. She was always nervous before these presentations but usually it was mixed with an equal amount of excitement and confidence. Tonight it was just mixed with equal parts of dread and nausea. She felt sick thinking about what Cam-Field would do if—when—they won approval for this project. And she was despondent about the soon-to-be end of her time with Bering.

The school's gymnasium was packed to the gills with standing room only. She glanced down at her watch, took a deep breath and walked up to the podium. "Good evening, ladies and gentlemen. On behalf of Cam-Field Oil & Mineral, I'd like to thank you all for coming tonight. And on a personal note, my assistant, Amanda, and I would like to thank you, and all the citizens of Rankins, for your warm and generous treatment. Your town is stunningly beautiful and we have so enjoyed our stay here." She was heartened by the solid round of applause.

She went on. "And now let's talk about the reason that we've all gathered here tonight…." Emily began by outlining Cam-Field's basic plan for the construction of the oil platform, storage facilities and pipeline. And while it was true, Emily then explained, that new unobtrusive structures would be built in and on the shore of the bay, jobs would be created, money would be pumped into the economy and virtually every aspect of Rankins would be improved in the process.

You're a big fat liar, Emily, she told herself. If she lived here she wouldn't want to change a thing. *These people are crazy if they agree to it,* she thought as she kept up a steady stream of corporate-speak.

And finally she added the frosting: upon approval of the final permits, Cam-Field would underscore its dedication to the future of Rankins with a donation of five million dollars for the hospital renovation. She reiterated their commitment to the community center and added that another million had been earmarked for the school system.

Forty-five minutes later, Emily was relieved to find that it was going much, much better than she had anticipated. Her voice sounded strong, her nervousness had subsided, her confidence felt revived and her words were making sense to her own ears. She didn't have the same enthusiasm for them anymore, but that was really irrelevant right now. Wasn't it?

"So, in conclusion I'd just like to add that in the development of this community's resources, Cam-Field will be dedicated to the health and well-being of the citizens of Rankins as well as the health and well-being of the landscape, the wildlife and all the unique aspects that make Rankins so special. Now I'd like to open up the floor to any questions or comments that you might have."

A young man stood up in the first row of the bleachers and Amanda passed him a microphone. He took it in one hand and raised the other in greeting. "Yeah, hi, um, about all these jobs? It sounds to me like a lot of them are going to need to be filled by skilled workers. How do you expect a bunch of fishermen and loggers to jump onto an oil rig and know what to do?"

"That's a very good question. Cam-Field has an extensive training program for its workers. It's a paid training program and the only requirements are that you are ready to learn some valuable new skills and willing to work hard." Emily briefly outlined the process.

She then successfully fielded dozens more

questions, and the audience seemed to have been tamed when she heard a new buzz from the crowd. She knew it was Bering before she even saw him striding purposefully and confidently up the aisle. She stepped aside as he approached the podium and his eyes flicked over briefly to meet hers, but she couldn't read a thing behind the glance. A seed of dread sprouted inside her and quickly blossomed as he began to speak.

"You know something I've always wondered? Why does everything have to grow, to change? To dramatically change? Really, think about it. Why do we need growth? Why do we need Cam-Field? What's wrong with things staying the same if we all like it the way it is? Nothing, I say. Because I think that everything is already pretty great around here."

That statement was met with wild applause and hoots from the audience.

"This is a very pretty picture that Cam-Field has painted here tonight. But that's all it is—a picture. And we all know that a picture is merely a very tiny slice of reality and often a rather inaccurate slice at that. I would like to take a few moments to show how Cam-Field's picture is flawed. I am going to start by pointing out a few problems and inconsistencies in these projections.

"The first and most glaring problem I'd like to bring to light are the eyesores that will be created right here on the shores of our bay—and in our bay—which essentially serves as our entire community's front yard. As it is now, when I and many, if not most us here, get up each morning, we are treated to the most gorgeous and picturesque view in the world—a clear horizon for miles teeming with wildlife. On any given morning I can raise my binoculars and see moose, wolves, caribou or bear along the shoreline or on the beach, birds on the water and in the air, whales surfacing, sea otters playing, and seals frolicking both on and offshore. Now if you will, imagine with me the view here in Rankins if Cam-Field moves in—a giant, hulking and ugly chunk of metal sitting right out there and obscuring these sights that we all love so much. I believe the word that Ms. Hollings used was *unobtrusive*. I'm going to show you exactly what Cam-Field's version of unobtrusive looks like." He paused and looked to his left. "Tag, would you start the slides please?"

It was all Emily could do to stand still and not react. She plastered a mask of indifference on her face and pretended to look interested in the photos, although she knew exactly what they portrayed. Photo after photo showed one oil rig, open pit mine or scarred landscape after another. She swallowed hard when he got to the photos of a toxic spill that had killed hundreds of birds in the mountains of Colorado. This particular incident had occurred fifteen years ago, when Emily had been working in the mail room, but she was familiar with the details.

The next series of photos showed a small oil spill off the coast of Texas, and then a larger spill that had occurred off the coast of California. There were studies about the toxicity of mine tailings, and of substances used in the extraction of certain minerals. She had to give Bering credit: once again, he'd done his homework. Emily could feel the community's confidence in Cam-Field wavering, but she was ready with her rebuttal. As far as the industry was concerned, Cam-Field had an excellent environmental record and she could recite it in her sleep.

"So we get a few jobs out of the deal? So what?" Bering was saying. "What happens to our fisheries if there's an oil spill? What happens to our wildlife? What happens to our tourism industry? What about people like

Abigail Cravens, whose bed–and-breakfast sits right on the dock and whose livelihood depends on the summer tourists? And what about Shay James at the Faraway Inn? And Tess and Mac at the Cozy Caribou? And myself and countless others? We all depend on the pristine beauty of Rankins for our livelihood, not to mention our quality of life."

The meeting went, thankfully, much smoother than Emily had anticipated. She felt that boded well for Cam-Field's cause. After Bering and the string of other opposing speakers had said their piece, Emily wrapped it up by reiterating Cam-Field's position and countering some of Bering's more damaging commentary. She urged any community members who hadn't received a copy of the proposal to pick one up at the door, where Amanda was manning a table with stacks of them and informational brochures.

Afterward, Emily spent time answering every question that was asked of her. She and Bering didn't have a chance to speak, and her heart constricted in her chest as she watched him walk out of the gymnasium without a backward glance. It was late by the time she and Amanda were finally able to go home— and they both knew they would be waking up Monday morning to face a very long day.

CHAPTER FIFTEEN

EMILY'S DAY WAS SHAPING UP to be just as long and exhausting as she'd anticipated—phone calls, emails, meetings. She was ready for it all to be over one way or the other. However, her anticipation for the coming evening was also partially to blame for her impatience.

She had decided something the night before while she'd listened to Bering rebut Cam-Field's proposal. Amanda was right. She was in love with him. And she couldn't leave Rankins without telling him. It was weird, she thought, how the realization once accepted needed to be expressed. She'd never been in love before, so she'd never understood what all the fuss was about. She was going to tell him tonight, after his surprise party.

It had to be tonight, because the town-council vote was tomorrow and she wanted to tell him before then. She wanted him to know how she felt before they had to face the consequences of the vote's results. It seemed

vital that she say it before the outcome somehow clouded its meaning.

They'd talked only briefly since the meeting, early this morning, just long enough for
Bering to invite her over later, after what he
believed was to be a simple birthday dinner
with his mom and sister. So when her cell
phone rang, she picked it up, thinking it was
him. It wasn't.

"Emily, dear? It's Franklin."

She cringed. Would this day never end?

"Hello, Franklin," she said evenly. "How
are you?"

"I'm quite fine physically, but otherwise
I'm a bit disturbed, Emily. I've just had a call
from Tom Watkins and he informed me that
the town meeting was rather contentious last
night. Is this an accurate report?"

Emily's brain shifted into work mode and
the implications of his statement sank in.
"You sent Tom Watkins here? To check on
me?" Resentment oozed from her tone and
she didn't care.

"He was in the neighborhood. I asked him
to stop by the meeting and see how things
were going."

"He was in the neighborhood of Rankins,
Alaska? Are you kidding me?" She spat out

the words. "There is no neighborhood here, Franklin. Rankins is it."

"He was in Juneau, Emily, and the last I checked I was still the CEO of this company, and there was no need for me to ask you. And from what I've heard, it was a good call on my part."

Emily could feel her pulse pounding in her temples. "Well, Tom has misinformed you. The meeting was spirited, yes, and it is true that we have faced a fair amount of resistance here. But I'm confident that we have the votes we need. The majority of the community might not be on board—although it is very close. This is a knowledgeable and sensible bunch of citizens here. But we have the number of town-council votes we need to get this passed, and that's what counts."

"Emily, I am afraid there is even more riding on this than you know. I have a bit of a situation here—"

"Franklin," she interrupted, "everything is fine here. I have everything under con—"

He continued to talk. "—which is why I'm sending Jeremy to help you out."

"What?" Emily nearly shrieked the response. "No!" She fought to control her tone. "Really, that's not necessary."

"He will be there sometime late this evening or early tomorrow."

"Tonight!" she shouted. "He's coming tonight?"

"Emily, there is no need to raise your voice. What has gotten into you? Yes, he will be there in time for the vote tomorrow. I thought it would be apropos to introduce Jeremy to the community at this juncture."

"Why?" Emily asked.

"Because if it passes, which I'm sure it will, then you and Jeremy will be working up there on the project together. Jeremy's requested it."

"THANK YOU, UNCLE FRANKLIN," Jeremy said after his uncle hung up the phone. "I really feel like the time is right now. I never should have balked in the first place. I've already got the ring. I'm going to ask her, and then we'll come home, get married and head back up to Alaska when the project begins."

"Hmm, frankly, Jeremy, I hope you're right, because after tomorrow, we're definitely going to need her back here as soon as possible. I don't understand exactly what's happening…." he muttered as he looked down at his desk.

Jeremy stood up and strode out the door.

"Kim" he shouted at his secretary as he approached his office. "I need the next flight out to Rankins, Alaska."

"Yes, sir," Kim said. "I'll book it immediately. Did you want that business-class or first-class?"

"What do you think?" he snapped as he stomped into his office and shut the door behind him.

KIM GLARED AT THE BACK of his door. "Pompous lowlife snake," she muttered under her breath. "A cheap seat it is," she said as she deftly began clicking away on her computer. "The cheapest seat available on the cattle-freight express..."

Then she picked up the phone and dialed. "Hey, Amanda, it's me, Kim. Guess who's slated to be on his way up north in just a matter of minutes?

"Mmm-hmm. Funny, I had a similar thought. Oh, yes, I can definitely do that." Kim chortled. "We are so bad, you know that? Absolutely, in the best way..."

"AMANDA, WHAT ARE WE going to do? Jeremy is coming up here." Emily paced back and forth in front of Amanda, who was perched on the edge of the couch, dressed and ready to leave for the party.

"Em—" Amanda tried to interrupt.

"Why would Franklin do that, Amanda? He's never sent anyone to help me on a job before. And Jeremy, of all people? The man is completely worthless. And now, of all times? I can't be babysitting him in addition to everything else I have to do. And he's going to be such a terrible spokesperson for Cam-Field. I can just see him strutting around like a peacock before the meeting. The town-council members are not going to be impressed. If they get a look at him before the vote in one of his expensive suits and his ridiculous shoes, they're going to vote us down because of that alone." She didn't need to remind herself that she used to be rather fond of that look herself. Now she liked comfortable jeans and layers of knit shirts and flannel and fleece and thick boots with traction on the soles...

"Emily!" Amanda barked, snapping her out it. "Listen to me. He will not be here before the vote."

"Yes, he will. Franklin said he was leaving today."

Amanda looked down at her shoes, which had begun tapping out a rhythm on the floor. "I happen to know for a fact that Kim couldn't get him out on a plane tonight. Well, she got him on a plane, but only to Dallas."

"What?"

"Yeah," Amanda murmured, her face twisted into a look of exaggerated disappointment. "Unfortunately, she could only get him as far as Dallas tonight. And then tomorrow he's getting on a plane that's going to Seattle, where he will again be delayed for quite some time. And then, in Anchorage there will be yet another delay and I just..." She shook her head sadly and said, "I don't think he's going to make it in time, Em. I'm sorry."

Emily was shocked at Amanda as her words began to register. She flopped down onto the sofa next to her. "I love you, Amanda."

"As well you should. Now, let's get going, because it's really bad form to be late for a surprise party."

BERING WAS DEEP in thought as he drove into the parking lot of the Cozy Caribou. He was also a little grumpy, as he'd wanted to spend the evening alone with Emily. It would be their last night together before the vote. And he wanted to savor these last moments before everything unraveled. But his mother had insisted that he meet her and Janie for dinner. The only reason she'd agreed to this small of a party was because Bering had threatened to not show up at all if she planned anything larger. So they'd compromised on a quiet dinner with just her, Janie, Tag and Shay.

Tag was standing outside the door when he arrived, and grabbed him in a bear hug. "Hey, happy birthday, cousin."

"Thanks, Tag. And thanks for coming tonight, man. I really don't feel like listening to Mom and Janie interrogate me about Emily all night. Maybe at least now they'll be on you about Amanda, too." Bering chuckled and slapped Tag on the shoulder as they stepped into total darkness.

"Why are all the lights out? Maybe they blew a breaker," Bering said as he groped around for the light switch.

"Surprise!" A crowd of people jumped out from under tables and behind the bar as the place lit up. Music came on amid cheers and more shouts of "Surprise!" and "Happy birthday!" His mom and Janie were instantly by his side.

Bering glared at his mother. "Mom, I thought you said we were having a quiet dinner?"

"We are," she said, "having dinner. It's just not going to be quite as quiet as I implied.... You're not mad at me, are you, honey?"

How could he be mad at this woman who'd given him nothing but love and support his entire life? "No, Mom." He leaned over and kissed her on the cheek and then Janie's, too, although he added a whispered threat in her ear.

He was visiting with a couple friends when he looked up and saw her. He gritted his teeth. She was wearing red. Her hair was swinging around her shoulders as she talked and gestured with her hands. Bering wanted to grab her hand and walk out the door and forget about the people, the party, tomorrow's vote and all the rest of this mess that they were tangled up in.

Then she met his eyes and smiled. Her entire being seemed to transform with that smile. And his heart swelled because he knew that it was only for him. He imagined for a moment that she shared a love for him as strong as he had for her.

He walked toward her and didn't stop until he was standing right next to her. She was talking to Cricket Blackburn, but thankfully, this time Bering didn't feel so much like punching him, especially when she reached up and threaded her arms around his neck and kissed him quickly and sweetly on the lips.

"Happy birthday, Bering." She whispered the words with her lips still touching his.

"It is now," he said as he grinned down at her.

EMILY HAD FUN, and in spite of Bering's initial irritation, she could tell that he did, too. He barely left her side, and anyone who had doubts about the status of their relationship before the party wasn't left guessing by the end of the evening.

"Well," Emily said several hours later as she followed him into his house. "No thanks to you, I got you something for your birthday."

"What do you mean, no thanks to me?" He slipped off his jacket and threw it on a chair. He went toward the fridge, opened it and removed two sodas. He unscrewed the tops and handed her one.

"What's this?" Her face lit with delight. Usually the only beverage Bering gave her outside the Cozy Caribou was water or some type of vegetable or fruit concoction that he whipped up in his blender.

"It's a special occasion," he said with a smile.

She put a hand on her hip. "Yeah, and you didn't even tell me it was your birthday."

He moved closer and kissed her softly on the lips. "I hope it's this sweater," he said. He set his bottle down and pulled her into his arms, splaying his hands across her back.

"You hope what's this sweater?"

"My present—I hope this is it. I like it. Where did you get it?"

"I ordered it online, and I'm glad you like it."

"I do. Now let's go watch a movie so I can admire you in it."

"I want you to open your present first." She removed the gift from her bag and handed it to him.

He peeled the paper away and opened the box. He looked puzzled as he peered down at it. "Emily, you can't regift this. I already gave it to you."

She smiled at him. "I know, but it's not quite the same. Look at it again—closely."

He stared at it hard for several minutes. Finally he looked up. "You did this?" he asked incredulously.

"I did."

"I've been trying to find out for weeks who did it."

Emily lifted her brows in surprise. "Well, you should have asked me—or Amanda."

"I did ask Amanda," he said. "She seemed

the logical person to ask, since Cam-Field donated it. Now that I think about it, she didn't actually say that she didn't know who'd drawn it...."

"She wouldn't," Emily said happily. "She was just protecting me. I didn't want anyone to know. She's a very good assistant."

He looked at it again and then at her as if he couldn't quite believe it.

BERING WAS HAVING a hard time. He couldn't reconcile the image she'd created in the sketch with who she was as a part of Cam-Field. He liked it, but it bothered him, too. He couldn't believe that someone who could see a picture like this and capture it so beautifully could just as easily destroy it. He was struggling to comprehend it. But for now he knew he needed to put it out of his mind and enjoy the fact that she'd given him such a precious gift.

"Emily, you're really talented."

"Thank you. But there's something I want to talk to you about, too," she said.

"Okay," he agreed. "Can I ask for something first?"

"Of course."

"A kiss," he whispered and touched his lips to hers.

"Thank you for this," he said. "I know exactly where I'm going to hang it."

"You do?" she answered. "Already?"

"Yep," he said. "Afterward, I kind of wished I hadn't given it to you."

"Bering!"

"Well, I didn't think you would appreciate it like I would, is all." He chuckled and rubbed a hand over his chin. "But who knew you had drawn it? I am in awe...."

"Bering, I—"

The chirp of his cell phone interrupted them. He looked at the display with a scowl. "It's Janie. I have to answer it," he said, but what he didn't say was that he knew it had to be important, because she wouldn't bother him tonight if it wasn't. At least it had better be....

"Janie, hey, what's up? Gareth? What? Have you called Tag? Okay, good. Yep, I'll be there as soon as I can.

"It's Janie. She's, uh, she's in labor. But it's still too early. I have to go and be with the boys while my mom meets her at the hospital." He grabbed his jacket and slipped it on.

"Is there anything I can do? Would you like me to sit with the boys so you can go to the hospital?"

"Um, maybe... Can you come with me right now?"

She put on her coat, grabbed her bag and they headed out the door.

EMILY SPENT THE NIGHT at Janie's, and Bering spent the night at the hospital. Emily had slept intermittently on the sofa. Bering had finally called her from the hospital around 4:00 a.m., but it was six in the morning before he felt comfortable leaving the hospital.

Now he was telling her that while Janie's condition had been extremely serious, she was currently stable and so were the babies. They had managed to stop the labor, but she was going to have to stay in the hospital for a few days and take it easy for the remainder of her term. Which meant the rest of the family would have to step it up to help her with the older boys.

"Mom has already written up a schedule so someone can pick the kids up from school every day. I have Tuesdays and Fridays."

"Bering, please let me know if there's anything I can do to help."

He wrapped his arms around her and hugged her. He buried his face in her hair. "Emily, you've done so much already. Staying here all night like this so I could be at the hospital…" He whispered softly, "Thank you." Then he pulled away and looked down at her.

She smiled warmly at him. "It was the least I could do. I'm so glad she's doing okay."

"How are the boys?"

"Worried about their mom. They were up late, but they are still sleeping. They were relieved that they didn't have to go to school. Why don't you go lie down for a while and get some sleep? I don't have to be at the office until ten."

Bering took her up on the offer and slept soundly until nearly ten when Emily came in to wake him. Tag was calling on her cell phone looking for Bering.…

BERING MET THE SENATOR at the Cozy Caribou. He shook his hand and sat down opposite him in a booth. "Jack, thank you so much for coming—I didn't expect you to actually show up for the vote."

"You're welcome, Bering. It's my pleasure—and a really good excuse to get out of Washington for a couple days. Tag told me about Janie. How is she?"

"Still in the hospital, but it looks like she and the twins are going to be fine."

"That's wonderful news. She's a strong woman."

"That she is." Bering nodded and waited for the senator to continue.

"The reason that I'm here, Bering, is that things have moved even faster than I anticipated. It didn't take much digging to piece it all together. And…long story short—there are indictments."

"Indictments?"

"Yep, this investigation has taken on a life of its own. And we have you to thank for that, Bering. The Department of Justice guys served Franklin Campbell and the CFO at their office this morning. But it seems that his nephew, Strathom, the senior VP, is on the run."

"On the run?"

"In transit, anyway. He was supposed to be here in Rankins last night, but apparently there was some kind of mix-up with his flight and he ended up in Great Skeet for the night. We're assuming it was unintentional."

"I would say so," Bering said. "They don't even have an airport up there."

Senator Marsh smiled at Bering. "Apparently, they have an ice field that's suitable as a landing strip. Word is he had to spend the night in an old maintenance shed. And now there's a storm moving in up there. But I'm here to hold a press conference and announce

the indictments before the town-council con-
venes. I tried calling your house and cell phone
several times during the flight and again this
morning but I couldn't reach you, which is
why I called Tag. We have notified the news
outlets, so I wanted you to be here for this."

"I see," Bering said weakly. His head was
spinning. He looked across the room and saw
that a pool table had been moved and a podium set up in its place. There were people
milling around with microphones and cameras. Just then another news crew came in
through the door and headed toward the
crowd. "I was at the hospital all night and
had switched it off. I saw that you called, but
I never thought…"

Bering hadn't even dreamed there were
going to be indictments. The senator had
told him about the investigation, but in Bering's experience, things didn't usually move
so quickly where Washington, D.C., was
concerned. He had assumed that the senator
would bog the project down in some type of
political red tape, but he hadn't been expecting this. He wished he had time to tell Emily;
still, it wouldn't make any difference anyway.
If the project was stopped—it was stopped.
And he knew Emily well enough to know that

she would not want something illegal to be going down within her own company.

"I almost feel sorry for Campbell's step-daughter. I wonder how she's going to take the news. Has she arrived yet? I've been curious about her—we haven't been able to pin any of this on her yet. It's easy to assume that the apple doesn't fall far from the tree, but as she didn't actually come from the tree... Who knows, right? The employees sure seem to love her, but it's hard to believe that she could have such a key role in the organization and not know anything."

Bering felt a cold numbness spread through his chest. "His stepdaughter?" he repeated, even as the notion began to seep into his consciousness.

"Yes, I assumed you knew. This Emily Hollings who's been running the operation here? She's Franklin Campbell's stepdaughter. And from what I've garnered, she is also Strathom's fiancée. Like I said, it's pretty hard to believe that she wouldn't be involved in some capacity, isn't it? But regardless, we're shutting this thing down, and someone is going to pay for this egregious and illegal activity."

Bering heard the words, but he couldn't quite bring himself to respond. He stood, but then remained motionless as Senator Marsh got up and strode across the room, stepped up to the microphone and began to speak. Bering watched the unfolding scene play out but he had no idea what to do about it. It was as though he was suddenly frozen in his shoes, unable to react as the probable repercussions of what he'd precipitated began crashing down around him.

"Good afternoon, ladies and gentlemen. I'm honored to be here this morning as one of your senators from the most awesome of all the states in our great union, Alaska, and happy to be serving in Washington, D.C., as an advocate for the town of Rankins. I know you were all expecting a vote from the town council at tonight's meeting, and I understand that passions have been running high on both sides of this issue for the last several months, especially so in the last few weeks. But I'm here to inform you that there will be no vote tonight or anytime soon, for that matter. As of this morning, indictments have been handed down alleging fraud, bribery and conspiracy against Franklin Campbell, the chief executive officer of Cam-Field Oil & Mineral, Damon Kryzinski, the chief financial officer, and Jeremy Strathom, the senior vice president of operations.

"As a result, the environmental-impact reports for the project here in Rankins have been subpoenaed, an investigation has been launched, thus rendering Cam-Field's operations here on hold indefinitely...."

EMILY HAD KNOWN that something was wrong before she'd even stepped through the door of the Caribou. Amanda had called in a panic right after Bering had left, informing her that news crews were arriving at the diner and that Laurel had called to say that Senator Marsh had arrived and was holding a press conference in regard to Cam-Field's proposed development project.

But she'd known, in her heart, before this. She'd felt at the town-hall meeting that things weren't right, and she'd felt it when Bering had asked her to cancel that last rally. And Laurel had sensed it, too. Things had been too quiet. She should have paid attention to those warning signs. Heeded her instincts. Clearly, she had allowed her feelings for Bering to cloud her judgment. But what did this mean exactly?

Emily's brain fought to make sense of the senator's words. Indicted? Franklin indicted? She felt as if she was standing on a thin sheet of ice that had begun to slowly crackle beneath her feet. She could almost feel the swirl-ing tentacles of icy water waiting to grab her and pull her under. Her stepfather wasn't ex-actly an environmentalist, that was true, but as far as Emily knew, he'd always done ev-erything by the book. She would have known if he'd been breaking the law, wouldn't she?

She saw Bering standing near the front of the crowd. How could he do this without even telling her? He could have at least given her the courtesy of a warning. And he hadn't even glanced her way. He was standing there look-ing tough and hard—as if he was made of stone. He'd made her care about him, and all so he could have her stepfather indicted and make a fool of her in front of this town that she'd come to love with all her heart? She'd been right all along—about not being able to separate business from her personal life. How could she have been so stupid? All her life she'd lived by a set of principles that had served her well in business, and now, the one time she hadn't listened—the one time she'd allowed her heart to intrude—she was paying for it big-time. She should have known better.

She was intensely disappointed with her-self. Her radar had been malfunctioning ever since she'd arrived in Rankins, and if she was any kind of true professional, she would have made allowances for that. She'd known that she wasn't at the top of her game—she should have bowed out and let someone else do this job. But her stupid pride had been at stake. Well, if it had been in shreds before, it was completely gone now, just…blowing away on the Arctic breeze. Not to mention the playing fast and loose with her heart—what a joke. She was the joke. Bering must be enjoying the laugh of a lifetime. But she had more important things to worry about than herself now.

Poor Franklin—Cam-Field was his passion, his baby, his lifeblood. And if anyone knew the truth of that, it was Emily. It dawned on her that she had no choice in the matter now. She had to do something. She certainly couldn't quit. It was true that she couldn't forgive him for promoting Jeremy over her, but she couldn't leave him to wallow in this mess, either. She had to help him. She had to help clean this up.

She turned and spotted Cricket Blackburn just inside the door. She went over to him, whispered in his ear, received a nod in return and then quickly left the restaurant before reporters noticed who she was or that she was there.

Franklin wasn't going to win any father-of-the-year awards, that was true, but he had given her a roof over her head, a quality education and a job that she loved, or had for most of her life anyway. Security—Franklin had given her security.

But Bering had given her love. And his family had shown her unconditional acceptance—or so it had seemed. And she'd thought that Franklin's betrayal had hurt. Injured pride was a surface wound compared to the icy-cold knife Bering had plunged into her heart. His betrayal cut so deep she was sure it would never pump warm blood through her body again. Right now, security didn't seem so bad.

"I'M STANDING RIGHT here. You can't ignore me forever."

Amanda sighed dramatically and looked up, not bothering to mask her irritation. "What do you want, Bering?" she said.

"Where is she?" he repeated again through clenched teeth.

"None of your business."

"Amanda. Come on. Give me a break. I need to see her."

"Yeah, well, she doesn't want to see you."

"Yes, I've gathered that."

Bering had called and called Emily since the meeting and she hadn't picked up even once. After the press conference, he had stayed, at the request of the senator, long enough to answer questions from reporters. Emily had left before he'd had a chance to explain, and now he couldn't find her.

"But I want to see her," he said.

"So what? I don't know what to tell you, Bering."

"Amanda, can you please help me out here? What can I do? What can I give you? Money? Anything you want."

"Help you out? Sure, yeah. You know what? I am going to help you out and," she added, her voice now infused with fake enthusiasm, "I'm going to do it for nothing. Now, under normal circumstances I would probably lose my job for this. But since you're the one who made it his mission to befriend Emily, bewitch her and then stomp all over her, I'm willing to risk it. So here goes— you're a self-centered, despicable dirtbag. And I suggest that you go find someone else to toy with, because Emily is done with you."

"Amanda, listen. I want to explain—"

"You really hurt her, Bering. If you had any idea what that woman has gone through in her life… She has never had anyone— Oh, never mind. That doesn't even matter. What matters is that you're a first-class jerk. There, see? Now I've done my good deed. And you don't even need to reciprocate in any way because I've done it purely from the goodness of my heart—"

"I need to see her, Amanda."

Amanda puffed out a stream of air, sat back and crossed her arms over her chest. "Why did you do this to her? You obviously knew you were going to win this thing, so why? It was cruel to get involved with her like you did."

The guilt he felt at her words was nearly overwhelming. "I didn't know all this was going to happen. After a certain point, I was... confident I was going to win, yes, but I didn't know...everything. I didn't know her stepfather was the CEO—I don't know how I missed that one, but I did. I didn't know the senator was coming to Rankins today, and I didn't know about the indictments. I knew an investigation had been launched, but that's it. And I know that Cam-Field has been investigated before and nothing serious has ever become of it. Amanda, I swear to you, I didn't know..."

Amanda stared at the wall behind him.

"Amanda—" Bering continued his plea "—look at me. I have to see her. I have to explain. It's not like you think. It's not what she thinks. I never meant to hurt her."

Amanda stared at him hard. "I love Emily,

but I've always believed that she works too hard, that her job is too important to her. To my knowledge, the only men she's ever dated have been business acquaintances and the only socializing she does always has something to do with Cam-Field. That smooth-talking rat Jeremy proved to be the worst of all. And the truth of the matter is that I've never seen Emily as alive as she's been these last weeks that she's spent with you, Bering. She's been like a different person—Emily, but better...happy."

"Then give me a chance, ."

She sat forward in her seat and opened the drawer in front of her. She took out a small manila envelope. "Here," she said and handed it over. Bering opened it and looked inside—a key. He knew immediately what it unlocked. Now if only the key to sorting out this whole mess could be acquired even half as easily.

Amanda lowered her voice another notch. "There is no doubt in my mind that she would not only fire me, but kill me on the spot if she knew I gave it to you. And as she's also an incredible person and my best friend, you'd better fix this, Bering. Do you hear me? Fix this."

"I'm going to try, Amanda. Believe me, I'm going to try."

CHAPTER SIXTEEN

BERING USED THE KEY to get into the house, but she was already gone. He didn't know why he was surprised. He knew the logistics that Emily was capable of. Some of her stuff was still there, but enough of her personal items were gone that he knew she was, too. The only thing he saw in her bedroom, lying on the floor by the side of her bed, was the scarf he had given her. He picked it up and stuffed it in his pocket.

As Bering walked to his pickup, he heard the familiar and unmistakable sound of a Cessna flying overhead. He stood outside in the freezing wind and he knew. He felt the joy drain from his soul along with the gradually decreasing hum of the plane.

"SO, ESSENTIALLY WHAT you're telling me here, Stuart, is that Cam-Field submitted environmental-impact reports with incorrect facts and improper documentation?"

"That's correct, Emily." Cam-Field's long-time attorney slid a paper across the gleaming conference table. "These are all the jobs where the paperwork was forged. Franklin's name is on the paperwork, but he claims, and we know, he did not sign them."

Emily shook her head in disbelief. "He didn't. He hasn't signed off on EI reports in years."

"I think the best course of action would be to try to pass the buck along to the local governments who approved the work."

"Play dumb, you mean?"

"Plead ignorance," Stuart corrected.

"What jury in the world is going to believe that a company as established as Cam-Field is going to make mistakes like this? Mistakes that we've never made before? And the CEO of all people? Any good attorney is going to point out that Cam-Field has filled out hundreds and hundreds of these reports over the years. And to have Franklin's signature on them—there's no way…"

"We're just going to have to show them how it can happen. Bad advice from inept local officials…" He continued to lay out a scenario showing how it could have happened but Emily had quit listening.

Inept… It dawned on Emily right then and there, as she perused the list, exactly what had happened. She didn't even need to think it through—it was like a picture coalescing perfectly in her mind's eye.

"Wait a minute." She spoke up and began talking it through quickly. "It's Jeremy—he was involved with every one of these projects. And they all happen to be projects that I was not involved with. I personally look over every EI report that's submitted when I'm on a job because local governments can tie up the process for months if it's not done properly—meticulously even. And they all have their own idiosyncrasies to figure out and maneuver through. So what I'm confused about is how these were all approved so quickly. It's not at all like most local governments that I've worked with. Oh, wait…" She shuffled through some papers and muttered under her breath.

"Excuse me?" Stuart said. "Moose—what?"

"I'm sorry, Stuart," Emily said and ran her fingers through her hair. "What I'm thinking here is that someone has executed some old-fashioned bribery. I would be willing to bet that if you talked to the officials who signed off on this paperwork, you would discover who's behind it all. And Jeremy is my bet."

Stuart seemed incredulous as he asked, "Are

you saying that Jeremy forged his uncle's signature on these papers? And bribed government officials?"

"I am." She nodded.

"But how can we prove..." He trailed off, and Emily could see the lightbulb flicker on inside his head. He nodded a few times before he spoke. "I'm going to have to dig a little deeper here, Emily. In the meantime, maybe you could talk to Franklin and see what you two can come up with."

EMILY GRIPPED THE RECEIVER in her hand, willing Amanda to pick up. She did. Emily breathed a sigh of relief.

"Amanda."

"Oh, Em, it's so good to hear your voice."

"Amanda, I'm so sorry I left you to deal with the chaos up there."

"Don't worry about that. It's my job. I'm good at it. How's everything there?"

"It's rough, to tell you the truth. From a legal standpoint, it doesn't look good." She quickly filled Amanda in on her suspicions.

"I knew he was a weasel, but this is so beyond what I could even imagine," Amanda said when she was through.

"I know. Franklin and I are meeting today to go over it all step-by-step. There's no way

Franklin knew about this. He has always insisted that everything be done properly."

Amanda agreed wholeheartedly, "No, this has got Jeremy's greasy fingerprints all over it. It doesn't jibe with who Franklin is. He loves the challenge of what this company does. Besides, if he was to do something like this, which we know he never would, he certainly wouldn't have put his signature on the documents."

"I agree. It's just proving it that's going to be the problem. How much longer before you can get back here?"

"Just another day or two ought to do it."

"Did you find it?" Emily asked and held her breath as she waited for the answer that she feared was forthcoming.

"No, Emily, I'm sorry. It wasn't there. I personally packed up the whole place and it wasn't there. I've looked everywhere. Are you sure you didn't take it with you?"

Emily squeezed her eyes shut tightly as a wave of disappointment washed over her. "Yeah, I'm positive."

"I'm sorry, Em. Do you want me to get you a new one?"

"No, no, it's…it was special."

Bering had called several times after the press conference but Emily had ignored every one. She'd raced to the office after leaving the meeting, grabbed her laptop and some paperwork. She'd then rushed home, stuffed her essentials in a bag and had taken off for the airport. But somehow, she'd lost her scarf.

After the conference, she'd wanted to get out of town as quickly as possible—both to get home for Franklin and to avoid Bering. When she'd seen Cricket Blackburn by the door, she knew that he was her quickest ticket out of town. Emily would always be grateful that Cricket had acquiesced right away to her request without an interrogation. His avoidance of the subject had lasted all through the flight. And in Anchorage he'd even arranged for a car and escorted her to the terminal with a quick squeeze of her hand and an assurance that if she ever needed another impromptu "sightseeing tour," he was available. She'd nearly broken down then, but had managed to hold it together. Then she'd literally walked onto a plane bound for San Diego. She hadn't even called Amanda until she was boarding the plane. One short layover in Seattle and several hours later, she'd landed and went straight to the office.

She'd barely left since then, except to briefly visit her mother, who was so distraught that Emily could barely get a word in edgewise. In between bouts of hysterical crying and smothering Emily in hugs—which was a new one for her—she'd pleaded with her, demanding that she resolve it all somehow.

"Do something, Emily. You know how he's always been able to count on you!"

Now Emily sat back in her office chair and tried to retrace her steps again in her mind.

"Emily, are you still there?"

"Yes, Amanda, I'm sorry. I'm distracted."

"Maybe if I asked Bering, he could have Janie knit you another one and—"

"No," Emily barked. "No, Amanda, thank you, but I don't want anything from him. I don't want to talk about him. I can't even think about him right now." Bering hadn't called again since the night she left. As soon as she'd left town, the calls had stopped. She'd been right all along, she realized bitterly— Bering had used her. He'd won, and now that Cam-Field was gone from Rankins. his business with her was done. too.

She'd known that when Cam-Field was finished in Rankins she and Bering would be, too. But she hadn't been prepared for it to end like it had. She hadn't been prepared for it to end at all. Because who was she kidding? In her heart she'd longed for the fairy tale. Even though she knew it couldn't possibly happen, she'd thought they would at least part amicably. Maybe even keep in touch. She'd even fantasized about him visiting her in California and her traveling to Rankins occasionally. She had been hoping that it would all work out somehow. How naive. How utterly lovestruck. It was embarrassing. It was worse than embarrassing—it was humiliating. It was heartbreaking. And what was worse was that she'd been a willing participant in the disastrous circumstances that were now her life.

"OKAY, FRANKLIN, WE have been over the charges set forth in the indictment, and we ourselves know your signature was forged." She thought for a second and then said, "But we have to prove that somehow. McFarland has a legal team working on it, but in the meantime I need to run something by you. It's not going to be easy to hear, I'm afraid."

"What is it?"

Emily looked her stepfather straight in the eye. "I think Jeremy is behind this."

"Emily, what are you saying?"

"It all adds up. He was involved in each of these jobs, and they all happen to be jobs that I wasn't working on. And I don't want you to think that I'm speaking from a case of sour grapes here, but his work has always been sloppy. He's managed to cover it up by constantly delegating virtually everything. But truthfully, Franklin, he doesn't even really know the industry. I would have thought in the years he's been with Cam-Field he would have learned certain specific things, but that doesn't appear to be the case. Anyway, I think it's why he chose jobs that I wasn't working on. It is no secret that I'm a control freak. I personally oversee every aspect of the process. It would have been impossible for anyone to get away with this malfeasance if I had been on these jobs."

He didn't say anything for a long while, so Emily continued, "The employees don't like or respect him and I—"

"Emily, this is a rather harsh way to speak about your fiancé, don't you think?"

Emily blinked at him dumbly for a few seconds. "My what?"

"Your fiancé," he repeated.

"What—Jeremy, my fiancé? Franklin, Jeremy and I are not engaged. Where in the world would you get that idea?"

"Why, from Jeremy. I know he hasn't officially proposed yet, but you do have an agreement, right? Jeremy reassured me of this only last week."

Emily laughed at the statement. "That's totally ridiculous. Why would he...? Jeremy and I broke up, and we weren't even that close to begin with."

It seemed so pathetic to her now that her relationship had been such with her stepfather that he wouldn't have been clear on something as important as her relationship status. It was even worse that Jeremy could have convinced him so easily that things were fine between them. She was still intent on sticking with the career change she'd decided upon in Rankins; it had just been delayed a bit. As soon as things were straightened out, she was going to tell Franklin that she was quitting and leaving San Diego. But for now, she was going to mend whatever she could of this relationship between herself and her stepfather. They could communicate just fine where business was concerned; they should be able to succeed on a personal level, as well.

Emily looked over at him and saw that his normally vibrant color had faded to a dull gray. She was afraid he might be cracking under the stress. He'd had some minor heart issues in the past. She sat forward in her seat and placed her hand on top of his, something she never would have done before....

"Franklin, are you okay?" But she knew

he wasn't okay. Emily could see now that he was angry.

He sat up straight and cleared his throat. He placed a hand on top of hers. "Emily, my dearest, I'm afraid I've made a terrible mistake."

Emily felt her heart sinking. She knew that if her stepfather was admitting to making a mistake then it had to be bad—very bad. She prayed it wasn't anything illegal.

"Here's the thing," he said. "Jeremy convinced me to promote him over you because he told me you two were going to be getting married. He assured me it was something you had discussed—that you had an agreement. He asked me not to say anything to you about it because he hadn't officially proposed. He wanted to 'do it right,' he said. Naturally, I was rather surprised, but also quite happy for you. Needless to say, your mother was thrilled that you were finally going to get married and live a 'normal' life." He grimaced before continuing.

"Now, I'll admit," he added with a halfhearted chuckle, "I was disappointed that you were choosing marriage over Cam-Field. That wasn't the Emily—the daughter—that I'd raised. But Jeremy insisted that you would still be a vital part of the organization. You

weren't going to give up Cam-Field completely—you were just going to become his
'second in command,' allowing you time to
take care of him and the children."

"The…the what?" Emily stuttered, gripping the edge of the desk in front of her. Her
heart was thudding heavily in her chest and
cold sweat had begun to form on her brow.
"Children?" she repeated, stunned. "Taking
care of him? What children?"

"Emily, I can't tell you how sorry I am."
He squeezed her hand. Had he ever held her
hand before? A few times maybe, once, she
remembered, when she was little and she'd
taken a fall off the ladder in the supply room
and she'd had to have stitches in her chin.

"I've been an unpardonable fool. I love
you, Emily. I know…" He swallowed heavily and went on. "I know that I haven't said it
enough to you over the years. But I know that
you know how proud I am of you. I've never
had a problem telling that much. You've
always made me so very proud. You know
that, right? How proud I am? My heart just
aches with joy when I think about the woman
you've become, what you've accomplished…"
He trailed off and Emily watched his Adam's
apple dancing in his throat. She was stupe-
fied. Was he actually on the verge of tears?

"It's a lie, Franklin," Emily said and slowly shook her head back and forth. "It's all lies," she repeated, not quite believing it, that Jeremy had stooped so low. She knew he was capable of laziness and stupidity and arrogance and general lack of character, but this… It was reprehensible. It was unforgivable.

"I can see that now," he said slowly. "You know, I wanted to ask you about it at the time, but your mother was so…ecstatic about the whole thing, and she and Jeremy insisted that a surprise proposal would be sooo wonderful." He raised his hands in frustration and then slapped them hard on the table. "I knew better. In my heart I knew better! But you don't think your own nephew, your own flesh and blood…"

"Franklin, this is all so unbelievable to me," she said. *Traitorous, conniving, bribing coward,* she thought. "Where is Jeremy anyway?"

JEREMY WAS IN one of the circles of hell. He wasn't sure which one, as he'd always found classical literature a complete bore. But he was definitely suffering hellish-type tortures— that was for sure. He was Jeremy Strathom III! And he'd been freezing his backside off for three days waiting for the snow to finally stop falling so he could get out of this uncivilized ice patch.

He had no idea how he'd ended up here in the first place. He was supposed to be in Rankins wooing Emily. And now, after he'd finally gotten through to Kim in San Diego, he'd learned that Emily was already back there. Why would Emily be back in San Diego already? He didn't know the details because the line had promptly gone dead and stayed that way. Things had either gone incredibly well or incredibly catastrophically. And knowing Emily, it could only be the former.

He couldn't wait to get back home. He had no doubt that she would say yes when he proposed. She was crazy about him—well, she had been until Franklin had announced the promotion. But an official proposal of marriage for a frigid ice queen like her would get her back on board the Jeremy train. He'd purchased a huge diamond, he'd turn on the charm and she wouldn't be able to resist him. Not to mention that it was the best thing for her career. It was the best thing for Cam-Field, and Emily always did what was best for Cam-Field.

"Mr. Strathom?" A young woman's voice pulled him out of his reverie. "The pilot says you can get on board now. But he said to make sure you got an extra jacket, 'cause it's gonna be pretty cold on there—unless you wanna ride with the cargo." She nodded knowingly and added, "But trust me, you don't want to be doing that."

"Cargo? It's a cargo plane?"

"Yes, sir, that's all we ever get here. That fancy plane you came in on was a pretty rare thing. It was carrying a VIP—our chief coming home from a conference in Anchorage."

Jeremy shook his head. He had no coat other than the one he was wearing, which was nothing more than a thin wool overcoat. He had no gloves, no hat—not even a handkerchief. He had no idea where his luggage was. "Um, would you by any chance have any spare clothing lying around? Or a blanket? Anything of any warmth will do. I could pay you."

The young woman shrugged her shoulders and looked him solidly in the eye. "Well, snow clothes are in pretty high demand around here. I tell ya what—why don't you tell me what you got for cash, and I'll see what I can do...."

As it turned out, even Amanda managed to make it back to San Diego before Jeremy. Emily screwed the top off a root beer and handed it to her. Yet another thing she missed about Rankins, she thought as a fresh wave of sadness overtook her—frosty, cold, birch-syrup-flavored root beer on tap from the Cozy Caribou. Would she ever quit missing that place, she wondered, and missing Bering? She willed herself to ignore the ache that had taken up permanent residence in her heart. She opened her own bottle and took a long swig. Then she proceeded to fill Amanda in on all that she'd discovered over the course of the past few days.

"Jeremy is actually planning to propose to you?"

"According to Franklin," Emily said. "Can you imagine anything so absurd?"

"Well, Emily, in light of your impending engagement, there's something else I think you need to know about Jeremy. He's…he was seeing someone else before we left for Rankins. Kirsten Leer—you remember her?"

"The agent from Dieter & Manning Insurance?"

"Yep, that's the one."

Emily shrugged. "That figures. No one needs that much insurance." She tapped her fingers on the tabletop, deep in thought.

"Why didn't you tell me this before? How long was it going on?"

"A few months at least, and I didn't find out until a couple days before we left. And I was going to tell you—I was just giving you some time to deal with the promotion and everything—but when we arrived in Rankins, you were so…not yourself. I decided it could wait awhile. And then you got your feet back underneath you and I was so relieved to see that, and then you started seeing Bering and I… It didn't seem important anymore. Em, I'm so sorry."

"Oh, no, Amanda—it doesn't matter. I'm not hurt or upset about that. I'm relieved. I mean, I obviously dodged a bullet. I'm a bit angry maybe, because of the way he used me. And of course I was devastated about the promotion, but really, when I think about it, I'm a better person after it all. But I am furious about what he's done to Cam-Field—to Franklin. I mean, that man has given him everything. I had to work so incredibly hard for everything I achieved. But Jeremy could have had it all without even trying."

She continued tapping her fingers as she stared off into space with narrowed eyes.

"What is it?" Amanda asked. "I know that look of yours."

"I... It's just that, why would he be proposing anymore? I mean, he already got the promotion. So, why would he need me now? I know he told my mother and Franklin that marriage was his plan but he didn't have to follow through with it. He could have just let time go by and eventually made some excuse about how it didn't work out between us. I mean, I assume that he didn't actually plan on proposing while he was getting involved with Kirsten, so why...?"

"I know why," Amanda said. "He couldn't do it."

"What do you mean?"

"He can't do the job without you, Emily. Now, granted, the staff may have been, um... how shall I say it?...uncooperative while we were gone. But my, uh, sources have informed me that the guy has been coming completely undone..."

Emily listened with fascination as Amanda filled her in on all that had transpired while they were away. Emily was impressed by the amount of information that Amanda had managed to gather—everything from Jeremy's tanking on the Argot job and the graphics staff's part in it to his medical diagnosis with irritable bowel syndrome.

"Amanda," she said, her voice filled with awe, "have you ever thought about a career in espionage?"

Amanda's lips turned up into a satisfied grin. "Just looking out for my best friend—who also happens to be my boss."

"What an idiot!" Emily said. "Amanda, why didn't you tell me he was such an idiot?"

"It took me a while to see it for myself. He was very smooth, and he's a good-looking guy if you like that pretty-boy thing, and he's a snappy dresser. He was talking the talk and putting in long hours, although now I'm certain he was in his office playing video poker and shopping for shoes the entire time."

Emily let out a disgusted snort of laughter. "According to the feds, he's supposed to be arriving today. What is taking him so long anyway?"

"Oh, unfortunately, he had to travel on a cargo flight full of live birds. Apparently there's some Native Alaskan village up there where they rehabilitate migratory birds that have been injured and then they let them go back into the wild. They've got this indoor setup for all kinds of birds and different weather conditions and everything. Isn't that interesting? But if Kim's calculations are correct—and I'm sure they are—he should be arriving in a few hours." At that she winked, toasted Emily with her bottle and took a deep drink.

CHAPTER SEVENTEEN

BERING LET HIMSELF into Tag's house. He heard a female voice and realized that Tag must have some company. He was surprised because his cousin hadn't dated at all since Amanda had left town. Well, he would make himself scarce very shortly. He just needed to pick up the mail that Tag had been collecting for him the past few days.

Then he was going to go home, take a shower and head over to Janie's. The twins had come early, but thank goodness not as early as they'd feared. They'd been healthy, if a bit fragile, at three weeks early, but now at three months they seemed to be thriving. He counted his blessings for that every single day. Janie, however, was battling a severe case of postpartum depression, and Bering was doing his best to help out any chance he could.

But when he walked into the kitchen, what, or who, he saw there stopped him dead in his tracks.

"Amanda?"

"Bering!" She gave him a quick hug and a kiss on the cheek. "Howdy, stranger."

"What are you doing here?" he asked.

"Visiting your cousin," she said, flipping a thumb over her shoulder. "And it's nice to see you, too."

"I'm sorry, Amanda. It is great to see you. Um, how are you? What are you…?"

"I'm good—great now that I'm here. And I'm here because someone had to fly back up to make a donation at the Chamber of Commerce banquet tonight. I volunteered. Cam-Field has decided to donate a million dollars to the hospital anyway—a philanthropic gesture of good faith or something like that."

"Oh, that's great. Is, uh, Emily," he stuttered, "did Emily come with you?"

"No, Bering, she didn't. I thought you probably knew…. She doesn't work for Cam-Field anymore."

Bering swallowed heavily and looked down at the floor. "Did she get married, then?"

"What? Married? No!" Amanda sputtered.

"Senator Marsh said she and Strathom were engaged. So I thought maybe she got married so she wouldn't have to testify against him. I know the trial is coming up…."

"That's silly. She would never marry that fool."

"Oh—"

"Bering," Amanda interjected sharply, "what are you wearing?"

Bering looked down at his clothing and let the relief sink in. Emily. Not married. Why did that make him so inexplicably happy? It wasn't as if he still had a chance.

He met Amanda's annoyed stare. "Oh, sorry...yeah, I'm a little dirty. I've been on a four-day guide trip—"

Amanda gestured at him impatiently. "Not that." She reached over and tugged Emily's red knit scarf out of his collar. "I'm talking about this." She snatched it off his neck.

"What?"

"Emily went crazy thinking that she'd lost this scarf." Amanda held it aloft as if it were evidence from a crime scene. "I tore the house and the office apart looking for it. Then she thought maybe she'd left it in the rental car. I had to search through an entire Dumpster, Bering, looking for it."

Bering stared at her in confusion. "But...I found it at her house. The day she left here when you gave me the key. I went there to see her, but she was already gone. I found it on the floor. I thought she had left it on purpose."

"Trust me, Bering. She did not leave it on purpose. She was devastated that she'd lost it. Almost as devastated as she was over you— Know what?" She grimaced and tried to correct her slip of the tongue. She plastered on a wide fake smile and continued talking. "We should go for a walk. Whaddya say? All that frigid, fresh air, Tag?" She gestured toward the door.

Bering was stunned. It couldn't be possible, could it? That she hadn't left it on purpose? That she'd cared enough about it…to want to take it with her?

"Amanda, are you saying that she didn't leave it? That she wanted it?"

"I think we should head toward the water, don't you? But let's stick to the sidewalk. Better safe than sorry, as I always say." She started marching on the spot. "I'll just get my coat and stuff and then we can head out. It's really not so bad outside. You guys said it was beautiful up here in the summer but I didn't believe it would be this—"

"Amanda." He stepped toward her and took hold of her wrist. "Please, just, please," he said in an urgent tone. "Tell me everything."

"I'm not supposed to talk to you, Bering." Amanda looked away from him and winced. "She made me promise," she added quietly.

"Amanda." He squeezed his eyes shut for a second, opened them and asked, "Do I have to beg…again?"

"All right," she said with a dramatic sigh. "I can't stand this anyway. She's…she was totally broken up about it—betrayed by her stepfather, betrayed by Jeremy and finally betrayed by you. A betrayal trifecta. But those things were nothing compared to getting her heart broken by you, Bering. Emily's never been in love before and you just—you can't imagine how awful it's been for her."

"Love! What love? I didn't know… She never said… And I…I didn't mean to betray her. And even some of the newspaper articles said that she and Strathom were engaged."

"Pfft," Amanda said with a roll of her eyes. "You believe everything you read in the papers now? She was in love with you—you moron."

"But…but she never said anything."

Amanda scowled at him. "And you did?" she said, her tone oozing sarcasm. "You mean she didn't reciprocate when you shimmied up her balcony with your mandolin and professed your undying love through poetry and song?"

"I…I… But the scarf…"

"I can't believe you gave up because of this stupid scarf."

"I don't understand... I thought... How is she?"

Amanda shrugged helplessly. "How do you think? She's been miserable. Slowly getting better, but the only thing that's kept her sane was helping to straighten out the legal nightmare that Jeremy created."

"Where is she, Amanda?" Bering's tone allowed for no argument.

"You're not going to believe it when I tell you."

Wow. It REALLY was one big boat, er, ship—whatever it was, it was big. Emily stared up at the cruise ship with a welcome sense of satisfaction. She'd survived. The past four months had been hell, but she'd made it. She'd done her part to untangle Cam-Field's massive legal knot. The charges against Franklin and the CFO had been dropped, leaving Jeremy on the hook for the entire fiasco.

But luckily, like Jeremy did virtually everything else with regard to his career, he'd done it badly. It hadn't taken the authorities long to prove that he'd been bribing local officials. The idiot had even used a company check when he'd first started the scheme.

His trial date had been scheduled, and in the meantime he was behind bars. Franklin had refused to post his bail, and Emily hoped he was having a fine time in his new corner office constructed entirely of steel bars.

Franklin had offered Emily her rightful position as vice president, and she'd shocked him and the entire Cam-Field staff by not only declining the offer, but by resigning, as well. Her mother had nearly passed out when she heard the news. Emily suspected it had as much to do with the fact that she wasn't getting married as it did with her resignation. Franklin had taken it surprisingly well. Emily knew it was partially because he didn't believe that she would stay away for good. He'd told her that he was giving her a leave of absence to think it over. But what he didn't realize was that she'd already thought it over, and she wasn't going back.

But she also now believed that he really did want to see her happy. That was the one good thing to come out of the whole ordeal— she and Franklin had breached some kind of emotional wall in their relationship. Emily felt sure that he loved her—he told her almost daily now. And they'd begun to talk and to discover that they did have things to discuss that didn't relate directly to Cam-Field. They still talked about that, of course, but he began to share things about himself and about her mother that she'd never known—about how her mother's childhood had been filled with poverty and neglect. Emily better understood her mother's neediness, and while it didn't make up for her lack of parenting during Emily's childhood, it was somehow improving her relationship with her mother, too. And that was the best that Emily could hope for, to move forward—in her relationship with her parents and in her life.

She'd applied for a job on one of the cruise lines that ran out of Houston, gotten the job, learned the job and now here she was, two months later, sitting in the sun preparing for the ship to depart yet again. She'd worked every single day for the past month, until her boss had finally insisted that she take a few days off. She wasn't looking forward to the downtime, because she'd discovered that the busier she wasn't, the more time she had to think about her time in Rankins—her time with Bering.

If only she could somehow work her way out of love with him. Sometimes it surprised her how much she still missed Bering. She supposed she should feel lucky, rather than extraordinarily pathetic, that she'd managed to make it to twenty-eight before she'd had her first experience with heartbreak. Poems were written about it and songs were sung, but she'd always assumed that they were speaking metaphorically and exaggerating for effect. They weren't.

She'd forgiven him for the most part, now that time had passed, for what he'd done. Maybe *forgive* was too strong a word, but she certainly understood why he'd done it. He'd warned her that he was going to do whatever it took to keep Cam-Field out of Rankins— she just hadn't been savvy enough to realize that he was referring to the indiscriminate shattering of her most important organ.

She might have done the same at one point in her life. It seemed so strange to her now that her job had ever been that important to her. She had definitely become a different person. Or was it that she'd just never known who she really was? Regardless, she was glad that the end result had saved Rankins from destruction and her stepfather from prison.

Emily glanced up from the book that she'd been staring at for the past few minutes and froze as she saw a familiar figure striding her way. What? No, it couldn't be… Emily stood up as he got closer, her book slipping out of her hands, tumbling onto her lounge chair and hitting the ground with a thud.

She squinted toward the advancing form. "Aidan?" she called out as he neared.

"Hey, Emily. They told me I'd find you up here."

Emily beamed and hugged him. "Aidan, what in the world are you doing here?"

"Taking a cruise. This is a cruise ship, is it not?"

"I can't believe you're here."

He looked down at her intently. "I thought maybe we could use some brother-sister time, and I haven't had a vacation in, what, three years? I'm all yours for the next two weeks. I figured I was due. I've never been on a cruise before. What's it like?"

Emily shrugged. "I wouldn't know, either. I've been working the entire time, but it seems like everyone is always having fun. This is my first one to enjoy like a paying customer."

BERING SPOTTED HER immediately. Even in the crowded room, his eye was drawn to her like a magnet. Again with the red—as though she knew he was coming for her. His lips slowly turned up into a smile as he watched her. She was wearing red and she was dancing. She was a really good dancer. Why hadn't he ever danced with her? He was going to correct that right now. But wait, who was that guy holding on to her like that?

"Amanda," Bering managed to whisper when he could finally speak. "Who is that?"

Amanda peeked out from behind him. "What the—" she exclaimed. "I can't believe it. I really can't believe it," she repeated. "He's actually here. That's—"

And in that moment Bering knew, and he started moving. It was Strathom. She was with Strathom. She'd actually gone back to him. But she couldn't. He wouldn't let her. Not now, not when he'd come so far and was so close to getting her back. He'd learned so much from Amanda on the way here— about her relationship with Strathom, about her family, her life—and he knew how difficult it all must have been for her.

But if Amanda was right and she really did care about him, he had to try. He had to convince her to at least hear him out. And he was hoping for more than that—he'd brought Amanda, Tag and Janie along in case there was any chance that Emily would say yes....

He strode across the long dining room and stepped onto the dance floor.

"Bering?" Emily said, shock registering

clearly on her face. "What are you doing here?"

He gently took hold of her elbow and guided her off the dance floor.

EMILY FELT AS IF her heart was going to explode inside her chest it was beating so wildly. What could he possibly be doing here? Had he come to get information out of her? She'd already told the authorities everything she knew. She was on the prosecution's list to testify if they needed her.

"I came here to talk to you, Emily. I need to tell you some things I should have told you months ago." He reached into his jacket pocket to pull something out, but paused for a moment as his eyes drank her in. They roved over her lightly tanned skin and finally settled on her wide gray eyes. "I, uh, I—"

Emily felt tears sting her eyes and she looked away.

"Emily," Aidan said as he approached them. "Is everything okay?"

Bering cursed softly and then spoke sharply without looking away from Emily, "Give us a minute—"

She looked at Aidan, wanting to reassure him. "It's fine, Aidan."

"Aidan?" Bering said, turning now to take

a good look at him. "Aidan... Oh, right, you guys look so much alike."

Emily huffed impatiently and pointed at him. "Yes, this is Aidan, my brother. Forgive my rudeness in skipping the introductions. Bering, what are doing here—" she blurted, noticing then what he was holding in his hand. "Is that my scarf? How did you...?"

"Um, I wanted to bring it to you. Amanda said you didn't leave it on purpose."

Emily swallowed down the bubble of hope that had started to rise within her. "You came all the way from Alaska to bring me my scarf?"

"Amanda said you were looking for it and I thought maybe that meant—"

"What, Bering? You thought it meant what?" Her voice was choked with emotion.

He stepped toward her and wrapped the scarf around her neck. "I thought maybe it meant that you didn't leave it on purpose."

She gripped the ends of the scarf and squeezed her eyes shut for a few seconds. She opened them and started to speak in a strangled voice. "Bering, no, I didn't. I—"

"Emily—" he began, but then fell silent as he stared deeply into her eyes. "I didn't know Franklin Campbell was your stepfather. I knew Strathom's name because of the research I'd done on Cam-Field before you ever showed up in Rankins. But I didn't know your relationship to him or to Franklin Campbell. Emily, I never would have let the senator make that announcement if I'd known…. And then I found your scarf lying on the floor and I thought that you'd left it…."

Emily reached for his hand and held it tightly.

"From the day we met and you stripped your clothes off in front of me…"

She still held on to one end of the scarf and Bering closed his hand over hers. "What are you saying, Bering?"

"I love you, Emily."

"Oh, Bering," she whispered. "I love you, too."

Bering tugged on the end of the scarf, gently pulling until she bumped lightly against his chest. He took her into his arms.

"My sister's a stripper?" Aidan looked toward Amanda and frowned.

"No, no, it wasn't like that," she said. "She was on drugs."

"Oh, drugs, yeah, of course," he said drily. "That explains it—a druggie and a stripper. Who are you people anyway?"

BERING WANTED TO get married on the ship, but Emily refused. They were lounging side by side on deck chairs outside her cabin, with the scarf resting on her lap. At least she'd agreed to marry him, though.

"Emily, I brought Janie and Tag and Amanda with me, and your brother is already here. Who else could you possibly want to be here?"

"It's not that, Bering."

"Is it your parents? Because they could meet us at the next port, too, and anyone else that you want—"

"No, no, that's not it, although that's incredibly sweet."

"What is it, then?"

"I want to get married somewhere that means something to me."

Bering sighed. "All right, as soon as we get back to San Diego, we'll make the arrangements. Is there a church or a country club or something that you have in mind?"

"Ugh," she said with a groan, "it would take months to plan a wedding like that."

Bering kissed her. "Emily, I don't want to wait months, but I will do whatever you want. At least then my mom could be there and maybe even some of my aunts and uncles and some cousins—"

"Bering, they can all be there."

"Yeah, I know. But it's not just the expense of flying everyone in—it's the logistics of it. Everyone getting time off work and kids out of school—"

"I want to get married in Rankins."

Bering bolted to a sitting position. "What? Emily, really? Are you sure?"

"There are three churches in Rankins, right? If we can't get one on such short notice, maybe we could get married at the VFW where the Rotary auction was held. Or the inn—does Shay do weddings? Oh, Bering, let's get married at the inn."

Bering kissed her again. It was too much. She was too much. The happiness he felt, after all the weeks of misery. It just couldn't be possible to have everything now, could it?

"Emily, that would be so...so...perfect. When are you going back to work at Cam-Field? Because that would give me time to pack some stuff and make arrangements and—"

"And what, Bering? Move to San Diego? Give up your business and your work with the Department of Fish and Game? You would do that for me?"

"Maybe we could work something out where I just give up the Department of Fish and Game stuff. I don't do it for the money anyway. I do it because I enjoy it and I find it interesting. But if I gave it up, then I could spend the winter here with you and then I could go back up for the summer—"

"No way," Emily said aghast. "And live apart all summer? And what about the spring fishing season and hunting in the fall? Are you crazy?"

"Emily, I'm willing to work something out. But I don't know what I would do in San Diego. I can't get a regular job—like in an office…"

Emily laughed. "Bering, the look of terror on your face is absolutely priceless." Then she said, "Why does no one believe that I'm not going back to Cam-Field? Franklin is still sending me a paycheck. I haven't even cashed them, but he still won't get the message."

She sat up and grabbed Bering's chin and turned his face toward hers. "I love you so much for your brave, albeit ridiculous, attempt at compromise." She feathered a soft kiss across his lips. "I want to live in Rankins, Bering. I miss it and that's what I want. I've never felt more at home anywhere in my life than I did there."

"But I thought you hated it."

She placed a hand on each of his shoulders.

"I did at first—or I thought I did. Until you…
and this." She tapped on his chest. "And this."
She leaned over and kissed his chin. "And
your family." She kissed his cheek. "And
your wolves," She kissed his lips. "And your
moose." She kissed him again. "And your
seafood, and your ugly, puffy clothes that
kept me impossibly warm, and the salt that
kept me from slipping on my own sidewalk,
and that fire in your cabin. I think I'd like to
honeymoon at that cabin or maybe Hawaii.

Bering shrugged. "Okay."

"Okay?"

"Emily, we can go anywhere you want."

Her look was pure delight. Bering felt her
happiness mixing with his, replacing the last
remnants of the piercing sadness that had
been a part of him for too long now.

"Anywhere?"

"Anywhere."

Emily smiled slowly and said, "You know
what? I would love to go anywhere with you,
Bering, as long as we can always go home to
Rankins."

* * * * *

LARGER-PRINT BOOKS!

GET 2 FREE
LARGER-PRINT NOVELS
PLUS 2 FREE
MYSTERY GIFTS

Love Inspired

Larger-print novels are now available...

ReaderService.com

Manage your account online!

- Review your order history
- Manage your payments
- Update your address

---

*We've designed
the Harlequin® Reader Service
website just for you.*

Enjoy all the features!

- Reader excerpts from any series
- Respond to mailings and
  special monthly offers
- Discover new series available to you
- Browse the Bonus Bucks catalog
- Share your feedback

Visit us at:

ReaderService.com